# She's a Sinner

## by

## Lynn Shurr

*A Sinner's Legacy, Book 2*

**She's a Sinner**

Cover Art by *Diana Carlile*

The Wild Rose Press, Inc.
PO Box 708
Adams Basin, NY 14410-0708
Visit us at www.thewildrosepress.com

Publishing History
First Champagne Rose Edition, 2015
Print ISBN 978-1-5092-0338-3
Digital ISBN 978-1-5092-0339-0

*A Sinner's Legacy, Book 2*
Published in the United States of America

**"Alix, would you like to dance?" Tom offered.**

"Oh, yes!" She shot to her feet.

Tille appraised her outfit. "You should have worn the black. You look like a Catholic school girl about to take her first communion."

The hurt that passed over Alix's face prompted Tom to say, "I think you look like a bride."

"That's what I thought—sort of bridish. Let's dance."

The music had turned frenetic, so not a chance of him holding her close. Tom went into what Dean called his war dance, among many other choice expressions. He jerked his arms over his flaming red head and lifted his long legs almost in time with the music. Dancing, not his greatest skill. Alix did the same. They circled the dance floor. Were people staring?

He noticed Vince Barbaro come out of the shadows and ask Tille to dance. Alix's sister had worn short black spandex that clung to her rear and cupped each braless breast held up by straps that crossed behind her neck. Vince watched her boobs jiggle as he did a few *Saturday Night Fever* moves designed to impress. She'd worn heels high enough to increase her mammary motion. Both seemed happy with their choice of partners.

The door to Mariah's Place opened letting in a shaft of low, long-lasting summer sunshine. As usual, the couple who entered stood there for a moment waiting for their eyes to adjust to the dark. The sunbeam illuminated them from the back as if they were surrounded by holy light, an anointed pair—Dean and Stacy…

## Praise for Lynn Shurr

"Shurr is a wonderful storyteller."

*~The Romance Studio*

~*~

"Lynn Shurr's sinfully delightful New Orleans Sinners series is sure to please both non-sports fans and sports fans alike. Do yourself a favor and dive into the world of the Sinners."

*~Farrah Rochon, USA Today Best-selling author of the New York Sabers football series*

~*~

"Very easy reads, well written, combined with conflict, believable plots and secondary characters that make the story come alive."

*~Jane Lange, Romances, Reads and Reviews*

~*~

"What I love about these books is that they appeal to any audience, not just those who love sports…Another theme I would say plays heavily into the books is love and acceptance. I love how deep and well written the characters are."

*~Juliette Brandt, Paperbacks and Frosting*

~*~

"Lynn Shurr stories have that distinctive Louisiana flavor…and make you eager for another taste."

*~J.L. Salter, author of Scratching the Seven Month Itch*

~*~

"The author has created a family full of surprises with the Billodeaux bunch. After reading just one book, I am eager to read more about this colorful family."

*~Rachel's Willful Thoughts, The Romance Reviews*

## Dedication

For Lauren Silberman,
female kicker,
who tried out for the NFL in 2013

# A SINNER'S LEGACY

The children of Joe and Nell Billodeaux
who fulfilled the prophecy that they would have
twelve offspring, this way, that way, all ways

Dean Joseph Billodeaux—Joe's illegitimate son by a one-night stand with a woman who planned to shake him down for money. He is adopted by Nell who believes she cannot have children of her own. Current Sinners quarterback. (*Wish for a Sinner*)

Thomas Cassidy Billodeaux—a redheaded son who enters the family through an open adoption with a teenage mother. His birth father is Joe's no-good cousin. He is a kicker for the Sinners. (*Wish for a Sinner* and *Kicks for a Sinner*)

Jude Emily Billodeaux—twin of Ann, conceived by in vitro fertilization using eggs purchased from Nell's sister, Emily. (*Wish for a Sinner*)

Ann Marie Billodeaux (Annie)—Jude's quiet twin. (*Wish for a Sinner*)

Lorena Renee Billodeaux (Lori)—First of Nell's little frozen babies to be born, one of the triplets. (*Kicks for a Sinner*)

Mack Coy Christopher Billodeaux—Second of the triplets to be born. (*Kicks for a Sinner*)

Trinity Billodeaux - Youngest of the triplets and named for the Father, Son, and Holy Ghost, smallest of the three and in need of a powerful saintly help to survive. (*Kicks for a Sinner*)

Xochi Maria Billodeaux—child of Joe's no-good cousin by a young Mexican woman. She is Tom's half-sister and is adopted into the family after the terrifying deaths of her parents. Her name means "blossom" in Aztec. (*Kicks for a Sinner*)

Teddy Wilkes Billodeaux—a child with spina bifida abandoned by his mother at Nell's health care center and adopted by the family. He believed himself to be Joe's natural son. (*Paradise for a Sinner*)

Anastasia Marya Polasky (Stacy)—daughter of Nell's sister, Emily, and a bogus Polish prince. She becomes a ward of the Billodeauxs upon her parents' deaths, but is never adopted by her own wish. She arrives on their doorstep the same day as Teddy. (*Paradise for a Sinner*)

Edith Patricia Billodeaux (Edie)—a normally conceived child, twin of Rex. (*Love Letter for a Sinner*)

Rex Worthy Billodeaux (T-Rex)—Edie's twin brother and future Sinner's quarterback, maybe. (*Love Letter for a Sinner*)

Chapter One

Rookie Day at the Sinners' football training camp in Metairie, Louisiana, and the May sun beat down unrelentingly upon the newbies, the wannabes, and the has-beens. Tom Billodeaux, placekicker for the team, thought Coach Marty Buck simply wanted to sweat the new guys for the hell of it since he'd had them dress out in full pads and helmets. At least, he hadn't called for stockings, too. Lots of hairy legs showed as the new recruits and a bunch of walk-ons ran through their drills. If they thought Coach paid no attention behind those dark sunglasses and beneath that red Sinners cap covering an ever-increasing bald spot in his white crew-cut, they would be so very wrong. Age had honed Coach Buck to stringy whipcord muscles and scored his face with lines as deep as crevasses, but the brain beneath the hat still contained every detail of running a successful football team.

Sitting squarely between his kicker and his punter, Marty Buck said, "What did you think of that one, Lightfoot?"

Brian Lightfoot, a punter known for his long kicks and elegant placement, shook his head sadly. "I pity the boy. That was a high school performance. He took three steps before making his kick, a big waste of time. My guess is he's a placekicker, but thought he'd give punting a try when he heard I announced my retirement.

Frankly, the rest weren't much better." Brian smoothed back his long dark hair made distinguished by small wings of silver on either side.

"Yeah, we got the usual mishmash—university players who weren't drafted, really young guys who aren't going to college, and some old dudes who want a few more years in the league. A few of the relics would do, but I don't want to go through this again next year. None of them have your talent."

Lightfoot regarded his nicely manicured nails. "Of course not. That would be very hard to achieve," he replied without false modesty.

"Take a good look the next candidate. What we have here is Ancient Andy Mortenson's grandchild." Buck referred to the Sinners' very first placekicker known for his strong leg and amazing longevity. Only three major kickers adorned the history of the expansion team, Andy, Howdy McCoy, and now Tom Billodeaux, well-schooled by his predecessor and stepfather and not going anywhere else anytime soon. He planned to play as long as those who had gone before and helped to earn five Super Bowl rings.

Tom felt free to comment about a possible rival. "Wouldn't Andy's offspring be trained in placekicking? He runs his own camp for kickers."

"Like Brian said, we only got an opening for a punter. Still, a punter with placekicking skills could be your backup."

"Don't need one." Tom shook his head hard enough to flick off some of the sweat that ran down his freckled, boyish face.

"You never know." Coach cupped his hand around his mouth and shouted, "You're up next, Lindstrom.

Let's see what you can do."

A lanky figure narrow in the shoulders even with the pads, but long in the leg trotted onto the field. A fringe of straight, pale blonde hair splayed out from the back of the black helmet. Around six feet tall with a light build, Tom estimated. "I'm not sure he could take a hit or throw a block if necessary."

"Some people would say the same about you, Billodeaux. Don't get your panties in a wad. We ain't looking to replace you."

"Where did this guy come from anyhow? I keep track of college kickers and haven't heard of a Lindstrom playing anywhere."

"Straight from the soccer field. No football experience," Coach Buck said. His kickers groaned. "Hey, hey, give the kid a chance like I did Lightfoot once upon a time."

"So true. Good legs," Brian said. "Long, nicely developed, but not bulky—and possibly waxed which is more than I can say for Tom." He regarded his own sleek, olive-toned limbs displayed in khaki shorts topped by a pink polo shirt. "I think I'm overdue for a manscaping."

"We ain't running a dating service, Lightfoot," Coach Buck growled at his openly gay punter. None of the team cared so long as he did his job and left them alone. All kickers were weird in one way or another anyhow.

"I'll have you know I'm in a committed relationship," Brian replied.

Tom leaned his red head across Buck. "Mama Nell would say just don't get hurt, Uncle Brian." Not that Brian actually was his uncle, but in the extended

Billodeaux family honorary relatives just seemed to accumulate. Lightfoot had been his stepfather's friend forever.

Coach Buck slammed his clipboard on his knees. "Could we get our heads back in the game? Lindstrom, you ready?" The black helmet bobbed. The coach gave the long snapper the signal. The football sailed through his legs and landed with a thwack into big hands that turned the laces outward. Taking two steps, the punter's left instep met the dropped ball firmly but not too hard and lofted it into the air.

Brian Lightfoot started his stopwatch. The football landed forty-two yards away, bounced twice and came to rest. "Hang time in the air four point two seconds. Classic."

"Could be a lucky kick," Tom said, unwilling to offer a compliment to a soccer player who hadn't paid his dues, even though he'd spent his own grade school years playing that game since Mama Nell wouldn't let her boys on a real football field before middle school.

"Let's see another one, Lindstrom," Coach bellowed. "Can you do any better?" The helmet bobbed. "Bolivar, give the kid a better snap this time, huh?"

The ball soared fifty yards before coming in for a landing. Brian checked the hang time. "Five seconds. Call me impressed."

"Jesus Gawd, a left-footed punter and a good one. I always wanted me one of those. Belichick works with 'em, and I can see the advantage—that reverse spin is bound to mess with the return team." Both men stared at their coach. Rare to see dour Marty Buck elated about anything. Mostly, he excelled at chewing players to bits for their screw-ups.

Tom felt he needed to point out a well-known fact. "Belichick says it's just a coincidence he has left-footed punters."

"My left nut! He'd do anything to mess with the other team. A left-footed punt is like water going down a toilet backwards in Australia. It confuses people. Now I got me one."

"I'd like to see one more punt," Tom said.

"You're a tough sell, Tommy, but why not? I'm lovin' this. Lindstrom, one more time." Coach signaled the long snapper again.

Another punt flew down the field clear to the five-yard line before coming to rest and bumping out of bounds. The special teams coach out on the field galumphed over despite his excessive bulk and delivered such a mighty slap of congratulations to Lindstrom's back that it pushed the kid forward a little. Brian Lightfoot fanned his handsome face. "Omigod! A perfect coffin corner punt. I've only done that twice in my entire career. If I weren't in love already, I'd be falling for the guy right this minute."

Coach Buck snorted. "No, you wouldn't. Lindstrom, come over here."

The new kid approached with the special teams coach trailing right behind with his wild gray hair flying and a big, shit-eating grin on his face. "I think we have ourselves a new punter," he announced before the two came to a full stop before Marty Buck.

"I'd agree," said Brian Lightfoot.

"You, too, Billodeaux?" Coach Buck elbowed his kicker.

"Yeah, I guess so."

Tom might only be a placekicker, but fans chanted his nickname when he came out on the field—Tommy the Toe, Tommy the Toe. He wondered what they'd call a phenom like the Lindstrom kid. He'd have to work closely with the punter. The guy would hold the ball for him. If he didn't already room with his brother, Dean Billodeaux the quarterback, on the road, they'd share accommodations. While the game went on, the two of them would be keeping their legs warm together apart from the other players. He swallowed his little spate of jealousy, stood, and offered a hand. "Welcome to the Sinners, Lindstrom. Exceptional work out there."

The answering grip was light and the palm a little soft and damp. Tom swore the nails were coated with a clear polish. Brian would approve, as he'd never been able to drag Tom in for a manicure. Maybe those long, tanned legs were waxed, but they could do the job.

The voice that issued from the depths of the helmet came out soft and low. "Thank you. That's a great compliment coming from Tommy the Toe. *Morfar* will be so pleased."

"*Morfar*?"

"That's Swedish for grandfather on my mother's side." Lindstrom unlatched the black helmet and revealed a face possessing strong, high cheekbones, a straight, slim nose, nearly white brows, wide lips coated with a pink gloss, and eyes as clear and blue as the sky over the fjords in high summer. All of this was framed by straight light blonde hair, blunt cut at the shoulders and wispy bangs hanging sweat-soaked across her heat-flushed forehead. "But please, call me Alix since we might be working closely together."

Coach Buck cackled. "I got y'all, each and every

one of you. This is Ancient Andy's granddaughter. I wanted her to have a fair shake."

Brian did his usual gallant shtick. "*Enchanté, mademoiselle*. A magnificent performance." Brian Lightfoot, his luminous dark eyes gleaming, bowed and kissed her somewhat large but feminine hand. The punter put her other hand to her cheek and blushed.

One thought ran through Tom Billodeaux's head as he stood aside watching. If Brian hadn't fallen in love with Alix Lindstrom at first sight, he surely had.

Chapter Two

"As far as I'm concerned you got the job, but we have to run it by the higher-ups," Coach Buck told the young woman. Coach pointed a certain finger skyward, whether indicating his opinion of the administration or thanking God for a left-footed punter was difficult for Tom to tell. "We'll be in touch. You can get out of here now."

"I'm done, too. I'll walk you back to the locker room and keep watch in case you want to shower," Tom offered with all the eagerness of a puppy with a new toy.

Alix Lindstrom shook her head. "Thank you, but I changed in the ladies' room and left my clothes there."

"We have a ladies' room?"

"Sure, for when the reporters come to watch practice or a scrimmage. Some of them got tits, you know. Surprised you haven't noticed, Billodeaux." Coach Buck barked out a laugh that caused his placekicker to go red in the face and curse his fair and freckled complexion.

"I noticed. I mean I'm not like Brian. Not that there is anything wrong with Brian. He selected the flowers for my brother's wedding." The more Tom babbled the deeper the crimson grew on his cheeks.

Alix helped him out a little by cutting him off. "Yes, I know that. The pictures in *Bride* and posted by

*The Knot* were so gorgeous. They really did have a fairy tale wedding."

His fear that his perfect woman might be a lesbian vanished. He doubted they pored over wedding magazines, but with same-sex marriage becoming prevalent, maybe they did. What did he know about it?

"I was in that wedding." Could he have been any smoother? Why didn't he just say, "Did you see me, huh, huh?"

"I noticed. You were the only redhead in the bridal party."

"Among the twelve kids in our family, I always stick out like a thumb hit by a hammer.

"I know."

Whether Alix knew how many children were in the Billodeaux family or was agreeing that he resembled a sore thumb, he couldn't tell. How to make his next move and not sound like a complete idiot? Coach Buck took care of that for him.

"You two get out of here. You're blocking my view of the field. Pick up your feet if you want a place on my team, you lazy bums!" he shouted to all the rookies and walk-ons in general. Action out on the grass became frenetic. "Take Lindstrom out to dinner, Tom. Show her the town. Talk up the team before she signs with someone else."

"Oh, I wouldn't do that. *Morfar…*"

Tom shook his head. "Show me the way to the ladies' room. I'll wait outside while you change. We can get that dinner someplace nice downtown." He grasped her elbow and escorted Alix away from the training field and all the ogling guys on it. She took the lead in showing the way to the ladies' room. Alix didn't linger primping, but appeared only minutes later with her makeup-free face washed and shining and her body clothed in an oversized and much worn Sinners jersey bearing a number one that nearly covered her shorts. The laces of her kicking shoes hung out of the side of a gym bag, that footwear having been replaced by a pair of flip-flops.

"Sorry, no shower in there. I have to get back to my room and do a better job of cleaning up if we're going out somewhere. I left my pads in the ladies' room. Is that okay?"

Tom suppressed a wince at the mention of pads in a ladies' room. The guys could craft some pretty crude jokes out of that. "Bring them out for me, and I'll see they get back. Where are you staying? I'll meet you there in an hour."

"I'm at the La Quinta on Veteran's Boulevard. Could we make that two hours and meet in the lobby? I really have to take a bath and wash my hair. I smell awful." She glanced at her pink-painted toenails.

Tom wrinkled his pug nose and took a deep sniff. "Nope, you smell better than any guy on that field even without the shower." He coaxed a smile out of her as wide as one of Julia Roberts. "But sure. Get the pads. I'll meet you there."

Alix delivered the bundle of equipment into his arms and set out for the parking lot with a wave. Tom trudged back to the locker room burdened with her gear. As he passed the field some card, probably Barton "Beef" Bolivar from special teams who was working with the rookies as center now that he had finished snapping, chanted, "Tommy's got a girlfriend, Tommy's got a girlfriend. He's carrying her pads."

The heat of a blush crept up the back of his neck, but he turned and answered. "Tommy's got a date and you don't, loser." Satisfied, he moved along. He'd carry Alix Lindstrom's pads any day. Heck, he'd even go into a drugstore and buy her some.

\*\*\*\*

Tom Billodeaux took extra care with his appearance. He realized he had a penchant for loud clothes that went with his trickster personality, but for the sake of Alix Lindstrom toned it down all he could tonight. Straightening his silk tie of silver and black stripes in the mirror, he doubled checked his pale gray summer suit with the black square in the pocket matching his shirt and hoped he didn't look too mafia. He'd shaved close and done the walk through a mist of masculine cologne as Uncle Brian had taught all the boys in the Billodeaux family. "Do not overwhelm, a typical adolescent mistake," Lightfoot coached. Nothing Tom could do about his flaming red hair and freckles unless he went girly and used dye or makeup, but that would be going too far. At least, he'd had a recent haircut and subdued his wild curls.

Which car to take? The old truck shared with his brother Dean as a teen, the big SUV, or Dean's dream car, the black Mustang convertible, left in his care while the newlyweds took that long delayed trip to Germany. Not the truck, and much as he wanted to, not the Mustang. Driving that would bring up Dean, and he'd have to confess he didn't own it. He could only be thankful his alluring quarterback of a brother was out of the country. If Alix fell all over Dean like most women, Tom wouldn't have a chance with her. You'd think marriage might end all that, but women still came on to

Dean—but not when his wife, Stacy, stood anywhere in the vicinity. She could ice all of New Orleans in August with a glance.

He grabbed the keys to the red SUV with the little Sinners devil on its rear and headed for the interstate, taking the exit for Veteran's Boulevard. Definitely overdressed for the budget motel lobby, he sat near the cereal dispensers for the free breakfast and waited for his dream woman to appear. Alix Lindstrom came through the door precisely on time, not making a man wait. Tom liked that.

He also liked what he saw. Her pale straight hair gleamed and rested on shoulders that might be a little broad for a woman but would seem frail compared to those in the Sinners' locker room. She'd darkened her light brows and lashes and outlined those big, blue eyes, making them even more striking. Her lipstick was a bold ripe peach color. She wore a sundress that tied around the neck. Its tangerine and blue swirled skirt ended just above the knees, and that still left plenty of her bare legs showing. Because her feet were encased in plain white flats, Tom figured Alix might be a trifle self-conscious about her height, but he still had a couple of inches on her. Not gorgeous like Stacy or model-perfect like Ilsa, the woman who had dumped him for Dean, Alix Lindstrom suited him just fine.

Alix greeted Tom with that wide smile, then a slight frown as she took in his attire. "Are we going somewhere formal? Friends told me Louisiana would be pretty warm this time of year, and I didn't bring much besides shorts and tees and this dress. I thought it would be okay for walking on Bourbon Street if we end up there."

"You look okay for anywhere, and we are dining on Bourbon Street at Galatoire's, one of the grand old New Orleans restaurants. They used to require coats and ties but have gotten it down to jackets now. Still, it is a dressy place, but you're fine. We have reservations. Shall we go?" He offered his arm, and she latched onto it lightly. Tom figured he was the envy of a group of German tourists raiding the fruit bowl on the counter. At the SUV, she didn't need any help getting in, but he gave her a hand anyhow. Manly Manners 101 as taught by his short Mama Nell who really couldn't get into an SUV or large truck without help.

He maneuvered the interstate again, got off on Poydras to point out the Dome where the Sinners played, and parked in the garage across from his condo. "Parking is hard to find here, but it's only a few blocks."

They braved broad Canal Street with its four lanes and streetcar tracks and penetrated a couple of blocks down Bourbon Street where they were seated immediately at a prime table by the window, supposedly the same spot Tennessee Williams used to dine. Tom had requested it; Sinners in the window, especially any named Billodeaux, were always good for business—not that Galatoire's wasn't always packed and noisy. The tuxedoed waiter appeared immediately with menus.

As they perused their choices, Tom mentioned their historic table. Alix replied, "*A Streetcar Named Desire*, right?"

"Yes, desire." He should have kept the heat out of his voice and lowered his eyes faster because he made her blush again. Alix hid her blue eyes behind the large menu. Tom rushed to a neutral subject. "We should have appetizers. Let's see, they have sweetbreads and escargot, that's brains and snails. The Oysters Rockefeller is really good."

Alix surprised Tom by wrinkling a nose so straight he was amazed it could scrunch up like that. "No thanks on those."

"Then, have the Galatoire's Goute. That's shrimp and lump crabmeat in sauces. I'll get the Oysters Rockefeller, and you can try one." Tom ordered a bottle of champagne as well, and it arrived icy cold at the table where the sommelier made a ceremony of opening the bottle and not spilling a drop. They decided on entrees of blackened redfish for him and pompano topped with crab, artichoke hearts, and mushrooms for her.

"Do you treat all the walk-ons this way?" she asked.

"Only the best punters. Coach told me to take you out, and believe me, you never disobey Marty Buck." Tom picked up the small loaf of French bread and twisted it in half scattering bits of crust across the table.

Alix dug into her portion. "So good."

She ate like an athlete with gusto, not a girl who always watched her diet, and he found that appealing, too.

As she devoured her shrimp and crab dish, she said between bites, "We don't have seafood like this in Wisconsin."

"Few places do. If you sign with the Sinners, you can eat it every night."

"What do you mean if? Who else would take me? I know *Morfar* called Coach Buck to get me a tryout."

Tom offered her an oyster on the end of his cocktail fork, and she tried it without hesitation, cupping her hand under it to prevent the green sauce from falling on her dress. "Delicious, but I don't think I want to try them raw."

"You will if you stay here. Coach really wants you on the team, and he has lots of pull. One thing you need to be careful of though. The guys upstairs are going to try to lowball you on the salary. They'll start around $250,000."

Her blue eyes widened. "That much?"

"For a punter like you that's an insult. Do you have an agent?"

"No, but *Morfar* probably knows some."

"Use mine. He manages Dean, too. He can get you a million, maybe more." Tom fished out the card he'd placed his pocket before leaving the condo. "I'll put in a word for you."

"Thanks. You really think I'm that good?" Alix deposited the card in a purse so small Tom wondered why women bothered to carry them. She had that in common with all girls.

"You are so good I'm almost jealous, but we'll work together and be together a lot."

She flushed a little. "I'll like that, but I've only had a year of practice. You see, I wanted to be on the next Olympic women's soccer team and didn't make the cut. I had Mia Hamm's picture on my wall since childhood. You know the one of her stripping off her jersey at the 2004 Olympics."

"Me, too, but probably not for the same reason," Tom said. "Awesome black sports bra."

"Yes, that's the color I always wear as a tribute to

her."

How he'd like to see her in that bra, any bra. She wasn't big busted, but seemed just right for her height and athleticism. Big boobs only got in the way in most sports. Tom kept that thought to himself as well.

"I hoped to get the chance do the same gesture, but that won't happen now. My main strength in soccer was in long, high kicks down field, but I'm not so great at scoring," she admitted as the waiter removed her empty plate. "I was in the dumps so badly at failing to make the team that *Morfar* put me in his training camp for kickers for an entire year. He only takes three students at a time at $3000 a head, so it cost him to instruct me in punting. He said the Sinners already had a great kicker, but he'd gotten wind of Brian Lightfoot's retirement. He thought I'd be safer, too."

"As a punter you won't have to worry about scoring, and you'll be making history as the first female NFL player." Tom didn't add he hoped to score and make his own kind of history with Alix Lindstrom. Dinner arrived within minutes, taking his mind off the randy thoughts.

Alix's pompano stared up with a dull dead eye through its coating of sauce and crab meat. Its crispy tail overhung the plate. "Do you want me to ask the waiter to take off the head and the tail?" Tom asked.

"Oh, no. I go fishing with my dad all the time, even out on the ice in winter. Trout is best served like this. The bones add flavor."

For the first time, he caught a whiff of a Wisconsin or maybe Swedish accent in the way she drew out that oh-no, but Alix proved not to be a squeamish babe. "You like fishing?"

"Sure."

"My father isn't too into it, but Connor Riley used to take us out in the Gulf on his boat."

"Imagine going saltwater fishing with two football greats. I've never been on the ocean before, the Great Lakes, yes, but not an ocean."

"It's a big boat. Those lakes, they are pretty great, huh?" After making a remark as idiotic as that Tom concentrated on his blackened redfish.

"Yes, we could trade fishing trips."

Good, she didn't seem to mind his inane conversation. "Here, try some of my redfish." He forked over a small portion.

"Oh, spicy!" Alix fanned her lips and took a large swallow of champagne. She wrinkled her nose again as the bubbles tickled, and she laughed. "Food up north is sort of bland."

"If you stay here, you'll get used to the flavors and come to love it red hot." Like me, he implied.

She took no notice that he could see, but said, "I'm sure I will."

They worked through most of their fish and shared sides of cauliflower au gratin and potato soufflé, but needed boxes for leftovers. Still, Tom insisted they share a portion of bread pudding.

"Doesn't sound all that great," Alix said. "And I'm very full."

"Once you've had it with praline sauce and vanilla ice cream, you won't ever forget it."

They managed to devour a portion between them. "I really need to walk that off," Alix claimed. "Can we stroll down Bourbon Street now?"

"Oh, we don't stroll here. We strut! But first, let's

take the leftovers to my place so they won't spoil. My condo is just across from the parking garage."

"Yes, it would be a shame to waste food like that."

They made the trek back across Canal as night set in, and people came out to enjoy the lessening heat of the day. Alix seemed impressed by his apartment and its location so near the French Quarter.

"Yeah, it's fairly big for one person. Dean and I shared it before he got married. Now it's all mine. I've been thinking of taking on a roommate. That person would have their own wing with two bedrooms. Dean turned his second bedroom into a game room, but that spare room would make a nice office or sitting room for someone. They'd have plenty of privacy with this big living room and the kitchen between us. Wall-mounted big screen TV, gas fireplace beneath. We don't really need a fireplace down here, but it adds ambience." Realizing he sounded like a realtor, he shut his mouth.

"Oh, we need them in Wisconsin in case the snowstorms take out the electrical wires. I love a nice fire in the evening."

"Top-notch appliances, too," Tom babbled as he put their takeout boxes in the fridge on top of several others. "You want coffee? I have this pod machine thing."

"No, thanks, but I'd love to cook in here. I bet you think a girl jock can't get a meal on the table."

Tom really didn't care if she could or not. He wanted to do all his cooking in the bedroom, so very nearby. "I'd eat anything you cared to make."

"Really, I'm a very good cook. Mom insisted. She said even the boy in the family needed to know how to make Swedish meatballs."

"Boy?" Could she be transgender? They weren't that uncommon in New Orleans, but Wisconsin?

Alix cuffed him lightly on the arm. "It's a family joke. Poor *Morfar* had only one child, a daughter, my mother Britta. She married Nels Lindstrom and gave birth to three more girls. When she was pregnant with me, she told both men this was the last and it better be a boy. I came into the world at a strapping nine pounds and looked so much like my grandfather it became a standing joke. So, I went hunting and fishing. I played soccer, basketball, and Little League baseball on a boys' team. I wore flannel and sports uniforms while my more petite, girly sisters dressed in ruffles and lace and took piano lessons. I guess I'm not very feminine because of that."

"Alix Lindstrom, there is absolutely nothing wrong with you." Tom wanted so badly to cup her face with his hands and swoop in for a kiss. Heck, their heights matched so well, he'd hardly have to bend his head.

"I appreciate that, but I must tell you I went to my prom with the girls' soccer team, not a date."

"Those high school guys didn't know what they were missing."

A pretty ordinary compliment, but she studied her flat-heeled shoes, blushed, and he loved it. After he'd been taken in and discarded by the sophisticated and conniving Ilsa, his sister's roommate, Alix seemed as fresh and pure as the land of sky blue waters. No, that was Minnesota. What did they call Wisconsin? The Cheese State? Oh yeah, the Badger State. Neither was too flattering.

"College was better," she said.

"For all of us. Believe me high school girls weren't

keen on red hair and freckles. Where did you go?"

"University of Wisconsin-Madison. I had a soccer scholarship and played some other sports for them."

"So a Lady Badger?"

"Just a Badger. They got rid of sexist terms years ago."

"Not here. Just warning you. You ready to strut Bourbon Street?" He half hoped she'd say, "No, let's stay in and light a fire."

"I can't wait!"

"Just a minute." In the face of that enthusiasm, Tom went to his bedroom, shed his jacket and tie, opened his collar, and rolled up his sleeves. No sense sweating any more than you had to on Bourbon Street or setting himself up for muggers by being too well dressed.

They descended into the bawdiest strip of the French Quarter where tourists roamed, college students newly released from classes raved, and hardcore drinkers staggered from bar to bar. Barkers beckoned passersby into strip clubs and drag shows. Good jazz clubs and superb restaurants abounded. One man with a large snake draped about his neck asked Alix if she'd like to stroke his python.

"Why not?" She relieved him of the reptile without any help and handed Tom her phone to take a picture. He obliged and shoved a few dollars at the snake handler, though he hadn't liked his tone.

They marched on dodging living statues of many varieties from tin men to cowboys and an excess of sidewalk tap dancers. At a souvenir shop, Tom ducked inside and returned with a fringed parasol striped in purple, green and gold—the colors of Mardi Gras. He opened it and demonstrated his strut for Alix by wiggling his skinny ass and taking grotesquely long strides while pumping the umbrella up and down. She laughed with her head thrown back and snapped another picture.

"You try it." He handed over the parasol. "Work those hips, lift those legs, stick out that chest!"

"I don't have much of a chest."

"What you have is great, and there isn't a person on this street who can beat your legs." She did her best to his applause and a few lewd comments from some drunken frat boys Tom really wanted to pop. He steered Alix away and into one of the better bars.

"You could probably use something to drink by now."

"After all that champagne, I doubt it, but it's still very warm outside. How about a martini?"

"Shaken, not stirred, right?" he said in his best James Bond accent. The bartender rolled his eyes, but Alix giggled as good as any girl.

The drinks arrived with a scrim of ice on the top and a plastic pick shaped like a sword impaling two olives immersed in the glass.

"Not bad," Tom said. "But I think the best part is the olives."

"Me, too. I've never had a martini before and wanted to try one. Really, I usually drink beer. Wisconsin has great beer—and cheese curds to go with it. Pretzels, too."

"And it has you. That's lots to be proud of."

Alix cocked her head at him. "I can't figure out if you are recruiting me or flirting."

"Maybe both. Ever seen a drag show?"

Alix shook her head.

"Then you're in for a treat." He paid for their drinks and escorted her to the best spot he knew for that kind of entertainment, Les Femmes Fatales. They settled at a table close to the stage, ordered beer for their two-drink minimum, but being a classy joint, it came in frosted glass mugs. A Cher impersonator took the stage and did a set followed by the lovely Diana Ross. The last to perform swayed into the spotlight wearing a long lavender gown studded with crystals that made it glitter with every movement, though the bodice rode low on two spectacular breasts. The long, blonde curls of an impressive wig draped over them. Following the theme, she had coated her lips with in shining lavender and wore contacts that made her eyes appear almost purple. Stalking the platform in killer stiletto heels and unafraid to show some leg with a slit up the front of her dress, she launched into a steamy song about jungle fever and repressed missionaries.

"Dolly Parton?" Alix guessed. "Though I don't think she'd do a song like that."

"Nope, Layla Devlin."

"Never heard of her."

"Hollywood is a cruel place. That song is from one of her movies. My dad did a cameo in one of her films, and she got a little obsessed with him. Mom warned her off, and she transferred to our previous quarterback. Nearly killed both my mother and his fiancée around eight years ago. She ended up in an asylum and never did another motion picture."

"Kind of sad. Now that you mention it I remember some of that from my movie magazines. I just forgot her name."

"Not really sad when you think of it from the Billodeaux point of view. I don't know where she is now, but I'll bet my dad keeps track."

The steamy ditty came to an end. Speaking in a low and husky voice, the chanteuse breathed into the mic. "Good evening, I'm Lilah Devine, and this is my tribute to the magnificent Layla Devlin wherever she is tonight. Lilah has not forgotten you, baby. But the two of you up front—naughty, naughty for speaking while I perform." She shook a rather masculine finger tipped with a long, lilac nail and bearing an enormous amethyst ring at them. "My first piece was the Academy Award nominated song from Miss Devlin's film, *Masai!*. Layla had great range in her acting ability. The next is the love theme from her western, *Savaged!,* in which she starred with New Orleans' own Joe Billodeaux." She waited until the smattering of applause died down before beginning a ballad of hopeless love.

Since both of them blushed at being scolded, Tom and Alix stayed silent for the rest of the performance. Lilah left the stage blowing kisses and paused near the wings to throw one two-handed into the ether. "For my beloved Layla."

They left soon after that uncomfortable event. Tom told Alix the rest of the story as they strode along the blocked off street that had become considerably boozier in atmosphere during their absence. "That guy was as obsessed with Layla as she was with football players. Supposedly, he provided her with the gun she used to assault the other women, but he swore up and down he'd given it to her to protect herself. Anyhow, no charges were pressed against him. In him, Layla at her best lives on."

"Even sadder." Alix studied her feet as they walked along side by side almost, but not quite, touching.

"Hey, New Orleans isn't a place to be sad. Want to go hear some really good music at Mariah's Place?

"I've heard of it—where all the Sinners players hang out. Don't think I'm ready for that yet." She checked her watch. "I have to be at the airport at six a.m. and should get some sleep. This has been a wonderful evening. I'm sold on the city. Just one more thing." Alix curved an arm around Tom's waist and pulled him close. She snapped a selfie of them together. "I need evidence because no one back home will believe I spent the night with Tommy the Toe. I mean went out with Tom Billodeaux." Her blush probably showed up on the second insurance shot.

"We'll do it again after you sign with the Sinners." He led the way back to Canal Street. "Say, you remember what I said about needing a roommate? You could stay with me for free since I own the place." Okay, it was his turn to flush when he recalled that Stacy said if you paid a woman's rent she was your mistress.

Evidently, Alix felt the same way. Her fine, fair hair flew as she shook her head hard. "I couldn't do that. What would *Morfar* and Dad say?"

"What do you pay for rent in Madison?"

"Four hundred a month when I lived there with a roommate. I'm staying with my family until I get a job."

"Believe me, you have a job. You can pay me that much if it would make you feel better." Four hundred— you couldn't get a closet for that in New Orleans let alone part of a luxury condo, but she didn't have to know. "I wouldn't intrude on your privacy. You could cook. I can eat. See, it might work."

She smiled at last. "I'll think about it if the deal goes through."

"It will. Say, you need to come up and get your food. I'll show you those two rooms and the bath."

"You keep my portion. I can't take food on the plane. If there is a next time, you can show me the rooms then."

Reluctantly, he steered her into the parking garage, keeping an eye out for the bag lady who sometimes lurked there and might put Alix off coming to New Orleans. Tom helped her into the SUV for the return trip to the motel. He walked her to her door and lounged against the wall wishing for an invitation to come inside—which he didn't get.

"I do hope I see you again, Tom."

He shot a finger at her. "You'll be at mini-camp in June. Mark my words. Your parasol. You'll need it for Mardi Gras." He turned over the gaudy little umbrella.

"Thanks for everything." Alix leaned forward a little, then seemed to think the better of bestowing a kiss and slipped inside her room.

Tom lingered while she turned the lock with a snick and rattled the door chain into position. Looked like the evening had definitely ended. No matter, he'd see her in May for sure.

****

Alix leaned her back against the motel door. She wondered if Tom still stood outside wanting to come in. The thought had flashed through her mind, but no. If she jumped into bed with a Sinner, some people would

25

assume she'd gotten the punting position by sleeping with the kicker. She released a deep sigh of regret. This whole thing would not be easy, and she so did not want to disappoint *Morfar*, not in his condition. He'd gotten the first call after she returned to the motel and been his usual subdued self. "*Ja*, sure, you'll get the job. You are my best student." Beneath that, she'd sensed his excitement. At home, her mother shrieked and her sisters squealed. Her dad delivered an austere, "Nice work." That was as good as it got in Wisconsin.

She hoped she hadn't spilled too much to Tom Billodeaux. Oh, she knew all about him and his family—more than she let on. Right next to her Mia Hamm poster, she'd hung one of Tommy the Toe taken after a sixty-one yard field goal that saved the game. He hadn't made the cover of the sports magazine, but his personality shone through from his wide grin to his tousled red curls, worn long and wild at the time. Though proud of his accomplishment, he'd stated modestly that he was happy to help the team get the win. So cute, very nice and supportive, just as she'd imagined. And interested in big, clunky her, if she wasn't mistaken.

Alix kicked off her flats and did a happy dance with her big feet on her way to a second shower. She'd be able to wear two-inch heels on a date with Tom and believed he wouldn't care if she went even higher! Please, please, please, let him be right about the Sinners taking her on as a punter.

Chapter Three

Exactly as Tom figured, Alix Lindstrom got her contract. His agent did squeeze an even million annually out of management for three years. In his opinion she was worth more. Acton "Action" Jackson, the hyperactive head of PR for the Sinners, all but did cartwheels across his office in ecstasy over the promotional possibilities, not that the Sinners' home games weren't always sold out anyhow. The man had a slate of interviews set up for Alix that began with her public signing and donning of a Sinners jersey bearing the number one in honor of her grandfather and extended all the way to the start of the season. She'd come back to town for the first event along with her parents and Ancient Andy, all of them put up at the Marriott so close to his place he could see it from his bedroom window.

If a kicker could kick himself, Tom would have done so for not getting her cell phone number during their evening out. He'd held the thing in his hands when he took her picture with the python and never keyed in his own. What's more, he could barely get near her for all the hoorah over the first female punter in the NFL, the first woman to play as well. Asked how he felt about this development by numerous reporters, he replied that Alix Lindstrom had great potential, and no, he didn't think her sex would be an issue for anyone on

27

the Sinners team. He might have lied a little about that last one because a few of the guys mumbled under their breath about the sanctity of the locker room, bad enough that female sports correspondents had to be accommodated, and how football in general should be a male preserve.

Others, he suspected, were getting ready to make their move on the attractive new punter. With that thought in mind, Tom crossed the street and tried to contact her first by having the desk ring her room. A gruff male voice, definitely not Alix, answered, "*Ja,* who is there?"

Judging by the heavy Swedish accent hardly diminished over the years, he was speaking to the iconic kicker, Anders "Andy" Mortenson. Tom's throat dried up a little. "Um, Tom Billodeaux. I'm trying to reach Alix. I'm down at the front desk."

"She is out shopping for summer clothes with her mother."

"Oh well, tell her I called to see how she's doing." Tom prepared to hang up but the voice on the other end boomed, "Wait, you will wait a minute. I will come down with her father, and we will have a cold beer in the lounge. When Alix returned to Wisconsin, all we heard was about Tom Billodeaux, nothing else. Time we meet in person."

"I think we did once when I was very little—before I knew I wanted to be a kicker."

"*Ja, ja,* Joe's redheaded boy. We are on our way."

Left without a choice, Tom went toward a bank of elevators hoping he'd chosen the right set. His hair would help them pick him out anywhere in the lobby as strongly as if he wore a rose tucked behind his ear.

When the two men emerged, he had no doubt they were Alix's kin. The younger of the two, a robust man of around fifty, had her height and a full head of white hair. Thick white brows sat above piercing blue eyes. He had the tanned, leathery hide of an outdoorsman and shoulders as broad as a bull elk. Nels Lindstrom offered Tom a hardy handshake, but not a smile.

Ancient Andy Mortenson, who had kicked for the Sinners until the age of forty-two, no longer resembled the man whose video clips Tom had studied. The thick head of blond hair had been replaced by a shining bald head and a face lacking eyebrows. Diminishing his height, he stooped forward, and his legs were uncertain enough to require the use of a thick cane that more resembled a cudgel. Still, in the broad cheekbones, wide mouth, and straight nose, Tom saw some of Alix. Andy also shook his hand, but more lightly and with a slight tremor. Even Tom's, "It's an honor to meet you, sir," didn't cause those Alix-like lips to break into a grin.

Andy Mortenson answered with, "Let's have that beer."

They moved to the dark and quiet of the lounge in the late afternoon far from the heat and traffic noises off the street that pushed inside every time the main doors opened. Under the glow of red-shaded lights, the men took seats at the bar with Tom pressed between Alix's menfolk like a sardine in a thick sandwich. Both frowned when the bar had no Blatz beer available, but they settled for Milwaukee's Best in a bottle. Tom ordered the same, exerting beer diplomacy. Each took a few sips in silence.

Tom restrained his usual urge to run off at the

mouth or say something glib. He waited. Finally, Andy spoke. "You're a real good kicker. You probably make real good money, more than I ever did."

"Thank you. That's a great compliment. As for the money, a good agent and inflation probably accounts for my income."

Nels Lindstrom elbowed Tom in the side in a not unfriendly way. "You set up my girl with a top-notch agent. He got her a good deal. We appreciate that, don't we, *Pappa* Andy?"

Andy nodded and the red lights of the bar traveled across his bald head. "As her fellow kicker, we expect you to keep looking out for her."

"I plan to do that."

"Good. Now about this room you offered her in your apartment." Alix's father helped himself to a large handful of peanuts from a small dish on the bar and did some seriously intimidating crunching.

"Just trying to help her get settled in the city, sir. I mean she'd have her own suite—bedroom, bath, spare room and use of the kitchen and living room. We'd have the floor to ourselves, and the building has great security." Tom wet his mouth again with the beer.

Andy nodded his approval. "*Ja,* we think it is a good deal for Alix so long as those rooms lock. Alix is an innocent girl come to a big city, never lived anywhere larger than Madison. New Orleans can be a wild and dangerous place, I remember." Still, a faint smile passed over Mortenson's face as if not all the memories he had were bad. "We would expect you to watch out for her off the field, too."

"Like a sister," Nels Lindstrom added.

"Sure. I'd be happy to do that. I know how to look

out for girls. We have six in our family." Tom grinned, imagining his six-foot tall Valkyrie who could punt a football the length of the field and probably send a man's nuts clear up to his throat if he gave her any trouble as an innocent girl. "My place is just across the street. You want to inspect it?"

"*Ja*, sure. Her mama will want to see it, too. When they get back."

The men shared another beer in silence before returning to the lobby. With excellent timing, Alix and her mother, engulfed in enough shopping bags to open their own boutique on Royal Street, struggled up the steps to the echoing main floor. Their men hurried to relieve them of the load, and all rode up in the elevator to dispose of the burdens, including Tom who had somehow acquired a long, zipped bag over one arm and a pink striped Victoria's Secret sack that exuded a heady scent and promised even more than that. He glimpsed down hopefully at the contents but encountered only black tissue paper.

Mrs. Lindstrom relieved him of his parcels first by hanging up the long garment bag, then whisking away the lingerie. She held up the bag of dainties. "We drove all the way out to Metairie in that rental car for these because Alix noticed a shop on Veteran's Boulevard on her last trip here—as if we don't have such places in Wisconsin—not that I could ever get her to go inside one before. Nothing but sports bras and women's Jockey shorts for her in the past. I tell you, put wings on my baby's back and dress her in some of these bras and panties, she would look as good as any of those underwear models.

The sisters must resemble their mother whose head

was covered in short, golden curls, at her age probably thanks to a good dye job, and whose body, a trifle on the plump side, would fit neatly under her towering husband's arm. The friendly in the blue eyes, now Alix had that. She also had a deep blush on her cheeks.

"Mom!"

"Only telling the truth, my little tomboy." Mrs. Lindstrom reached up to ruffle her daughter's hair. "Always straight as a board, and she'd never let me perm it. Jeans and athletic shorts, tees, and flannel shirts in her closet. Cleats, running shoes, and flats on the floor. But today, we put a dent in that signing bonus with a whole new wardrobe. She doesn't believe me yet, but she will need those special occasion dresses. And in a city like this, we could find her size even in shoes! That is no small accomplishment."

Mr. Lindstrom and Ancient Andy had dumped their loads of clothing on a bed and subsided into two chairs on either side of a window that almost had a view of the Mississippi River. A tall black vase full of red roses sat on a table between them. It bore a gold ribbon reading, "Welcome to New Orleans, Alix." While Tom shifted from foot to foot amid the chaos, the other men waited silent as the north woods in winter for the feminine hustle and bustle to subside. Eventually, it did.

"We're going on over to Tom's place to check out those rooms, Britta. It's not far if you want to come along." Nels Lindstrom rose up and stretched, then helped Ancient Andy to his feet.

"Of course, I want to go along." His wife regarded the piles of bags still on the bed. "I don't know how we're going to get all this home."

"If you approve my place, Alix could leave the stuff there," Tom offered.

"Maybe." The mother reserved judgment. "Let's go see what you've got to offer."

Because of Andy's slow pace, they made it only to the neutral ground on Canal Street and had to wait for another change of the light, but eventually they got to the brownstone condos on the corner. Arturo, the doorman, smiled pleasantly at the herd of Wisconsonites traversing his lobby in Tom's company to the elevators, though he raised his eyebrows at one of his most interesting tenants. Undoubtedly, he recalled Ilsa, another tall blond, whom Tom had given free rein to come up to his place and lived to regret it.

Relieved that his cleaning lady had just been there in the morning and that he, thanks to his upbringing, was no slob, Tom watched Britta Lindstrom examine not just the suite of rooms offered to her daughter, but his as well. She seemed to pace off the distance between the two sets of rooms as if wondering if it would be sufficient to keep the two roommates comfortably apart. Alix trailed her, shutting doors behind them. Her face seemed to have turned a permanent shade of red. Tom still thought she looked beautiful.

After a cursory glance at the spare bedroom and bath, the men settled themselves on the brown velour couch in front of the large, wall-hung TV and gas fireplace and made themselves at home. "Built-in recliners, nice, eh *Pappa* Andy? Let me put your feet up." Nels provided that service for his father-in-law whom the walk across the street seemed to fatigue greatly. He began flicking through channels with the remote.

Meanwhile, his wife inspected the kitchen. "What I wouldn't give for a refrigerator this size! Though I do have a freezer for all that deer meat and fish the men bring home. Granite counters, very nice, and a dishwasher, but it is good to see someone washes out his own cereal bowl and coffee cup." She pointed at the strainer where Tom's early morning dishes dried on a rack. "Nothing sours living with a person more than being messy. I remember that girl you shared an apartment with your sophomore year, baby. She left a peach pit sit on the arm of the couch for a week and just piled dirty dishes and pans still half full of food in the sink expecting you to clean up after her. I don't think that will be a problem here."

"I do have a cleaning lady," Tom admitted.

He received a sharp glance from Britta Lindstrom. "Would you expect my daughter to pay half her wages, or do you think Alix will take over those duties?"

"Neither, ma'am. I've been paying Krayola all alone since Dean left. It's no problem."

Britta sighed. "Imagine having a cleaning lady. Not that they ever do as good a job as I would." She patted Tom's cheek. "Ma'am, I do love these southern manners. Nels, *Pappa*, have you spoken to Thomas about what we expect of him in the way of behavior?"

"*Ja*," came the reply from two throats.

"Good. We'll take the rooms. *Pappa*, you just wait here while we go get those new clothes. That walk-in closet is to die for, Alix. Then, maybe dinner. I'm thinking seafood."

She led the others from the apartment and loaded them up across the street. Arturo's eyebrows went up even higher when they returned laden with women's clothing bags. Tom stopped Alix from climbing aboard the elevator. With her arms still draped in shoe bags, he marched her over to the doorman.

"This is Alix Lindstrom. You might have heard of her, the Sinners new punter. She's going to be rooming with me for a while. Consider her my teammate just like Dean."

"Yes, sir. Whatever you say."

"That should take care of any nasty stories," Tom mumbled as they turned for the elevators again.

"There have been nasty stories?" Alix asked.

"All Dean's fault. Don't worry about it."

He treated them to a glorious seafood dinner and offered to drive them to the airport in the morning. Mrs. Lindstrom demurred. "No, no, you've done enough. A limousine service is coming for us, but we'll be back in two weeks with the rest of her things in time for that whatchacallit."

"Mini-camp, Mom," Alix replied, her voice strangled with embarrassment as it had been most of the evening.

"Yes." Britta held out her hand to Tom. "Now that I've met you, I know you will take care of our girl as if she were your own sister. Thank you in advance."

Her grip was quite firm for a small, older woman. Tom shook and wished dearly that he hadn't given his word to the entire Lindstrom family.

Chapter Four

The caravan hauling Alix Lindstrom's goods
arrived after a three-day drive from Madison. They
could have made it in two and a half, but turned in early
every night out of consideration for Andy's health
issues since he could not be discouraged from making
the journey. While Alix drove her stretch following her
father's truck which towed a small trailer, she kept
wishing she rode with the men instead of in her Ford
Escape containing her mother riding shotgun and her
two sisters, Rika and Tille, in the rear chattering away.
They could have flown down and spared her the agony
of their company.

But no, Mom called it their last road trip as a
family and equated it to the many times they had driven
Alix to various athletic events and stayed to watch the
games. Britta Lindstrom's eyes grew a little misty, and
Alix caved. Her mother immediately perked up and
began earmarking the stuff she should take along to her
new apartment. This included the slipper chair in Alix's
bedroom because men never thought to have a place to
sit down to put on their shoes, the high school desk
purchased especially to give her enough leg room, and
an entire box of Pyrex casserole dishes because Mom
noticed Tom didn't own any.

"The place is already furnished," she protested.
Secretly, Alix enjoyed the idea that she would be

sleeping in Tom's former bed since he'd moved into his brother's suite. Why change anything? She'd get her own place someday.

"But so very masculine and rather sparse. I am certain you don't want that hideous red and green plaid bedspread. Let's go to Bed Bath & Beyond and get something more feminine with sheets to match." And so they had.

They settled on a sky blue duvet embroidered in white with a matching dust ruffle and enough coordinated throw pillows to take up half the bed after Alix vetoed anything pink or flowered. Though her mother tut-tutted about the price of king-sized sheets, she bought two sets in white and pale blue and fresh bed pillows, too. "Curtains," her mother said. "We'll have to take down those red ones." Off they went to another department to select those and some dotted Swiss sheers that would let in the light but slightly obscure the view. The words "throw rugs" sent them in another direction. "We need them to bring the room together in case the carpeting doesn't match well."

The trailer preceding them carried more linens and kitchen goods than furnishings. As Alix drove past the exits for LSU in Baton Rouge, Tom's alma mater she recalled, she felt as if she were going off to college for the first time instead of joining the NFL. Once out of the city traffic they made better time passing through woodlands that crowded the road and eventually came to a vast cypress-studded lake that set her sisters to looking for alligators though they only saw egrets, blue herons, and gulls. Traffic clumped up again as they approached the airport exit and remained heavy into heart of the Big Easy.

Arturo welcomed them with a wide smile on his brown face. "Mr. Billodeaux's new roommate has arrived. I'll let him know. You can park in front of the building until you unload, then you'll have to move across to the parking garage. A space is provided for your car, but there will be a fee for the other."

"That sounds good to me," Alix said as the men, wasting no time, opened the trailer and handed sackloads of bedding to the women. Her father shoved the large plastic bag containing the duvet into her arms.

"No sense wasting a trip up," he remarked and gave her mother the two bed pillows. "*Pappa* Andy, you go with them and tell that young man to come down and help with the desk."

"If you need help…" Arturo began.

"Oh, no. You can see I brought my crew with me." Smiling tightly, Alix started for the elevator and crashed directly into Tom. It couldn't be called a chest bump, not with a huge folded duvet between them, but close enough. She seemed doomed to be flushed for the rest of her life.

Tom simply grinned. That smile, she'd seen it in photos and on film, puckish as if he plotted a practical joke. Now he directed it at her and asked, "May I take that?"

"I'm fine. It isn't heavy. You could help Dad with the desk."

"Didn't know you'd be bringing furniture, but hey, Dean and I moved four girls in and out of so many dorms and apartments we lost count. I have experience." He went to heave one end of the desk out of the trailer and showed more muscle than she would have figured his long, lean body possessed. The women stepped aside to let the furniture-bearers and Ancient Andy go first, angling the desk inside the elevator. Rika Lindstrom, the eldest daughter, squeezed in with the bag of sheets and a mattress cover just before the door closed. The others waited for the next car.

By the time they arrived, they found *Pappa* Andy ensconced in a recliner. Rika was already in the process of briskly stripping Tom's former bed of its plaid spread and red sheets. Having deposited the desk in the spare room, he stood bemused in the doorway of his old quarters. Rika winked at him. "You're cute, but this bedding is ugly."

"Now, Rika, young men think red sheets are sexy. Fold it all neatly. He can take it to the Goodwill or the Salvation Army." Mrs. Lindstrom stuffed the fresh bed pillows into pale blue cases and then into shams matching the new bedspread. Tille dropped her load of throw pillows on the floor next to her mother.

"Tom, you ready to bring up the chairs?" Nels Lindstrom asked.

"Ah, sure."

"Tille, come along and get some more bags since the others are making up the bed. No lagging," Nels ordered.

A second trip yielded up the slipper chair and the one that matched the desk plus sacks of what Tille called Alix's Uglies, her usual garb: flannel shirts, worn jeans, tees, snow and hiking boots. Her mother had packed a parka with fur around the hood she'd never need in Louisiana but might take on a trip to Antarctica someday. "Please put that stuff in the back of the closet. I'll get to it later," Alix begged as her sister began piling her sports bras and Jockey shorts into the top drawer of a large oak dresser. She thanked her recently very lucky stars that Tille hadn't chosen the second drawer where the Victoria's Secret purchases were stashed, still wrapped in black tissue.

Tille opened the walk-in closet, turned on the light and goggled at the array of new clothes hanging there. She chucked the black trash bags in her grip and began pawing through the largess. Seizing a gown from the bar, she held it up before her. "Can I borrow this? You hardly ever wear dresses."

If Tille got her hands on the item, a very chic black cocktail dress that would be the last Alix ever saw of it. She kind of liked the garment even if she doubted she'd ever wear it. Mom had picked the gown out claiming it showed off Alix's now-famous legs. "It won't fit you, Tille."

"Well, it might be a little too tight in the bodice since I've got more up top." Alix's sister glanced sidelong at Tom. "On me it would be a midi-dress, but I think it could work."

"Put that back, Tille. Alix paid for all her new clothes. Let her get a chance to enjoy them," her mother said.

"Go get the boxes," their father ordered.

"Set those down in the kitchen," Mrs. Lindstrom directed. "Nels, before you leave lift the mattress so we can get the dust ruffle on. See how it's all coming together with the light oak in this room?" The men nodded but declined to comment.

Tom stepped up after positioning the slipper chair by the window. "I'll take care of that." He heaved the large mattress off the box springs and leaned it against a wall.

"Strong." Tille gave him a coy look with her big, blue eyes.

Tom simply smiled and assumed a body builder pose. "Kickers have to stay in shape, too."

"I guess that's why Alix has all the muscle in the family. I could never move that mattress without help. Alix would be able to do it. She's great at heavy lifting. We're sisters, but we couldn't be more different." Tille held out her arms as if to display her petite body clad in short shorts and a pink stretchy tee covered in sparkles that molded to her full round breasts. She shook long, flaxen ringlets over her shoulders and stayed posed, waiting for Tom's comment.

He knew how to be a diplomat. "The Lindstrom girls are a bunch of beautiful women. They take after their mother."

Mrs. Lindstrom shot him a pleased look. The older sister, the one with a wedding ring on her finger and a little extra baby weight around hips covered in yoga pants, smiled at the compliment and swished her high, curly blonde ponytail with pleasure. "I had a baby girl six months ago, but I'm almost back to my original size three."

Andy Mortenson, having escaped the recliner on his own, leaned in the doorway. "*Ja*, all we get is girls in this family."

"You know you love her, *Morfar*," Rika said.

"I do. Named Isabel after my dead wife. All of them little curly heads except my Alix."

"*Pappa*, you should be resting. Would you like orange juice? I'm sure Tom has some," Britta Lindstrom fussed.

"Beer?"

"Not with your meds. Please sit down. Everyone else haul."

Haul they did, until the granite kitchen counters were covered with boxes, the fluffy white throw rugs had been unfurled in Alix's bedroom, the bed drowned in throw pillows. Tom had helped take down the drapery rods to hang the sheers and new curtains. "See how nice this looks. You can sit here in your slipper chair and look out on the world, but you should have a little table right here, too, for your coffee and magazines. That's what I would do," Mrs. Lindstrom said.

"Mom, the view is of the parking garage," Alix countered. "I won't have that much time to sit around."

"More than you'd think. We don't have practice every day. Um, looks nice—like I never lived here at all." Tom fingered a ruffle on a cushion. "Lots of pillows."

Mrs. Lindstrom explained, "This one has arms for sitting up in bed. This is a bolster for putting under your neck. The rest are just for pretty or to prop up your head when you have a cold. Well, let's get that kitchenware unpacked, then we'll be done. Plenty of empty cupboard space as I recall."

Ruthlessly rearranging the shelves, Britta had the mixing bowls and bundt pans, the casserole dishes, a good set of cookware, and canned goods containing Wisconsin delicacies put away in no time. She paused at the very end to ask Alix whether she wanted the *ebelskiver* pan and rosette irons up or down low.

"Low, I guess. Really, I don't see myself doing much baking."

"I don't know. Those skiver things sound pretty

delicious." Tom's lips quirked into a smile.

"She should make them for breakfast tomorrow. Now, I put some hornsalt in with the spices, not that these boys had much but chili powder and hot sauce. I did find cinnamon, but you'll never be able to get hornsalt here." With a final flourish, Mrs. Lindstrom took the last item, a small deeply carved wooden box, from a carton and placed it reverently on the counter. "All of my mother's recipes and also mine."

Despite her frustration over the chaos she had unleashed and her deep desire to be alone with Tom, Alix moved forward and gave her mother a fierce hug that lifted her off her feet a few inches. "Maybe I will find time to cook."

"That would be great! As an officially adopted Cajun, I eat almost anything." Tom's grin broke free.

"Oh," said Tille. "Alix knows that. She downloaded Joe Billodeaux's deep fat fried turkey recipe off the internet to put in her album, didn't you, Al? She's been filling scrapbooks on your family for years and years. Didn't you bring them along, Mom?"

"No. When Alix has a place of her own, I'll insist she take all her stuff just like I did when Rika married. Teenage things, you know."

"I mean you should see them, Tom. I thought she gave that up when she went to college, but I caught her cutting out articles on Dean and Stacy's wedding last year. And, she put her selfie with you in the album, too. Once she said she wanted to be part of your family and not ours. Quite possibly you are rooming with your stalker."

Alix went red in the face again, but not with embarrassment. She seized some of the colorful little cushions off the brown velour sofa and pelted her sister with one after another, showing she had a fairly strong and accurate arm to go with her legs. "You, you and Rika are why I wanted to be part of another family! What were you doing in my room, prying into my business?"

"Mom, make her stop!" Tille tried to dodge another barrage but lacked Alix's coordination and caught one cushion square in the face.

"What did I ever do to you?" Rika asked.

"Plenty, and you know it. You told your college friends I wanted to be a boy and saved my babysitting money for a sex-change operation."

"I was joking." Rika got a pillow thrown hard to the chest, a long delayed retaliation.

"Enough!" Nels Lindstrom bellowed. He restrained his daughter's mighty arm with one of his own. "Tom, she's a good girl and a great kicker, but push her too far and she does have a temper. No more, the three of you. Settle down now, and we'll get some dinner."

Rika seemed pleased by that. She pushed back some sweat-soaked curls that had escaped her ponytail. "I probably walked off five pounds unloading that trailer. What did you have in mind?"

"I can have pizza delivered if y'all are tired," Tom offered.

"Y'all, that is just so cute I could pinch your cheek—and those freckles…adorable," Mrs. Lindstrom said, whether to diffuse the tension in the room or because she really meant it. Alix suspected both.

"But Alix has been raving about the seafood. She printed out the menu from Galatoire's and circled all the foods you ate. I'll bet it's in her album. Can we go there? I mean even Wisconsin has pizza parlors," Tille whined and teased at the same time, something she was obviously adept at doing.

"I'd like something spicy, but not Italian. I weaned Isabel just before we came on this trip and now I can have anything I want to eat," Rika added. Her mother sent her a not too subtle signal by pointing at her own breasts. Rika glanced down at her blousy top. "I'm leaking! You hit me with that pillow and now I'm wet! Oh, God! Where is my suitcase?" She ran for Alix's room and slammed the door.

"Still in the car," Alix shouted after her. "Guess I should get it since this is all my fault, as usual."

"Yup," said Nels Lindstrom. "Exactly like having all the girls at home again."

Their *Morfar* had managed to sleep through most of the turmoil or pretended to, but the bang of the door woke him. "Someone say pizza? Fine with me, but I'd kinda like some oysters. You know a good place nearby, Tommy boy?"

"I do. Let's get that suitcase and once Rika is ready, head out."

Alix only nodded but couldn't help admiring Tom's coolness in a tense situation, exactly as she'd imagined him to be.

Chapter Five

At the Acme Oyster House on Iberville, Tom shared a tray of raw oysters with Andy who slurped them happily from the shell. "Come, Alix, be brave and try one," her dear *Morfar* chided. Alix would for him—and Tom.

"I did tell her she'd be returning here to live and would have to eat them sooner or later." Tom spiked one with a couple of dots of hot sauce and held the shell to her lips. "Just let it slide down. Eat a cracker afterwards if you must."

Alix let the gray gob slither down her throat—cold, salty, with a spicy tang—not so awful that she needed to grab a saltine. Anything Tom offered, she would eat. Tille immediately begged to be fed, though she frowned when her grandfather handed her one of the shells. Evidently not what she had in mind, but she ate it and declared the oyster delicious as she shoved a cracker into her mouth. Alix smiled with satisfaction knowing Tille well enough to sense she'd rather have spit it out. At last after years of merciless teasing, she was getting back some of her own.

"You'll all be sick. It warns you right on the menu that raw oysters can make you ill. With your low immunity, you shouldn't be taking a chance," Britta reprimanded her father.

"Oh, eat your Boo Fries and let me alone. I ate

plenty of raw oysters here in my day."

Rika freed a fry from the other appetizer topped with brown gravy and cheese. "I think these would be pretty popular in Wisconsin. My husband would love them."

Their entrees arrived, oysters in various forms from charbroiled to fried to encased in French bread for a po-boy. They ate hearty, all but Tille, and still had room for the bread pudding Alix insisted they must try. She captured the check by reaching over Tom with her big hand when it arrived, though the waitress placed it in front of her father. "My treat."

"Oh, Miss Big Shot," Tille pouted.

"Yeah, I can afford it." Alix made no apology. The men seemed impressed, and none of them denied her the honor of picking up the tab.

Their group stepped out into a sultry evening. Tom held the door for everyone from slow-moving Andy to the gaggle of women before he moved after them. A rawboned wreck of a woman emerged from the alley where oyster shells piled up in crates and flies buzzed around the remains of the feasts and accosted him. "Hey, hey, how about a BJ, Big Red? Only fifty dollars. I give the best because I don't bite. Right here behind the boxes."

The woman, her gaunt face partly obscured by badly scratched designer sunglasses and a heap of straggling light brown dreadlocks that covered her shoulders, smiled. She exposed her missing upper and lower front teeth that left a convenient penis-sized hole in her grin. Large, loose, pendulous breasts swayed beneath a purple T-shirt with a tiger logo on it. The animal appeared to be moving restlessly as the woman bobbed back and forth. Tom shook off her dirty-nailed grip. "No, thanks."

"For ten, you can see my titties. Big Lou has spectacular tits." She spit a little saying spectacular and started to peel up her soiled shirt, exposing a fish white, sunken belly between a set of ribs that could easily be counted one by one.

Tom removed a fifty from his wallet. "Take a break and get a good meal somewhere." He forked over the bill trying not to touch her.

"You Billodeauxs got money to burn," Big Lou sputtered through her broken dentition, but she snatched the money without a word of gratitude and shoved it down the front of her gray sweat pants all the way to the crotch. Giving Tom an obscene smile, she claimed a stolen shopping cart with her belonging and went on her way back to whatever hellhole she emerged from each day.

Tom turned to his horrified companions. "Sorry about that. New Orleans has its share of meth addicts and crack whores. Usually the police try to keep them out of the tourist areas."

"But she *knew* you," Rika said, almost implying he'd been one of her customers.

"The Billodeauxs are pretty well-known in New Orleans, and I sort of stand out in that group." Tom ruffled his red hair. "Lou hid in our parking garage for a while. She'd jump out from between cars and make lewd offers to my brother Dean and me. Probably other people, too. Arturo saw she moved along, but she knows we're good for a few bucks out of pity."

"Well, bless your kind heart," Mrs. Lindstrom said.

"You shouldn't encourage her, not in front of my

daughter. I'll expect you to shield her from people like that," Nels added.

"Dad, I'm all grown up. I know about drug users and prostitutes. We have some in Madison," Alix rushed to say, though her voice seemed faint after the raunchy encounter.

"Not like that. The cold keeps the crazies away. They all come south. She might attack you someday. You can't tell about people like that. I'm glad I don't have to live here," Tille claimed.

"She's not interested in me," Alix retorted. "Only Tom."

Tom applied his diplomatic skills again. "It's been a long day. Y'all are staying at the Marriott again, right?"

"Yup," Nels replied, still tight-lipped.

"Why don't we walk you there and then I'll take Alix home? I mean back to the condo. How does that sound?"

"Good." Her *Morfar* leaned wearily on his cane.

They set off and delivered Alix's family to the hotel. With a relieved sigh, she took his arm as they crossed Canal Street. "Thanks for putting up with them."

"No problem. You haven't met my family en masse. Believe me, we have issues, too."

"About those scrapbooks, I'm really not a stalker. I mean, I haven't even tried to friend you on Facebook. I am a member of your Sinners' fan page, though. But I never ever thought to contact you." Alix looked down at the brick sidewalk passing beneath her feet after making this confession. Their strides matched so well they walked in sync.

"I had a hard time in adolescence, no thanks to Tille and Rika. I used to imagine how nice it would be to belong to a family where everyone was very different, but still loved and supported each other. The fan magazines always featured your family, keeping track as it grew to twelve children. What did your dad say, 'This way, that way, all ways?'"

"Yeah, a prediction made by an old *traiteur,* an herbal healer some say had second sight. My mom wouldn't believe her until it all came true." Tom paused before the door to the condos and raised her bent head with his fingers. "Every family has its own kind of crazy. With mine, it's too much drama. Don't worry about it."

Her pulse raced faster in her long neck. Alix lifted her eyes to his. Tom leaned forward—and Arturo opened the door for them dumping a gust of cold air into the street.

"Ah, thanks, Arturo. Great timing." Tom motioned Alix to go ahead.

"My pleasure, Mr. Billodeaux," the doorman smirked.

As they rode up in the elevator, Tom said, "We could make popcorn and watch a movie. We have a good selection in the game room. You're welcome to use them anytime and anything else in there. If you don't want to sit out in the living room, there is a TV and DVD player in the armoire across from your bed."

"Give me a rain check on the movie. I think I'll just shower and turn in. I told my family I had to check with the Sinners office tomorrow and fill in paperwork, but we'd get together for dinner. That way I can avoid sightseeing with them."

"Plenty of sights, but you have lots of time to take them in. I can show you around when you want unless you really don't like that sort of thing."

"Oh, I'd love to tour New Orleans, just not with them. Mom and Rika will complain about the heat. They don't like to walk. Tille wants to shop until she drops, and the men get bored. Dad and *Morfar* will find a bar to kill time and upset Mom. *Pappa* Andy really shouldn't be drinking, but she fusses over him too much and that only makes him more stubborn."

"What's wrong with him?" Tom let them into the condo and turned on the lights.

"Liver cancer. The doctors removed the lobe with the tumor in it, and he underwent chemo. That left him weak, hairless, and more cantankerous than ever."

"Jesus, that's bad. I had two beers with him that day you went shopping. Your dad didn't say anything."

Alix squeezed his hand lightly. "Not your fault. My father feels a man must live his life as he wants and won't interfere. Tom, *Morfar i*s counting on me to succeed at being a punter. It's part of the legacy he wants to leave. I can't fail him."

He squeezed her hand right back with more strength. "Andy Mortenson is already in the Hall of Fame. He shouldn't put so much weight on you."

"Just help me to do my best."

"I will. Tomorrow you should check in. Then, we'll go to the training facility and work on our legs. How does that sound?"

"Like a perfect day. Thanks." Alix leaned over and gave his freckled cheek a small, sisterly peck before she went to her room. That shouldn't scare him too badly—just in case he had doubts about her being a stalker.

\*\*\*\*

Tom awoke to an amazing aroma that wafted down his hallway and seeped under his bedroom door. It beckoned him to leave his bed where his dreams had been disturbing—having sex with Alix in his old bed while a movie ran on the DVD player and being kicked hard in the nuts by her for even suggesting it, both possible outcomes. Should he shower, shave, and dress before appearing in the kitchen where he heard the clanking of dishes indicating either Alix had arisen, or his cleaning lady arrived exceptionally early?

Krayola had caught him in a bath towel more than once and seemed to delight in the sight. His morning woody having deflated at the thought of the housekeeper, he slipped nude from the covers and rummaged for a clean pair of plaid pajama bottoms, found his slippers under the bed, and drew on a dark green terry robe that didn't clash with his red hair and showed a little chest. Skip the shave but brush the teeth, he decided. Some girls liked the scruffy look, but none of them appreciated morning mouth. He sauntered casually to the kitchen.

"Hey, you're up early. Smells great in here."

Damn, Alix was fully dressed in worn jeans and a T-shirt from some athletic department in Wisconsin. Even her long toes were covered in old sneakers. All his baby doll nightie hopes evaporated. Maybe he should have dressed, too. Still, she gave him a brilliant smile.

"Plaid. You match your old bedspread," she chirped.

"Ah, you want me to put on some clothes?" he asked out of consideration.

Alix bent over an odd little pan covered with deep depressions. She carefully turned a ball of dough with what looked like a knitting needle. "No, you're fine. I've seen my dad in less than that. He's a boxer shorts, sleeveless T-shirt kind of guy. If we're going to be roomies, I guess we can't be too formal. I'm cooking you *ebelskivers* this morning to make up for all the chaos I brought into your life. Sit down and try some with a little powdered sugar."

She withdrew a basket lined with a cloth napkin from the oven and put it on the dining room table already set with dinnerware, utensils, large glasses of orange juice, and a small bowl of powdered sugar. Tom piled half a dozen of the little donut-ball looking delicacies on his plate, covered them with snowy sugar, and speared one with a fork. Red juice ran out of the side. "It's bleeding," he joked. "Sure you cooked it enough?"

"Oh, no, that's lingonberry jam stuffed inside. Mom left three jars of it in the cupboard. I hope you like them."

She actually looked as if she feared he might spit it out. Even if an ebelskiver tasted like a ball of shit, Tom vowed he'd get it down. But no, the dough was light and sweet, the jam a nice surprise. He popped another into his mouth as Alix tended to the cast iron pan on the range.

"These are great. Kind of like beignets. They seem like a lot of work. What time did you get up to start them?"

"Oh, an hour ago. I would have made coffee, but wasn't sure how to work the machine." She dumped the new batch into the basket and started another round by filling each hole in the pan with batter. "Eat them while they're warm."

"I think this might be the kind of breakfast where the cook eats last, sort of like waffles. I'll get the coffee. It's easy once you get the knack of it. I always have it on the strong setting because that's how we like it here."

"Same in Wisconsin. Let me finish this batch, then I'll sit down."

Alix added dabs of jam to the bubbling batter and applied her knitting needle in turning the *ebelskivers*. Tom brewed two mugs of coffee and took them to the table. Finally, Alix joined him, bringing along more of the pancake balls. They dug into breakfast. A little lingonberry juice dribbled down Tom's chin. Alix leaned close, reaching out with a napkin to capture it—and the damned doorbell rang. She snapped back into the upright, uptight position.

"Probably my family."

"No, someone who knows the entry code." As Tom listened to the little beeps, his mind ran through the possibilities. Dean and Stacy were still abroad. His folks would be at the ranch running Camp Love Letter for sick children…unless they planned a surprise visit, but Mom never did that. She said young people should have their privacy. Had he changed the code since his brief affair with Ilsa? Dear God, he hoped so. Who?

His sister burst inside, all big, bright dark eyes and a curvaceous figure encased in a swinging purple dress. Unfortunately, she didn't follow Mama Nell's rules. "Rise and shine, Tommy. I brought scones from the coffee shop—but I see you don't need them."

Both he and Alix stood up. He pulled the tie on his

robe a little tighter. "Ah, this is my new roommate, Alix Lindstrom. She's going to punt for the Sinners. Alix, meet—"

"Xochi Billodeaux! I'd recognize you anywhere from your pictures. Tom saved your life from a Mexican drug lord when you were both small children." Alix's face shone with the light of the star struck. "That was so smart and brave of him."

"Actually, stupid to run away to Mexico in the first place, but she was worth saving," Tom said. "Want some of these *skiver* things. Alix made them. They're delicious."

"Sure, the scones will keep. Nice to meet you. Smart of Tom to take on a—roommate—who can cook."

"Here, sit next to Tom. Let me make some fresh for you." Head bent, cheeks flaming, Alix dashed back to the kitchen.

Tom lowered his voice. "Thanks for embarrassing her. Maybe you weren't worth saving."

"What am I supposed to think? You didn't say a word to anyone about this arrangement. Here you sit in your robe and slippers like the lord of the manor, and she's slaving over a hot stove. I'm surprised you didn't send her down to the newsstand for the morning paper. How long has she been here? Say, these are good." Xochi forked up a second *ebelskiver*.

"She only arrived yesterday, and I didn't ask her to make breakfast. She wanted to do it." Tom's voice dropped even lower. "Since you're here, what do you see?'

Xochi waved her brown hands in front of her face in a mysterious way, closed her eyes, and flung back her long, black curls. "I see my brother is besotted by another tall blonde he hardly knows."

"No, I mean really. Do your woo-woo thing with the auras. You used to say Ilsa glowed orange, all ambition."

"Okay, fine. From the quick glance I got, she burns with a vibrant blue light."

"Is that good?"

"Blue is the color of adoration. Couldn't be for a scruffy redhead like you. You need another haircut. Must be from lucking into a plush condo in New Orleans."

"Cut it out, Xo. Do you see anything bad?"

"Nothing dark about her. I don't think a person having darkness within could cook such light and wonderful food."

Fortunately, Alix only heard the last part of the sentence as she bustled in and dumped more *ebelskivers* into the basket. "Thank you. Have a fresh one. Put only a little powdered sugar on it, not as much as Tom did."

"He's used to beignets drowning in the stuff. Make him take you out for breakfast tomorrow." Xochi ate three more and downed the coffee. "I need to get to work. Great meeting you, Alix. We'll be seeing a lot of each other. The family will definitely want to meet you. And if this arrangement doesn't work out, I live just across the street and have a spare room."

"I think you are running late, Xo. Let me walk you to the door." Tom pulled back his sister's chair in case she intended to say anything more to screw up his plans. He took her arm and helped her along. At the doorway, he leaned in and said, "Maybe I should change my entry code."

"What, you don't want me to water your plants when you are away?"

"I don't have plants!"

Xochi wetted a finger and rubbed his stubbled chin. "You got some jelly there."

"I know! As my favorite sister, do you think you could keep this quiet for a while, just until we see how it goes? Give Alix a chance to settle in and get used to me."

"I suppose, but you know Dad will be coming down for the mini-camp. Alix has been all over the news, and he'll be curious to see how she does."

"I'll run across that field when I must."

Xochi smiled up at her brother with a warmth that said she favored him, too, among all her siblings. "Tom, she could do a lot worse than you. Good luck."

He closed the door and hurried back to Alix and the cooling *ebelskivers* figuring he could eat a dozen more. "Alix, sit down. Let me serve you another cup of coffee. I'll get dressed, and then we'll go over to headquarters."

Chapter Six

Best workout ever! They ran side by side on the treadmills, not talking very much, just companionable. Alix wore her running shorts under her jeans, and he could see the shadow of her black athletic bra under a fresh white tee. She'd put on better shoes for exercising. Simply seeing her peel out of her jeans and that slight shadow of the bra seemed as good as a striptease to Tom. Now he watched her work the rowing machine, waiting his turn since the gym had only one. He swore even her sweat smelled good—at least better than any guy in the place.

Alix finished up and turned the machine over to him, but rather than stay and watch the bunching of his muscles, which weren't all that bad, she headed for the weight room. He'd told her he did power squats, leg presses, and extensions in there as part of his routine workout, to which she'd replied, "Sure, that's what I do, too." Tom guessed he couldn't blow off the rowing and tag along after her. Way too obvious that he wanted her attention.

By the time he finished and entered the weight room, his view of Alix was blocked by the fortress-like pair of shoulders owned by fullback, Vince Barbaro, who observed the new punter's every move. Alix extended her legs against the pedals and raised the weights, hold one-two, drop, hold one-two, drop, in a steady rhythm. When she paused to suck up some water, Barbaro moved in with a broad, smarmy smile and extended a hand the size of a small canned ham.

"Hi, Alix, I'm Vince Barbaro, your personal protector. I'll see none of the return team guys get at you on the field."

Alix shook and gave out the usual nice to meet you. Jesus, the man had the most perfect tan Tom had ever seen. Even when he'd served as a Camp Love Letter lifeguard, Tom had to slather on the sunscreen to protect his fair skin and build a tan gradually over the course of the summer to the point where he no longer looked like a freckled albino if there was such a thing. It the fall, his brown faded quickly, and his spots popped out again with a vengeance.

Tom inserted himself into the conversation. "Hey, Vince. What are you doing in town? Looks like you've been somewhere sunny."

Alix's personal protector flashed his smile again, even whiter than usual displayed on the background of that tan. It went well with those dark eyes and thick, black hair of his, too. "I've been relaxing at that private island your dad recommended off the coast of Mexico. He used to treat the whole team to a week there when the Sinners had a good season. How come Dean doesn't do that? I mean we won the Super Bowl for him last year."

"Distracted by Ilsa having his baby and getting married to Stacy around the same time, I'd guess. His plate was full to overflowing." Tom defended his brother. "I'll put a bug in his ear. We can still get a trip in before summer training camp. You guys deserve it even belatedly, but why exactly are you here?"

"Coach called me in for mini-camp. He wants Alix to get used to players coming at her to block her punts." Vince turned to Alix again. "But don't you worry your pretty head about that, little lady. Just do your punts. Vince got you covered."

Oh, she didn't like that sexist comment. Alix narrowed her wide blue eyes and replied coolly, "You do your job, and I'll do mine. We'll get along." Tom rejoiced.

"Yeah, I guess." Vince flexed his impressive tattooed guns displayed prominently by the wife-beater he wore. "Since I'm here, I might as well do some bench presses. You want to spot me, Tom? Or maybe not. With the weight I lift maybe you couldn't raise it if my grip slips. I'll get a trainer." He whammed Tom between the shoulder blades in farewell and shoved him forward several inches. "I keep forgetting what delicate flowers you kickers are."

As Vince sauntered off, Tom mumbled, "Fullbacks!"

Alix stopped extending her legs. "Are all the team members like him?"

"Most of them are good guys, maybe a little crude. I really think Vince wanted to impress you."

"Not working. Anyone can look at me and see I am not little and hardly a lady." She scrunched that straight nose again, a habit he found totally endearing, especially since it implied Vince stank.

"You're great the way you are." Tom rushed on lest she be offended by the compliment. "Well, I'm going to do some planks. They're good for the core development."

"I know," Alix replied with a hint of exasperation.

"Right. Call me when you want to switch." Tom stretched his length on a nearby mat and did his best to present his long, lean line supported by the smooth muscles in his arms. He conjured coming upon Alix doing planks in their apartment. He'd kneel between her legs, slowly peel down her exercise shorts and reveal her firm, white buttocks. Tom switched to rocking planks, flattening his body on the mat and raising his head and feet to discourage the reaction in his pants to that fantasy. He willed himself not to look her way, but she spoke, letting him know she was watching.

"You could probably do yoga really well, Tom. It's also good for the core. I'll show you some of the moves."

"At home, maybe." He glanced around to make sure no one heard, but the weight room was lightly populated during the off-season. The guys would be working out somewhere, maybe in their home gyms or at a posh resort. He doubted any of them did yoga—but he would if Alix showed him the positions. The things he'd do for love.

Wearing a sweatband around his brow, Vince Barbaro tossed his long black hair sending flecks of sweat into the air as if he were advertising a Stallone movie. Hell, Tom's own hair grown out turned into a curly red tangle that didn't toss at all, let alone like a stallion's mane. Vince, buckled into a safety belt, squatted and pressed a free weight of amazing size. Raising the dumbbell over his head, he sent Alix another blazing smile. She didn't acknowledge it. Tom had that going for him. Yoga, why not?

"Want to switch now?" Alix asked.

"Sure." Tom sprang from his prone position and went to the machine where Alix wiped the seat with a towel before he took his place behind the weights. He doubted any of the fellows bothered, but probably the trainers did it for them. He'd never really noticed. Having a woman around could certainly make the training center a nicer place. He did his extensions while watching Alix plank out of the corner of his eye. She did the usual, then segued into a side plank, long body held up sideways on one arm and the other arm raised high. The sports bra girdled her breasts, but Tom could still see the soft swell of them under her tee. He lost his rhythm and the weights crashed down. Every male eye in the place stared their way—if they hadn't been watching Alix already.

"Side planks, good for hip strength." Alix flipped to do her other side away from him. That only made him concentrate on her buttocks again. He closed his eyes and quelled his desire with the weights.

"I think we've done enough for today," he said after a while. She'd gone into some of her yoga poses, positions he couldn't imagine doing—limber, so limber. "You want to get lunch and maybe do some sightseeing this afternoon, a carriage ride, eat some beignets?"

Alix toweled her face. "I want to get a shower and guess I'll have to go back to the apartment for that."

"For now..." He wiped himself down. "Let's swing by the locker room on our way back."

They did. The Dome's locker room turned out to be under construction. In the rear, plumbers installed a private shower in a large cubical with a locking door. Of course, the décor ran to red and black, the team colors of the Sinners. The commode was an ebony throne and the sink an inky raised basin with arching golden fixtures. A boxed mirror framed in curlicues leaned against one wall and a rack of makeup lights waited for installation.

"*Pour vous*," Tom intoned in his best French accent. French always worked when Brian Lightfoot wanted to impress the ladies. He gestured to the elegant dressing room. "Let it never be said the Sinners aren't going all out for you. Next thing you know Dean will want the same accommodations in his contract."

Alix took in her private space. "Dean doesn't seem like the type, at least during his interviews."

"Just joking. He isn't." Great, she appeared totally impressed by Dean, more than by the private bath. He guessed there was no sense in mentioning he'd suggested the makeup lights because his sisters had them in their bathrooms. "The place will be finished well before the start of the regular season."

"It's wonderful."

"So, shower, lunch in the Quarter, and sightseeing? If you want to avoid the heat, we can go to the aquarium."

"Afraid not. I forgot to tell you I have an interview again this afternoon. The PR man, Mr. Jackson, said to be sure I dressed and acted like a girl since last time I was wearing a jersey with *Morfar*'s old number on it. Do you mind that I'm number one? I asked for four, but he wanted to play up the connection to my grandfather."

She seemed sweetly concerned that he would be jealous or angry. Tom gave her his best grin. "I don't care. I always thought the great Ancient Andy was the first kicker for the expansion team, then Howdy

McCoy, then me, number three. The others had long careers with the Sinners, and I hope to have the same. How about you?"

Alix shook her head. "I don't want to punt until I'm past forty. I'd like to have some children way before then."

Tom imagined them, all tall and lanky, maybe strawberry blondes, some with blue eyes and some with Billodeaux brown, a blending of their genes. "I hope you have as many as your heart desires." He refrained from using the old come-on line, "I want you to have my babies."

He hit the right note. She rewarded him with a smile that could melt Arctic ice. They headed back to the condo.

****

Alix primped. It wasn't her style, but she did. Six dresses lay on her bed, three more than she'd ever owned before. She couldn't decide which. She'd blown her long blonde bob dry and parted it on the side with the bangs brushed across her forehead for a different look and put on one of the new bras that pushed her breasts together in the center giving her more cleavage that she really didn't want to show off. Now, she stood here in the matching bikini panties unable to decide which to put on. The black dress her sister coveted— really more eveningwear. Peach chiffon, pale green, lacy white, and one of those illusion outfits with a beige silhouette inside of the dark brown that was supposed to make a woman seem slimmer, not that she needed to be thinner. And the powder blue. Really, she should have consulted with Rika or Tille, but couldn't bear the thought of their comments. Everyone told her she looked great in blue even if it was a flannel shirt. This one had a flared skirt that hit slightly above her knees. She put it on, no stockings in this heat.

Alix checked her makeup in the mirror. Brows and lashes darkened, eyes outlined in smoky gray, and lips coated in a deeper pink than her usual gloss. Mr. Jackson didn't want her to fade out on the screen he said. Shoes, white wedges they'd actually had in her size! The saleslady deflated her delight a little by saying they carried bigger sizes and widths to serve the large transvestite population. Alix turned red, and her mother sucked in her breath before reprimanding the woman. "My daughter certainly is not a transvestite. She's a football player." Thanks, Mom. That made everything better. But the shoes were great!

Tom sat in the living room flipping through channels. Alix made her entrance. "Am I girly enough?" She held out her arms and enjoyed watching his eyes widen.

"You're gorgeous. I'd take you anywhere."

"Would you?" She waited, hoping he'd make a date with her, not just a casual offer to show her around.

Instead, he checked his watch. "You'd better get going. Traffic is always bad in the city."

"Guess I should."

He walked her to the door and opened it. In the wedges, she stood eye to eye with him, nose to nose, lips to lips. He swallowed and his adam's apple bobbed in his long neck. "We could go to Mariah's Place tonight. That's where all the Sinners hang out, but most of them will be out of town."

"I'd like that." She should have lowered her eyes

modestly, but she just kept staring into the dark depths of his.

"I mean, your family can come, too. The music is good."

So, not a date. Honestly, she'd forgotten about *Morfar* and all the Lindstroms for a moment, still in town, still butting into her new life. "That would be great, thanks."

The Sinners weren't taking any chances of her getting lost on one-way streets. They'd sent a car, and Arturo bounded out to open the door for her. Unaccustomed to such service, she'd have to ask Tom about tipping the man. So much to learn.

At the television studio, she found the interview conducted by an angular woman named Bess Harding who asked her nothing much about football and everything about being the new kid in town. Did she find New Orleans very different from Madison? What kind of dumbass question was that?

Alix put on her Swedish accent a la *Morfar*. "*Ja,* sure. It's colder in Madison even this time of year." Bess tittered. At least she understood Alix was being sarcastic.

"So how are you coping with the heat here?"

"By sweating and drinking lots of water." Bess, pencil-thin and garbed in an illusion dress something like the one Alix left lying on her bed, adjusted her stylish red wig and laughed at her statement as if it were the soul of wit and not just common sense.

"Are there any men in your life?"

"An entire team of them called the Sinners." That drew more cackles.

"Where do you like to shop?"

"Anywhere that carries my size." Alix stood up to emphasize her point and made her interviewer look like a stick figure beside her. "I'm a very big girl."

"And most attractive. I don't think you'll be playing football very long before some man snaps you up. So, any tattoos?"

"Um, no."

"Will you get one with the Sinners' logo?"

"It's only a three year contract, not a lifetime commitment, so no," Alix replied.

More inane questions followed. The worst part was trying to figure out what to do with her long legs and arms. She finally folded her legs under her chair, placed her hands primly in her lap, and prayed for the interview to end. At last, it did.

Her interviewer stood up, coming to about Alix's shoulder in height, and said, "Nice job, kiddo. You have a sort of innocent charm. Try to keep it. Don't get hardened like me." Up close Alix could see the deep lines and crow's feet the makeup artist worked hard to conceal. That same person had amped up her own face until Alix feared she'd be taken for a streetwalker when she left the studio. Fortunately, the car awaited her— and Tom at home.

Chapter Seven

"Oh, I can't believe we're here!" Alix breathed. "Mariah's Place—it's famous." She inhaled deeply as if absorbing the atmosphere of cigarettes long turned to ash and beer on tap as their group stood just inside the door letting their eyes adjust to the dimness and their ears to the throbbing of the music.

"It's more of a dump than I thought it would be and stinks of smoke," Tille said, maliciously crushing her sister's enthusiasm.

Ancient Andy peered around. "Pretty much as I remember it, but not as hazy. They called the place Bennie's back then."

"Howdy McCoy bought the club for his mother. No smoking allowed anymore since Mariah is using oxygen for her COPD. Too bad we missed her opening act. It's something to behold. Come on, you have to meet my step-grandmother." Tom led the way.

He'd learned that leading Swedes was not like herding cats, which ran off in all directions, but more like moving boulders. They'd gone to gorge on seafood again, this time at Ralph's and remained until the last fish bone was sucked clean and dessert consumed by all. Hence, the music had started about a half hour ago and a few couples had hit the dance floor.

Walking around them, Tom approached Mariah at her private table, the one with an empty chair dedicated to her deceased lover, Billy. With her big breasts shored up by numerous thin straps, she held court there in her outrageous white wig and a long silver gown with a slit in the front that showed off her legs clad in opaque tights and ending in glittering mile-high heels that would have killed anyone else her age. Tom introduced the Lindstrom clan. Mariah studied them with watery blue eyes. She'd had to abandon her bright green contacts because half the time she couldn't get them in and refused to ask for help.

"I remember you." She nodded at Ancient Andy. "You were a big deal kicker in your day, an inspiration for my boy. Me, I'm more famous now than I ever was." She watched Andy throw back his stooped shoulders and pretend he didn't need the heavy cane. "You can sit in Billy's chair. What are you drinking?"

Andy lowered his bony frame into the seat. "Aquavit if you got it."

"Tommy, see if Jackson has any." She nodded toward her fat, bald bartender, another fixture of the place.

"*Pappa,* no!" Andy's daughter protested.

Mariah gave her the steely eye. "Sweetheart, why don't you go dance a polka with your husband? Let the man live this life."

"That's what I say." Nels led his plump wife onto the dance floor and held her close for a slow spin around the room.

Behind the bar, Jackson wiped the dust off a bottle of golden liquor and removed two chilled shot glasses from the refrigerator. He screwed them into a bowl of crushed ice and drew two tall dark beers from the tap. Loading it all on a tray, the bartender delivered the drinks personally.

"Here you go, Mariah." With a nod toward Andy, he displayed the bottle of aquavit. "Linie okay?"

"*Ja*, sure. It's Norwegian, but very good."

Jake poured two shots and left the bottle on the table. "Honor to meet a legend like you, sir," he said before returning to his duties. "Let me know if you want anything else." The old man nodded, beamed, and shook hands.

Back at the bar, Tom slipped the bartender a twenty for delivering the rote message and summoned the three sisters who looked lost to an empty table.

"Where will Mom and Dad sit?" Rika questioned.

"I can't believe that old crone spoke to them that way," Tille fumed.

"That's my grandmother you're talking about. In fact, the whole team loves Mariah. She's one tough cookie and doesn't waste words or breath. As for the table, I'll shove two together."

"I'll help," Alix volunteered at once.

"I can do it. Don't get your pretty dress dirty." Tom thought she blushed—hard to tell in the darkness. The dress was pretty, white with transparent sleeves that showed off her toned arms and a loose filmy skirt edged in lace that swayed as she walked. Its top fit snugly, but not too tight or too low. The square-cut neckline exposed just a peek of the tops of her breasts. She had worn her white flats again and a necklace of tiny freshwater pearls. All of it modest and lovely, exactly like her.

Tom managed to fit the tables together without tipping over the atmospheric red candles in their votive holders or spilling basic condiments like hot sauce, red pepper flakes, and Cajun seasoning on the black tablecloths. The elder Lindstroms sat gratefully after their short romp.

"Tell the bartender to put any drinks you want on my tab. Alix, would you like to dance?" Tom offered.

"Oh, yes!" She shot to her feet.

Tille appraised her outfit. "You should have worn the black. You look like a Catholic school girl about to take her first communion."

The hurt that passed over Alix's face prompted Tom to say, "I think you look like a bride."

"That's what I thought—sort of bridish. Let's dance."

The music had turned frenetic, so not a chance of him holding her close. Tom went into what Dean called his war dance, among many other choice expressions. He jerked his arms over his flaming red head and lifted his long legs almost in time with the music. Dancing, not his greatest skill. Alix did the same. They circled the dance floor. Were people staring?

He noticed Vince Barbaro come out of the shadows and ask Tille to dance. Alix's sister had worn short black spandex that clung to her rear and cupped each braless breast held up by straps that crossed behind her neck. Vince watched her boobs jiggle as he did a few *Saturday Night Fever* moves designed to impress. She'd worn heels high enough to increase her mammary motion. Both seemed happy with their choice of partners.

The door to Mariah's Place opened letting in a shaft of low, long-lasting summer sunshine. As usual, the couple who entered stood there for a moment waiting for their eyes to adjust to the dark. The sunbeam illuminated them from the back as if they were surrounded by holy light, an anointed pair—Dean and Stacy, who were supposed to be in Germany until the end of the month. The tourists gaped.

Tom thought, *Oh, shit!* In a minute, Alix would want to meet and drool all over his brother, the famous quarterback, but she simply kept dancing with a joyous abandon that matched his own.

As the door shut, Dean and his bride of almost a year slipped alongside the length of the bar and took their usual seats at the very end around the corner in the deepest of shadow. Dean, no seeker of attention, preferred to go unnoticed. He never managed that. He'd barely put his fine behind on the stool when Sinners' fans began lining up with cocktail napkins to sign. Tom and Alix finished their gyrations as the music came to an end. Getting it over with, Tom asked, "I guess you want to meet Dean and Stacy."

"I'd love to! First, I need the ladies' room. I must powder my nose. Heck, I have to pee. Be right back." Alix peeled off toward the neon restroom sign.

Tom avoided the Lindstroms' table for the moment and went to say hello as the last of the Sinners' followers dissipated like fog on the Mississippi, leaving behind a mist of encouraging words. "Almost had us another Super Bowl." "We'll get it next year."

Dean greeted his brother with that dazzling smile he didn't mean to be sexy. It simply was. "Hey, bro. Glad to see you practicing your dancing. You looked like two whooping cranes mating out there."

Stacy, his blonde, brainy, and voluptuous wife, pressed Tom's hand. "He means that in a good way. Whooping cranes are beautiful birds. They mate for life."

"No, he doesn't. I couldn't dance as well as Dean if they offered me another million on my contract."

"Who's the babe?" Dean asked. Stacy elbowed him. "I mean the attractive and very tall young lady."

"Our new punter, Alix Lindstrom. That's her family at the table. Ancient Andy Mortenson is sitting in Billy's chair."

"No!" Stacy gasped. "I've never known Mariah to allow anyone to sit there."

"I don't know. She seemed to sense a kindred spirit. What are you doing back two weeks early?" He thought he'd have more time to impress Alix before Dean's light shone upon her and transmogrified her into another adoring female.

"After studying German all winter, Stacy was pretty fluent with four weeks of endless conversation with everyone she met, so I thought I'd come home for mini-camp. I have to work off all that bratwurst and German pastry. Every dessert over there comes with real whipped cream." Dean patted his stomach as if he had a paunch instead of a wall of tight muscle beneath his white dress shirt open at the collar to show the strong column of his neck and rolled up on the arms that launched his perfect spiral passes. "Besides, I was curious about the new punter. She even made the news abroad, mostly shots of her in a Sinners' uniform. Cleans up nice."

"She does. You ought to see her at the gym." Tom caught a glimpse of white out of the corner of his eye. "Here she comes. Try not to enchant her, Dean."

Stacy, possessive, put a hand bearing that famous yellow and pink diamond engagement ring on Dean's arm. "This prince already has his princess."

Alix didn't bother to wait for a formal introduction. She arrived and shot out her somewhat large hand. "Alix Lindstrom, your new punter. I'll try my best for you."

"That's all I ask," said Dean as he shook. The errant black curl that always flopped on his handsome forehead did its thing. Women adored that hank of hair. Stacy pushed it back into place.

But Alix's sunny blue eyes didn't stay on Dean's darkly handsome Cajun face, dwell on his sculpted lips, or move downward to his broad shoulders and chest. Instead, her wide pink lips formed an O as she glimpsed the rock on Stacy's finger. "Is *that* the engagement ring? Of course it is! There are no others like it. May I see it more closely?"

"Certainly." Stacy held out her hand for the inspection.

"Your wedding was out of a fairy tale. I admit I clipped your pictures from *People* and *Us*."

"Sit down and I'll tell you what went on behind the scenes." With a pleased smile on her lovely face, Stacy motioned to the stool on her far side. Rarely did someone want to speak to her and not Dean even though she spoke five languages.

"I guess we aren't going to be talking football," Dean said.

"Nope, girl stuff. Come meet the family." Inside, Tom's fear melted away. The Titanic had met the iceberg and didn't even leave a dent.

Naturally, Dean charmed them. He gave lurking Vince Barbaro a hearty handshake and extended that to Nels and Britta Lindstrom. He signed napkins for the two sisters, and when the music began again, the Super Bowl winning quarterback took chubby Rika, who used to be a size three, out on the dance floor for the thrill of her life. God, Dean was so smooth, but Tom noticed he'd asked the married one, not the sister who panted for his attention.

Back at the bar, Stacy still regaled Alix with nuptial details. At one point, Alix put her hand over her mouth and giggled. Must have been the story about Prince Dobbs, a Sinners wide receiver with a bad reputation, showing off his new religious tattoos to the guests—or maybe the one about Ilsa pawning Dean's month-old son off on Mama Nell. The kid promptly threw up on the napkin placed to shield her pale blue silk suit. Good times, Billodeaux family style.

Doing his duty, Tom raised his russet eyebrows and held out his arms to Tille. A disappointed quiver passed over her pouty lips, but she rose and followed him out onto the floor. Tom felt no need to hold her close for the duration of the slow song. Like an old-fashioned suitor, he kept Tille at arm's length and managed to stay off her toes. He tried a little conversation, but her eyes were so busy tracking Dean who had just spun Rika in an elegant twirl that she failed to answer. To his relief, Vince, doing his he-man bit, cut in by tapping his shoulder. No loss there. Tom headed directly toward Alix, the flame drawn to the beautiful white moth instead of the other way around.

"Mind if I interrupt your conversation for a dance?"

"Oh, good, a slow one." Alix got up and apologized to Stacy. "I want to hear more, but I guess we'll be seeing each other again if this is where the

Sinners hang out."

"I know we will. We'll have to go salsa dancing with Xochi's crowd, you and Tom, me and Dean."

"I'd like that very much."

Finally, Tom took her into his arms, not much distance between. She fit him so handily he failed to trip over his own feet as he often did with shorter women like Tille. They drifted along in perfect harmony. He might be a redheaded woodpecker, but Alix was a swan. Half a dance, only half a dance, and the music ended.

Tille approached with a cross expression on her baby doll face. "Mama says we have to leave. *Morfar* is drinking too much, and Dad thinks Vince is feeling me up."

Probably right on both counts. Tom suppressed his sigh of frustration and plastered on his jolly grin. "I'll walk you to the hotel and make sure Alix gets safely to the condo."

"No, no, we'll see her home first. It's just across a street. You been a great host, paying for dinner and drinks and bringing us here. You stay and enjoy the rest of your evening," Nels Lindstrom insisted.

Tille and Rika deposited their autographed napkins in their tiny purses. "Wait until I tell my hubby I danced with Dean Billodeaux! He'll be so jealous," Rika raved as the group started to move.

"Yeah, he'd probably like to dance with Dean himself. Thanks to Dad, I didn't get the chance," Tille moped.

"I had a wonderful evening. I met Stacy and danced with Tom," Alix said softly.

"Now, I don't know about a guy who has his own

bar tab, Al," her mother said as they stopped by Mariah's table to pick up *Pappa* Andy who swayed a little getting up and needed his cane to steady himself.

"Maybe Andy should spend the night. I have an apartment upstairs," Mariah suggested.

"Certainly not. We will take care of him ourselves," Britta Lindstrom said.

"Anytime you're in town, Andy, come by. I'll save your seat."

"*Ja*, sure, Mariah. I'd like that very much. We must leave in the morning. Long drive back to Wisconsin, but see you later."

The old kicker wobbled out shored up by his son-in-law and daughter. Tom stared until the last wisp of Alix's white dress flew into the night and the portal closed. Sinking down next to Stacy, he ordered a beer. Dean returned to his wife's side and did the same.

"What did you think of Alix?" Tom ventured.

"Nice kid. I hope she's as great a punter as the papers claim she is," Dean said matter-of-factly.

"Oh, Dean, can't you see Tom is smitten? He doesn't care how she kicks." Stacy shook her gorgeous blonde head.

"Language majors. What kind of word is smitten when talking about a man in lust?"

"In love, Dean. She isn't Ilsa, right, Tom?"

"So very right. Now what am I going to do about it?"

"Take it slow right now. She has a lot to adjust to at the moment," Stacy counseled.

"A month? Six months? A year? I don't think I can do that last one."

"Maybe a football season, but I think you'll

recognize the right time.'

"Lord, I hope so before someone like Vince moves in on her."

"Hey, you already have a head start since Alix is living with you," Dean said with one of his blinding grins.

If Tom had been a red wolf, he would have raised his hackles. "She's renting half the condo! You can't call that living together. She's my roommate. So, Xochi ratted me out already."

"Don't get upset. She only told me, not the whole family. I felt compelled to tell my husband—your brother and best friend—no one else." Stacy ruffled his curly hair to calm the beast.

"You know Dad will show up sometime during mini-camp. He always does. I'd give him a heads up about the situation to keep it from getting weird," Dean said.

"What, like you dating your cousin?"

"Exactly like that. And Stacy isn't really my cousin, and you know it," Dean retorted with some irritation. "Let Dad in on your arrangement before the tabloids get wind of it."

Tom finished his beer and slapped the heavy glass mug against the black marble counter. "Thanks for all the unsolicited advice. Maybe Alix is home by now. We can watch a movie together. See you later." Smitten, Stacy as usual had chosen the correct word.

Chapter Eight

Mini-camp began and the bleachers filled with sports reporters as usual, but they weren't assessing the first round draft pick running back or the strength new blood brought to the defense. All eyes stayed glued on Alix Lindstrom, first female punter in the NFL. Coach Buck had her decked out in full pads despite the heat. He had no intention of allowing her to be damaged as he commanded the Sinners return team to charge at her as she completed each punt. His reasoning—she could not flinch and flub those kicks. Not to mention how Marty Buck relished watching his own men cope with the new spin on punt returns.

Tom kept a sharp eye on his roommate. Vince Barbaro did his job protecting the punter, throwing blocks at anyone who got too near. They ran down the field a few yards together after each punt, very cozy, too cozy. Tom suspected the linemen had been instructed not to hit her, an illegal move, roughing the kicker, but shit happened on the field and those penalties often helped the team. He'd been downed more than once when the opposition tried to block his extra points and field goals. Alix did well both in the length of her punts and the steel of her nerves. Dean, who'd come out to work with the new running back, gave Tom a thumbs-up. He couldn't have been more proud if she'd been his own sister—not what he desired at all.

Coach called for a break, and Tom showed Alix how to make snow cones from the ice pile kept to cool off the big linemen. He doused a cup full of chips with a flavored sports drink after inquiring whether she wanted orange or lemon-lime. They sat side by side enjoying the treat while other players took theirs straight from the bottle.

"You did really good out there, showed no fear. That's important."

"I played soccer against some really tough women—and we didn't have all the padding and helmets. Besides, *Morfar* had me study your tapes. He'd say, 'See how Tom just swings his leg a few times to stay loose when the other team calls a time out to ice him. Never works. They should not bother.'" Alix licked at her orange snow cone with flicks of her pink tongue.

"You studied me? I'm flattered." Her lapping tongue drove him crazy with thoughts of what it might do applied to parts of his body. He really should take a dive into the snow pile to cool off like the linemen.

"You and Howdy McCoy and, of course, my grandfather. I have to admit my thighs burn right now."

Burning thighs, she had to say that. Not helping him keep his composure. "You won't be doing so many punts in a game as you are today. Lots of time to rest your muscles between kicks though you want to stay hot—I mean, warm."

Alix gave him an enigmatic Mona Lisa smile. You never knew what women were thinking. That was the trouble. Alix brushed her damp bangs to the side. Even with her light blonde hair sweat-soaked to brown, he found her attractive.

"Tom, get your ass out on the field and do some kickoffs for the return team," Coach shouted.

Tom's turn to show off, and he did for Alix who sat on the bench watching him drive ball after ball into the end zone. "No, no, no! Not so deep. I want them to practice running the ball back, not taking a knee," Marty Buck hollered. He set the next few down on the twenty-yard line and threw in a few directional kicks to provide more challenge. For a while, he forgot all about Alix Lindstrom.

Then, Coach switched him to doing field goals for the defense to block. "Lindstrom, get out there and hold for Billodeaux."

She trotted across the field and knelt before him, the start of another fantasy. Tom suppressed that one and instead gave gentle instruction. "Laces out of course. Hold the ball with your left index finger. This is the angle I want." He covered her hands with his and positioned the football to his liking. What he didn't like was letting go of her. "Don't worry. I won't kick you."

"I'm not afraid of that. I held the ball for my grandfather's students all during my training. He said that came under the punter's duties on most teams."

"Okay, then. Bolivar, we're ready for the snap."

Barton "Beef" Bolivar, the snapper, caught the ball Tom tossed him. "About time." He sent it shooting through his legs with such force, Alix bobbled the ball and the defense came roaring to retrieve it. They knocked her over in the scramble. Tom helped Alix up. "You okay?"

"Fine. I can take my knocks, but that wasn't a good snap."

"Yeah, I saw. Beef, we need a better one."

This time the snap came crisply, but not too hard. Still rattled by seeing Alix hit, Tom shanked it. Beef Bolivar sneered, "Either Tommy the Toe is out of practice or his holder is no damn good."

"Nothing wrong with that hold or the snap. I wasn't concentrating." Tom smiled, though he wanted to knock Bolivar in the teeth for that remark. "This is what practice is all about. Let's see your best, Beef. Alix, get ready." He did several more field goals, all perfect, from various places on the field before being waved back to the bench. Alix followed and settled down right beside him just as Brian Lightfoot used to do, but Brian's presence never made him want to put an arm around his shoulder and give a hug. Instead, he only said, "Good job out there."

"Thanks." They slurped more snow cones and took turns kicking into the net until practice ended.

When the whistle sounded, Coach Buck announced, "Lindstrom, to the showers. You got fifteen minutes to clean up, then the press conference. The rest of you hydrate or something."

Alix hurried off. Dean took her place beside Tom. "She's good, really good, but I think we have a problem with Bolivar. He's a resentful SOB. Wants to be a starting center, but he's not above trying to make a teammate look bad. Want me to have a talk with the special teams coach or Marty?"

"They saw what he did. No sense in getting into the middle of it. She'll have to cope with worse." Tom studied the hands clenched between his knees.

"That shank, you were more shaken than she was about being knocked down. Anytime you want me to hold for you, just ask."

Dean knew him better than any other man on earth. Only ten months apart in age, they didn't remember a time when they hadn't been adopted brothers. "Thanks. Great to have you back."

Side by side, they waited to use the showers at the practice field until Alix emerged fresh and clean with her wet hair slicked back behind her ears and dressed in the same gown she'd worn to walk the French Quarter with Tom. Captured immediately by the press, among them more female reporters than usual, she disappeared into the demanding mob.

****

The Sinners' general manager, Mitch Michener, emerged from his air-conditioned office and arrived in time to hand Alix onto the low platform set up for the press conference. He used all the right words: history making, big asset to the team, forward thinking management. Then, he popped a few antacids, his candy of choice, and turned the mike over to Alix soon buried in a barrage of questions.

"Were you shaken when the defense knocked you down today?"

"No, soccer players get knocked down, too. It's not the first time for me."

"Ever served as a holder before?"

She patiently explained about her training with her grandfather and sneaked a glance at her wristwatch. This had to end soon.

"What's your favorite color?" chirped one of the women.

Alix started to say blue, but came up with a better answer. "Red and black, of course."

Or maybe just red. She spotted Tom at the rear of the group, hard to miss with his blazing red hair, curly and damp, and his height. Her lips curved into a small smile. He waved. She returned the gesture without a thought. Eyes swiveled and sought him out like heat-seeking missiles. "Tommy the Toe," a few people chanted.

"Come on up here," Mitch said in a way Tom should consider as an order.

He complied and took the chair next to Alix. "Sorry," she wanted to say, but feared the mic would pick it up. She let one arm dangle beneath the red-skirted table. Tom did the same. They squeezed hands while he deftly fielded lots of questions about working with a woman, and got a laugh when one reporter asked if he worried about her mood swings.

"Hey, I'm the guy with five sisters and a sister-in-law. I can handle a mood swing of any dimension. Actually, Alix has proved to be the most even-tempered football player I've ever met. I mean some of these guys can throw a better hissy fit than my baby sister." He grinned at Dean and some of the other players who had stayed around for the circus. Tom squeezed her hand again and released his grip. For a moment, Alix felt alone and unprotected up on the dais, but he'd quickly deflected all the attention away from her with humor.

As the reporters moved on to privacy issues, Mitch described the specially built bathroom area in all its opulence. Tom chipped in that he'd suggested the makeup lights and reused the quip that their quarterback might want the same put in his contract to get another laugh.

Dean said good-naturedly, "I certainly do. I can never get this curl to stay off my forehead." Dean tucked his lock of hair back into place and mugged for any cameras turned his way. He'd gotten to be a pro at more than football.

The GM offered a brief chuckle and went on to more important matters. "We will also be holding a sensitivity training session for the men." In the back of the crowd, Beef Bolivar and Vince Barbaro groaned loud enough to be heard up front.

"Anyone not attending will be fined." Mitch glared at his players and crunched another antacid.

"Maybe Alix needs a special class of her own on how to deal with uncouth guys," Tom suggested, going for the joke again. Damned if Mitch didn't pick up on it.

"Say, not a bad idea. That's all about Alix, folks. We'll let Coach Buck take the stand with our new running back." With a gesture he'd never made to any other football player, the GM, sweating in his suit and tie, offered a hand to Alix to help her from the stage.

On the sidelines, PR person Action Jackson patted her on the back. "Good job. You never get flustered, do you?"

"It's not in the nature of Swedish-Americans to fluster," Alix replied. Except when Tom paid her a compliment. He came to her side more supportive than a sports bra, more understanding that most of her female soccer teammates. She sure hoped he wasn't lumping her in with his sisters and that he meant the things he said about her looks. Hard to tell when he turned so many things into a joke.

Dean joined them. "Let's get out of here fast.

Either of you need a ride?"

Alix answered quickly. "No, I came with Tom."

"Yeah, we're saving gas by carpooling," Tom claimed. "Besides, I'm used to big city driving, and she's not."

"Right, you two millionaires drove a few miles in a big, honking SUV to save gas. Maybe you just enjoy each other's company."

She'd kept her cool on the field and on the platform. Now she blushed. What would Dean think about the fact they hadn't gone out for pancakes this morning as Tom suggested? She'd made him scrambled eggs with grated cheese, half and half she found in the fridge, and a pinch of fine herbs from the bottle her mother left in the cupboard. As minute sausages browned in the skillet, Tom toasted a half a loaf of whole wheat bread and slathered on the butter. He declared toast to be his only culinary accomplishment. She doubted that since the Billodeauxs were famous for their huge barbecues often featuring whole pigs or deep-fried turkeys. He said things that simply made her feel good like, "Love these eggs. Dean never cooked for me."

They arrived at the parking lot, and as soon as Tom clicked the lock, Alix climbed into the passenger seat unaided like any good buddy. She didn't want Dean to make another remark, but oh, how she wished she were petite and feminine, the kind of girl Tom might lift by the waist to help into the car. If he ever tried that, he'd probably sprain his back. Alix put down the window to let the sweltering heat escape just in time to catch the last of the brotherly conversation.

"Heads up. I had a call from Dad while you were

on the platform being a celebrity. He's arriving tomorrow to watch practice," Dean said.

"Is the whole gang coming, too?"

"Nope, you're in luck. Mom doesn't want to sit in the sun all day. The triplets are on lifeguard duty for Camp Love Letter, and he says Edie and T-Rex will just get bored and whiney."

"Did you tell him?"

*"Moi?"* Dean poked a finger at his own chest. "I thought I was sworn to secrecy."

What secret? Alix pondered that while Tom circled the huge red SUV with the little devil on its tail and Dean roared off in his black Mustang GT. She shouldn't probe if he didn't want to share it with her. No matter. Tomorrow, she'd meet the legendary Joe Billodeaux.

Chapter Nine

Tom's cell phone rang as he set the table for breakfast. He tucked it under his chin and poured the orange juice. Nearby, Alix flipped pancakes made from scratch on a griddle and monitored the bacon she'd put in the microwave. "Oh, hi, Dad. No, we're—I'm not at the practice field yet. Where are you? Well, as Mom would say, watch out for the speed traps. See you soon."

He could have, should have, told him about Alix living at his place but not when she was standing right there with a plate of steaming pancakes in her hands and a wide, happy smile on her face. "I can't wait to meet your father. I'm sorry all the Billodeauxs aren't coming. I mean I wasn't listening in yesterday, just caught that part of the conversation."

"Don't worry about it. It's no big deal." Tom forked a huge pancake from the platter, topped it with another, buttered the mound, and drenched it with warm syrup. He cut out a triangle and ate—light and heavenly with a hint of an extra ingredient. "These are so great. What do you put into them?"

Pleased, Alix said, "Vanilla. That makes them special. Sorry, the bacon is a little overcooked. I'm not used to your microwave yet. It's always better done in a pan, but this way is less messy and saves time. I don't want to be late for mini-camp. When will your father arrive?"

"Three hours if he obeys the speed limits, so make that two and a half. I like extra-crispy bacon, any bacon really." He got that smile again. He'd never met anyone happier in the early morning than Alix, certainly not Dean. She appeared to spring out of her bed and into her clothes ready for action.

A little shyly, she said while concentrating on her pancakes. "If you ever want to talk about anything, I'm a good listener. *Morfar* says I don't gab as much as most women."

"I've noticed. When I walk into a room where my sisters are all talking, I feel like a weasel entering a henhouse. The clucking just gets louder."

"When I enter a room back home, my sisters are usually talking about me. At least, I think so. With me coming into the world last and several years younger, Tille felt displaced and Rika always was bossy and likely to find fault with anything I did. She's a little better since she became a mother. You seem close to your sisters."

"Closest to Xochi, but I get along with practically everyone. In such a large family it pays to be a diplomat, but we each have our own groups within the group. Dean and I have always been together. My twin sisters had each other from birth. Stacy and Teddy are tight and so on down the line. Xo is my favorite female sibling, same no-good birth father and our shared adventure in Mexico as kids." Tom bit into a piece of slightly burnt bacon, which crumbled all over his robe and caught in his chest hairs. He opened his robe farther to brush the crumbs away. Alix followed the motion of his hand with her eyes, and he willed himself not to flush because when he did, it was a full body experience.

Alix stood up abruptly. "I'll make more bacon less well done."

"No, sit and eat. We need to get going shortly."

Alix stuffed the remains of her pancake into her mouth and polished it off by chugging a glass of milk. "I only need to clean up the kitchen."

So she didn't have dainty manners, he could care less. "Just put everything in the dishwasher. Krayola will take care of the rest."

"A good, seasoned cast iron griddle can be ruined by soap and water. I'll wipe it down and be ready to go."

"We own a seasoned griddle?"

"My mom left it along with several bundt pans in case I want to bake."

"Cake is good."

"Maybe after we finish with camp I'll have the time." Alix tossed greasy paper towels into the trash and stowed her precious griddle. She hurried toward her rooms leaving Tom to polish off the bacon without a clue as to what spooked her.

**** 

What had she claimed about Swedes not getting flustered? Not so! Watching Tom brush those crumbs from his chest had sent a surge of desire straight to her nether regions and an imaginary flash of her licking the bits from the curly orange fuzz surrounding his nipples directly to her brain. After that, sex on the dining room table. Not that she'd ever done such a thing, but she'd be willing to try with Tom.

The perfectly handsome Dean unsettled her a little,

but Tom with his upturned nose and freckles was as friendly and nonthreatening as a troll doll she'd kept on her dresser as a child. If she jumped him, she'd violate his trust in letting her rent rooms from him. Every day she arose early and fretted over what to wear to breakfast. She owned no sexy nighties, only her new underwear, and slept in an oversized tee. Maybe the sundress yesterday had been too much, but were her khaki shorts, long enough on other people but kind of brief on her, and loose sky-blue polo shirt too little to be attractive? Men had it so easy, jeans and a T-shirt for casual, a suit and tie for formal. The piles of her discarded choices littered the white throw rugs in her bedroom.

If a guy wanted to ask a girl out, he did. If she asked a guy, she'd be considered aggressive or an easy lay. Yeah, yeah, women's equality for all it was worth. Look how the lawyer had tried to make poor Stacy seem cheap when she faced her attacker on the stand. All the papers, both legit and sensational, had covered the trial. Dean had stood by her. Alix had a feeling Billodeaux men did that well. But how to let Tom know she'd like to go farther than roommate with him? Too soon, she'd have to wait.

Though still leery of the traffic, Alix offered to drive, and Tom let her. She steered her Escape through the early morning traffic out of the city to Metairie where the lanes ran four across and she had to cut off another driver to make the exit. Tom sucked in his breath but didn't say a word about women drivers. At the training center, he walked with her to get her pads and helmet.

Already out on the field, Vince Barbaro tracked the

length of Alix's long, bare legs, up her lean torso and straight to her chest with his eyes. "Hi, Alix." He gave her a finger wave. She waved back.

Tom leaned in. "Be careful of Vince. He's not as sensitive toward women as I am." Concentrating on Alix, he collided with the bulky chest of Beef Bolivar coming out of the locker room.

"Watch it, Billodeaux!"

"I don't think I made a dent in you, Beef. Wait a second, Alix, and I'll see if it's all clear for you to go in there. If not, I'll bring out your pads and helmet."

Beef didn't move out of the way. "You two girls get together on what to wear this morning?"

Alix hadn't paid much attention to Tom's attire but now noticed he'd put on khaki slacks and a nearly identical polo shirt in a darker shade of blue. Tom gave the long snapper a grin that seemed almost feral, but his words were mild enough. "We did because we're besties. You know, you make a better door than a window."

"Yeah, Bolivar, you're stopping traffic. Save your blocking for the line." Behind the man, Dean Billodeaux backed up his brother. Bolivar moved aside and away without further comment. Dean handed Alix her gear. "I put it by the door just in case you needed to be in and out quickly. Sadly, I think some of the Sinners do need Dr. Funk's sensitivity training."

"That was so nice of you. I'll go change in the ladies' room and be out on the field in a few minutes. See you there, Tom."

As she turned back to her changing area, she noted most of the guys were working out in shorts and loose T-shirts today. No sign of reporters around, no press conferences planned. Coach Buck had announced he'd had enough of that BS and closed the camp to the media. Mostly, they'd be doing drills and running routes the schedule said, no contact anticipated. Only she had been required to cover up so completely in the relentless heat and humidity of a Louisiana June. Already sweat trickled between her shoulder blades, ran down the curve of her back, and into her shorts. The jerseys were hot and the pads uncomfortable, but she'd do what she had to do to make *Morfar* proud.

Minutes later, she was doing leg stretches next to Tom so much more lightly attired. "How come I have to wear the full regalia in this heat?" she asked.

"I can think of several reasons. Management doesn't want you accidently hurt in practice, Coach thinks you should get used to the gear, and both don't want you to be a distraction."

"How so? Mostly we stand on the sidelines kicking into the net and eating snow cones."

"Yes, we have the best jobs in football and the most long lasting, but you are a good-looking woman, Alix Lindstrom. The uniform covers that up."

Genuinely puzzled, she said, "I'm not that great, not like Stacy who is gorgeous, or Xochi who is dark and very beautiful."

"Or Ilsa, thank God," Tom muttered.

"The mother of Dean's son?"

"Let's just say pretty is as pretty does and forget about it."

Alix was out on the field sending her best left-footed punts to the return team for practice and working hard to get used to Bolivar's hikes when the area went quiet. The great man had arrived, Daddy Joe Billodeaux in person. He paused to greet Coach Buck, nodded in agreement to something, and soon began to warm up his arm by tossing a football back and forth to Tom. Rounding out the family scene, Dean trotted over to receive a manly hug and took over that duty. How she wanted to abandon hers.

Though steely gray of hair, Joe had stayed in shape and still possessed a charisma she could feel way out there on the twenty-yard line. Easy to see where Dean got his dark good looks and that curl hanging on his forehead. Her mother might say the older man could put his shoes under her bed any day, but to Alix, he was the man who had created a family of twelve kids, this way, that way, all ways, and still ran a camp for seriously ill children every summer. Judging by Tom and Dean, he'd raised his brood well. That fact impressed her more than his five Super Bowl rings. Oh, to be a part of his clan.

Bolivar's snap caught her in the chest but bounced off her pads. She'd probably have a bruise under there tonight. "Pay attention, Lindstrom!" Beef hollered at her. She nodded, got ready for the next one and executed her perfect coffin corner punt, putting on an exhibition for the great man and his sons watching from the sidelines.

Coach Buck signaled her to come in. "Lindstrom, we need you to kick punts the guys can return in practice, but since I got you over here, meet Joe Billodeaux."

Aware her hair would be a sweaty mess, Alix took off her helmet to shake the hand of Tom's father. "I'm very excited to meet you, sir."

"Good to hear I haven't lost my appeal to women,"

he joked and made her blush.

"I mean I've followed your great career and read the stories about your family. I'd like to meet each and every one of them, Mama Nell and the twins and triplets and Teddy."

Joe Billodeaux gave her the smile that made women swoon. "We'll have to invite you to our big Fourth of July bash at the ranch, then. Right, Tom? It's my grandson's first birthday, too, so a really special event this year."

"Absolutely, Alix has to come. I call dibs on her for the dragon boat races, Dean."

"Is Adam Malala here? I want to find out how many pigs he wants for the pit." Joe searched for the big Samoan cornerback.

Coach Buck shook his old white, but still ornery, head. "No, mini-camp wasn't mandatory for him. He's still in Samoa with the family. Guess he'll be back in time for the Fourth."

"Tell him I'm counting on him. Okay, let's get this show on the road and give Dean a break."

Joe strode out on the field and called plays for wide outs and the new running back. He could still lob those long spirals into the slot—if the receivers were in the right place to catch them. Alix accepted a rest and a snow cone while Daddy Joe dominated the field for a while. Much to her surprise when he finished, the elder quarterback returned to sit beside her.

"Can I make you a snow cone?" she offered. "I'm getting good at that, too."

"Let Tom get it. I want to welcome you to the Sinners. From what I saw, you are going to be a big asset to the team. I hope everything works out for you.

So, are you all settled in New Orleans? Tom, you getting that snow cone?" Joe repeated as his redheaded, adopted son lingered nearby.

"Right on it!" Tom raced to the snow pile, filled a cup, and slopped an orange sports drink over it. He returned in time to hear his dad say, "You find a nice safe place to stay? I always make sure my girls have good protection. New Orleans can be a dangerous place."

"Oh, Tom is taking care of me so well. He offers to take me to breakfast, but…"

Tom thrust the snow cone at his father. Part of it sluiced off onto the ground. "I think we should take Alix out to dinner tonight."

"Oh, I'd be glad to cook," she offered.

"No, no, our treat. Galatoire's? Nope, didn't bring a jacket. Maybe Court of the Two Sisters," Joe suggested. "We can wait for the heat to die down and eat in the courtyard."

"I'd love that."

"Good, I'll get reservations for seven-thirty. Now, tell me—"

Tom cut into the tête-à-tête between Alix and his father. "I'm going to do some field goal practice. You need to hold for me, Alix. Let's go."

"I'll see you later, Mr. Billodeaux," she said as Tom fairly yanked her away.

"Joe—for heaven's sake, call me Joe," Tom's dad shouted after her.

She was on a first name basis with a hall-of-famer. That tickled her down to the very bottom of her cleats. Tom didn't seem to be on his game and missed from forty yards and thirty yards, fine at twenty, and then as if to prove something, hit one dead on between the goal posts at fifty. "I can go longer," he told her.

"Yes, I know. It's only practice."

After that expression of her faith in him, things went smoother. At lunch, Joe spread himself around, sitting next to one of his favorite receivers of the past, Jakarta Jones, and giving out tips and suggestions to other players who crowded at his table. He bid farewell to his boys at mid-afternoon.

"I'm going over to my apartment to shower. No more locker rooms for me. Alix, do you want me to pick you up around seven?"

Tom jumped in with, "We'll meet you at the restaurant, okay?"

His dad cocked his head, but merely said, "Sure, see you then."

"Your father seems really nice," Alix said.

"He can be very charming, but you never want to see him or Dean with their game faces on, believe you me."

Laughing, she asked, "Show me your game face, Tom."

"Not sure I have one." He did his best to look mean and threatening, which only made Alix laugh harder.

"Sorry, sorry, it's the freckles and upturned nose. You simply don't look fierce, more like an angry leprechaun about to shout 'begosh and begorra'," she said.

"Let's see you do any better," he challenged.

Alix narrowed her eyes to slits of blue and thrust her chin forward, lower lip puffed out. She attempted to channel her grandfather on a bad day.

"That's—that's adorable—like a pouty child,"

Tom said as if he searched for the right words.

"I tried to imitate *Morfar*. Don't ever let him hear you say that." Both of them burst into laughter.

Coach Buck noticed and probably decided they were having too much fun. "If you two are done making faces, I want Barbaro to show Lindstrom how to throw a block in case she ever has to execute one. See she doesn't get hurt."

"Right, Coach. Come on, newbie." Vince picked up a pad and held it in front of him. "Dig in. Hit me hard as you can."

Alix did her best and got a "worst you can do?" from her personal protector. "I'm glad you aren't protecting *me*. You hit like a girl. Again on the count of three."

That irritated her. She pushed as hard as she could into the pad. Vince didn't budge. Gathering all her strength, she hit him again. This time he yielded a few inches.

"Okay, you got to do that every time. It won't stop a real football player from running right over you, but it might slow him down enough for me to come to your rescue. Again!"

Come to her rescue? Alix rammed into him, hurting her shoulder a trifle, and pushed Vince back a foot.

"Now you got it, babe. One more time."

Alix gritted her teeth and gave it to him again, another solid hit. "There you go, dude."

Vince gave her a toothy white grin and simply held up the pad again.

At the end of their session, Coach signaled for her to hit the showers first. Alix straggled in bone-weary and not too sure which she hated more, Vince Barbaro or football.

\*\*\*\*

Tom waited by the entrance to Alix's suite of rooms. He hadn't set foot past the threshold since she moved into the place. Not like her to dawdle or be late, and they planned to walk to the restaurant. He called down the hall, "You ready yet? It's ten after seven."

"I can't decide what to wear!" she called.

"How about the bride dress? That's pretty."

"No, what if I spill something on it in front of Joe? Besides, the neckline is too low. I guess the illusion dress maybe."

"Sounds great." Tom shrugged though no one lurked around to see. What did he know about women's dresses? And what the heck was an illusion dress anyhow? Whatever she wore, she'd look great in it— that he knew for sure. "It's seven-fifteen."

"I know, I know."

Alix emerged in a garment with dark sides and a beige center shaped like a woman's figure. It reminded Tom of Halloween skeleton costumes, but he knew enough not to say so or they'd be here until ten p.m. The skirt was slender and short enough to show off her endless legs. Good enough for him.

Alix stared at her shoes. "My mom said I should get the beige pumps because they go with everything, but I think the color makes my feet look big. Of course, my feet are big. Should I change to something black?"

"Your feet are fine, so are the shoes. Let's boogie. We're going to be late."

"Oh, I wouldn't want to keep Joe waiting."

That moved her forward, and they finally got out

the door, but not before Alix remembered the matching handbag she'd left on the bed and dashed back to get it. "I don't think I've ever had a matching handbag before. Mostly just backpacks and gym bags."

"I still don't own one. Whatever shall I do?" Tom put on his best Blanche DuBois southern accent and fanned his face with his hand. "Stop stressing. My dad doesn't really notice women's clothes unless they are indecent or on my sisters or both."

Out on the sidewalk, Alix hobbled along far differently from her usual athletic stride. "You okay?" Tom asked.

"It's the cracks in the sidewalks and the places with bricks. I'm not used to high heels and..." Either the ever-present heat or her own embarrassment made her flush.

"Might a gentleman offer a lady his arm?" Tom paused to bow with a flourish.

"I would gladly accept that offer."

Alix linked arms with him and steadied herself as they passed the elegant shops offering antiques, silver, and jewelry on Royal Street, so different from Bourbon. They arrived on the dot, not that Joe Billodeaux watched the time. He'd been holding court in the bar, signing autographs and visiting with old fans, not forgotten ten years after retirement. Never to be forgotten in New Orleans. His smile blazed when he saw them arm in arm, but Tom's dad made no comment. They followed the hostess to a courtyard table and ordered amidst the lush greenery, flowers, strings of lights, and the sound of water trickling in the fountain. Veal Oscar for Joe, tenderloin of beef for Tom, and corn fried catfish for Alix who couldn't seem to get enough of fresh Louisiana fish. Joe ordered turtle soup all around for starters.

Alix hesitated. "You really do eat turtles here? I'm not so sure…"

"*Mais*, yeah, *cher*. Us Cajuns eat everyt'ing. Even the zoo got signs naming where dat animal come from, its name, and how to cook it. And we do it good, good. Besides, we only eat da mean snapping turtles, not da the cute ones." His dad had launched into what Mama Nell called his cute Cajun routine.

The joke was old, but Alix smiled and tried the soup. "It tastes like beef," she said, surprised.

"And sherry. Dat's the best part, don't you know." Oh, Joe was on tonight.

Tom refrained from rolling his eyes since Alix appeared to be enjoying every minute of the routine and every mouthful of food.

As the meal came to an end, Daddy Joe declared, "We started with sherry in the soup. Let's stop with brandy."

"Oh, I don't really drink much hard liquor, only beer and wine," Alix said.

"You'll like it in this form—Strawberries à la Ray."

In the twilight, a chef ignited fresh strawberries soaked in strawberry liqueur and brandy. The blue flames reflected in Alix's eyes as they danced over the dessert. When the fire died down, the cook poured the entire mixture over vanilla ice cream that immediately began to puddle. Alix dug in as happy as a child eating candy, grownup candy. He could have watched her perfectly natural joy all night. He did the little ritual of fighting to pick up the check, but let his dad win this time.

As Joe signed the credit card bill, he said, "Want to hit a few clubs or just go over and visit with Mariah?"

Alix stifled a very wide yawn behind her hand. "If you don't mind, I'd just as soon turn in. While hitting Vince Barbaro was in some ways very satisfying, it did wear me out and give me a sore shoulder. Good thing I don't kick with that part of my anatomy."

Joe immediately retracted his offer to go clubbing. "Believe you me, I understand sore shoulders. We'll walk you home, then I might spend a little time visiting with Tom. I don't get to see enough of my boys these days."

"That won't bother me at all." They started off along Royal Street with Alix in the middle, sometimes having to split up for groups of tourists barging in the opposite direction, but finally crossing broad Canal Street. Arturo happily opened the door for them with a cheery, "*Buenos noches,* Miss Alix and the two Mr. Billodeauxs. Good to see you again, sir."

"*Gracias* and have a good evening yourself," Joe replied. "Alix, you have a place here, too?"

"Yes, she does," Tom interjected before Alix could open her mouth. He got to their entry first, punched in the code, and held the door for her.

"Certainly you are welcome to join us, Alix, if you don't mind a lot of family and guy talk," Joe said as she just kept walking past the huge sofa off toward Tom's old rooms.

"No, you have your chat. I'm going to try out those directional nozzles on my shoulder in that amazing shower, then go bed. Frankly, I'm relieved mini-camp is over, and I have some time to heal and get to know the city better. So great to meet you, Joe. See you in the morning, Tom."

While he didn't particularly like the dress, Tom did appreciate the way it clung to Alix's hips as she moved away. When he finished staring, he found his dad's eyes studying him.

"I think we need to talk about more than who you're going to pick up for the Fourth of July bash, son. Sit down."

"Look, I offered her my old rooms. I can watch out for her like I promised her family. She's paying rent and does most of the cooking. Nothing going on between us. I haven't set a foot across her threshold," Tom blurted in one long, revealing breath.

"Don't pee on my boots and tell me it's raining. You want that young woman."

"Okay, I won't deny it. How did you know?"

"You watched her eyes when they flamed the dessert, and you stared at her behind when she went down the hall. I was a quarterback. I know about reading the eyes. Just make sure you don't mistake her for another Ilsa. Alix used to be exactly my type, only with a bigger rack and much less innocent."

Tom tried a deflecting technique. "But you ended up with a tiny brunette."

"Yes, I did." As he'd hoped, his father's eyes took on a faraway look. "I decided I needed a more wholesome kind of woman, but let me tell you, those little ones can surprise the hell out of you. I chased after Nell, but in the end, she jumped me, dumped me, and took me back again. Lots of energy in small women."

"Please, no details!" Tom clamped his hands over his burning red ears.

Unfortunately, that plea caused his dad to return to the previous topic. "What I'm saying is Alix is the type of blonde you marry, not the kind you fool around with and end up getting slapped with a paternity suit."

"Hey, that happened to Dean, not me. Being dumped by Ilsa for Dean was a very lucky break. Before you say it, I'll go slow and be careful."

"Good. Now, if you want to talk more about your emotions, call your mother. You bring Alix to the Fourth of July celebration. Ilsa and Beck will be there for his first birthday party. Just as well you bring a date in case she decides to double back and pick off another Billodeaux. A woman like that can be pretty persuasive."

"Tell me I don't have to pick up her and the kid."

"Don't forget the kid is your nephew."

"Beck is great. It's Ilsa I like to avoid."

"No, just pick up the twins in Baton Rouge and get Teddy in Lafayette. Ilsa said she'll be bringing Prince Dobbs. No way to keep him out, not with his parents invited."

"Won't be a problem for me. I do pity Dean."

"It's his own fault, just as Dean's birth was mine, but I've never regretted him or adopting you. I couldn't have two better sons. Aw hell, I'm getting old and maudlin. Throwing those passes today made my shoulder sore as well. Since all your bedrooms are taken, I'll go back to the apartment for the night and head out in the morning."

"Want to come over for an *ebelskiver* breakfast? "

"Huh?"

"It's a Swedish beignet sort of thing Alix makes."

"She cooks, too! No, I don't want to intrude on

your domestic bliss. Expect a call from your mom. Just keep your hooray rod in your pants and if it escapes, don't forget the rubber raincoat, boy." He rubbed Tom's red curls as if he were still a lad and ended with the hug and the words, "I love you, son."

Chapter Ten

For two quiet weeks, Tom had Alix mostly to himself. They enjoyed breakfast together each day. Could she ever make an omelet and home fries to perfection. After that, off to work out or go for a long run side by side. Come home, wash off in separate bathrooms, unfortunately, and take in the sights via carriage or riverboat. They visited the massive white alligator and cute sea otters at the aquarium or strolled around the Audubon zoo to watch the tigers and polar bears cooling off in their pools. He usually paid for dinner in one of the French Quarter restaurants both plain and fancy since she cooked something nearly every day. They were in no danger of running out of places to eat for a long time. What had his dad called this?—oh yes, domestic bliss. Too bad it didn't include any kind of sex.

Tom anticipated all that bliss would disappear with the brevity of a sky rocket on the Fourth of July with Alix's full exposure to the Billodeaux family and its many honorary members. It began to extinguish when he stopped the big, red SUV in Baton Rouge to pick up his twin sisters who seemed to be perpetual graduate students at the university. Not identical but close enough with their large dark eyes and mops of curly black hair, Jude and Annie clambered their short selves into the back seat. Jude promptly reminded him he'd arrived fifteen minutes late. He retaliated by asking if she wanted to take a few minutes and to go inside to change because their low-riding short shorts and bare midriff tops were sure to set off their grandmother. "That navel ring better be a clip-on, Jude."

"Holy shit, Tom, you sound just like her," Jude shot right back.

"Language," he said, primly.

"He does Mom pretty well, too," the milder Annie replied.

"Okay, both of you are on your own. I'll stand around and say, 'I told you so.' Jude and Annie, this is Alix Lindstrom, the Sinners' new punter."

Alix's blue eyes shone as if she were meeting major celebrities. "I'm so happy to meet you. You're both so cute and petite."

"Small but mighty like our mother, and don't you forget it, Tom's giant girlfriend," Jude snarled.

Alix turned around and studied the hump of the Mississippi River Bridge in the distance as if memorizing a geography lesson. The back of her neck burned red. Annie reached up and put a hand on her shoulder. "I'm sorry about that. Jude is sensitive about being height challenged."

"Um, so am I, about being tall," Alix murmured.

"Yeah, I can't see over you," Jude said, and Alix promptly slumped in her seat.

Burned up, Tom announced in his best Daddy Joe impersonation, "I tell you me, one more smart remark out of you, Jude Emily Billodeaux, and I put you out by da side of da road for da gators to eat."

Jude answered right back. "Then you'd be in trouble for making me hitchhike to the party in these shorts. Okay, sorry. I'm only tired of being dominated by tall blondes, first Stacy, then that obnoxious Ilsa."

"Well, Alix isn't either one of them, so leave her alone."

"It's fine, Tom. Sort of like having Tille in the car. Jude doesn't know me yet, and I hope she'll like me when she does." If a mild answer turneth away wrath, Alix had just delivered one. She stared straight ahead as they approached and crossed the bridge spanning the wide river without one glance downward at the barges being pushed by tugs far, far below.

"We're both going to like you," Annie swore. "Jude is just pissy because a guy she wants is dating a tall blonde right now. She can't get his attention without jumping up and down."

"Anybody I know?" Tom asked.

"Nope," they replied in unison, giving a hint that he probably did.

Tom drew on his patter about the great Atchafalaya Basin when they reached the causeway across the swamp. He pointed to the place where an oil well blew out and to the vast number of jagged stumps sticking out of the water where once giant cypress grew before being logged out early in the twentieth century. They passed Breaux Bridge, Crawfish Capitol of the World, and moved on to Lafayette where his adopted brother, Teddy, sat waiting patiently in his wheelchair. He rose up on his crutches to allow Tom to stow the bright red chair and accepted help getting in beside his sisters. Annie gave him a shoulder hug and introduced Alix before Tom got the chance.

Treading carefully lest she step on any more toes, Alix said, "I know you are a sports reporter and an announcer, too."

"Only for the local paper and games, but I'm building my resumé. Any chance of an exclusive interview?" Teddy asked with a most appealing smile on his face. His fine, blond hair hung in his blue eyes giving him the appearance of a shy child.

"I've been interviewed so many times lately, I don't think there is anything left of me that's exclusive, but sure if you can think of any new questions."

"Great. I'll get in touch." Teddy settled in for the short remainder of the trip.

By the time the group arrived at Joe Billodeaux's huge country home, Alix had regained some of her shine. Knox Polk, the ranch manager and guardian of the gate, nodded his grizzled head and waved them on. As Tom turned the SUV down the live oak-lined drive, she whispered, "Lorena Ranch, I'm really here at Lorena Ranch," so quietly he figured only he heard over the conversation in the backseat. Knowing he had to get it over with, he parked by the kitchen door and led Alix inside to meet Mawmaw Nadine, the grandmother who loved her family fiercely but wasn't above telling them all their flaws.

Nadine labored at putting a two-inch topping of meringue on a vast pan of her notable bread pudding. Spatula still in hand, she opened her arms wide. "Tommy, give your Mawmaw some sugar." Dutifully he pecked her soft, lined cheek and bowed his head over her still thick, white hair to receive his hug. Not two seconds later, Nadine turned her strong features and dark, dark eyes on Alix.

"A new girlfriend?"

"The Sinners' punter, Alix Lindstrom." He might

as well get it over with. "She's renting my old rooms at the condo."

"That so." Mawmaw appraised Alix from her red painted toenails to the top of her light blonde head.

She'd worn sandals that exposed her long toes, khaki shorts, and a long T-shirt with a patriotic smattering of glittery red, white and blue stars. The neckline had a V, but it didn't go down very far. A blush spread across Alix's cheeks and she blurted, "I'm sorry, I should have brought a hot dish. I have lots of recipes, I just didn't think."

"*Cher*, this time you a guest. You like bread pudding?"

"Very much. I've had it several times in New Orleans."

"Mine is better. If you can cook, I give you the recipe. Looks like Tom is filling out some finally. He always was a scrawny kid. You could never feed him up enough. Your doing?" Mawmaw's eyes roved Tom's body and made his face light up like a red lantern.

He'd also worn khaki shorts and sandals, but with a fitted black tee that clung to his chest muscles and showed a small tuft of red hair between his pecs. At the time he dressed he thought it passed for sexy. Now he found himself checking for nonexistence rolls of flab. He hurried to say, "Alix is a great cook, like you. What's this?" He raised the lid on a covered dish and immediately slammed it down again with a sharp snort from his pug nose as if he'd inhaled a deadly gas. "Sauerkraut. Ilsa is here already."

"*Mais*, yeah. Who brings sauerkraut to a Fourth of July picnic? All you got to do is dump it from the can into a dish. That ain't cooking. That's lazy," his grandmother pronounced.

"Actually, sauerkraut is great with roasted pork. We eat our share of it in Wisconsin. I have a recipe for sauerkraut balls made with cream cheese and sausage. You'd never know you're eating it. Next time, I'll make some," Alix promised, so eager to please it hurt Tom's heart. What would Nadine's always-unbridled tongue say to her next?

Those dark eyes glittered in their net of wrinkles. "You got a kind heart when it comes to—sauerkraut." Turning them on Tom again, she said, "Has Alix met Ilsa yet?"

"No."

"Well, she's here with that not so charming Prince in the den. You might as well get it over wit'. Beck is still my great-grandbaby, my *cher bébé*, no matter what." As Tom and Alix moved toward the hall, they exposed the twins and Teddy standing behind them.

"You better go on upstairs and put on some clothes before your daddy sees you two—or anybody else does for that matter." Using her hands to gesture as always, their Mawmaw scolded so hard that meringue from the spatula flew through the air and stuck to their scanty tops.

"Sure, now we have to change," fumed Jude, who stomped by them looking at if she'd just come inside from a blizzard. Annie followed in her stormy wake as always.

Mawmaw Nadine held out her arms again to Teddy leaning on his crutches, waiting his turn. "Come here, honey, and give me one of your bear hugs."

While his grandmother received her homage, Tom

steered Alix to the vast living room/den where Joe Billodeaux's many trophies and awards filled all the crannies and his large family gathered regularly. At the moment, it was occupied by three people: Ilsa Beckmann, mother of Dean's illegitimate son; Prince Dobbs, a wide receiver for the Sinners, who claimed a miracle recovery from a gunshot wound the previous year; and the huge, black bulk of the Reverend Revelation Bullock, hall-of-famer cornerback and fulltime AME minister.

Prince held Ilsa on his lap in one of the big recliners. Tom noticed the placement of his hands, one dangling over her very prominent breasts clad in clingy red and the other wrapped possessively around her bare waist. Her long legs curled beneath his and her nearly white hair drawn up in a high ponytail mingled with Prince's head of short, light brown dreads as she pressed her face against his tawny cheek. He'd worn a sleeveless muscle shirt that displayed both his well-developed biceps and his once obscene and violent tattoos, now converted to an elaborate Celtic cross on one arm and a portrait of a dreadlocked Jesus on the other.

Obviously, the three had been discussing theology of a sort because the Rev said, "Son, it's hard to enter heaven with a beautiful blonde on your lap, especially one you're not married to."

Prince waved the hand perched on Ilsa's breast. "She's my woman now. We got a big announcement to make today. You'll see. Since I met Christ face to face, I plan to found my own church, the Temple of the Dreadlocked Jesus just like I got on my arm because that's what he looks like, ain't no white man."

The Rev pursed his big lips and steepled the large hands that had once stripped footballs from opponents like a bully stealing candy from a baby. To Tom, he appeared to be praying for patience. "First, you must learn humility before you can lead others to Christ."

"Sure, sure, I got humility. Learned it after being on the injured reserve for months and months, but now I'm back and ready to play," Prince Dobbs assured the minister.

"Hate to interrupt, but I wanted to introduce you to Alix Lindstrom, our new punter, since you weren't at mini-camp, Prince." Tom tried to keep the sarcasm out of his voice. "You, too, Ilsa."

Prince stood, all but dumping Ilsa on her ass, but she managed to regain her feet fast because she excelled at quick recoveries. "My, my, you are going to improve the looks of that team one hundred percent, you pretty thang." He reached out to grasp Alix's hand, but Tom stepped between them as if searching the room for a lost object.

"Where's my nephew on his first birthday? Hiding out?"

"Ach, no, he is *mit* the ponies. Daddy Joe says he is not too young to ride. What do I know? I am no farmer," Ilsa said with her German accent. She shrugged her pale shoulders, beautifully exposed by the red top that tied around her neck. Her white shorts were only slightly longer than the twins' and rode even lower.

"Rancher," Tom corrected. "We'll go watch him ride."

"So," said Ilsa as her cold, pale blue eyes lasered in on Alix. "You are with Tom? He is such a funny boy to play *mit* and all over freckles. You understand what I mean?"

"I'm not sure I do."

"Come on. You haven't seen the horses yet or the rest of the place. We'll go out by the front door." He grasped Alix's hand and towed her into the hallway again. Might as well tell her exactly what Ilsa meant now and get it over with, though for the moment Alix seemed to be awed by the shining burgundy floor tiles, the sweeping staircase to the second floor and the excessively sparkly chandelier hanging in the foyer, all chosen by his dad before his mom's better taste intervened. They exited through the large front door with its beveled sidelights and came out on the many-pillared verandah.

"Gravestones?" Alix said, her eyes wide and riveted on two small markers by a rustic bench.

"The family's pet dogs."

"Oh, Macho and Titi. I remember now. Where is everyone else?"

"Only bodies we have buried here," Tom joked. "But if you mean the living, probably over by the corral or the barbecue pavilion. It's early. The place will get a lot more crowded by noon."

"Ilsa is right. You are funny."

And freckled all over, as the German woman knew only too well. Tom took a deep breath. Here goes. "Yeah, Ilsa knows all about me. We were lovers before she figured out American football and the amount of money quarterbacks get paid. When Dean and Stacy broke up, she moved right in on him while he was still smarting and dumped me. I blamed Dean at the time, but I see it differently now. I had a lucky escape.

Unfortunately, she's in our lives forever. Anyhow, that's how she knows about the freckles all over." He gestured to his body but kept his eyes on the ground not daring to raise them to Alix.

"Oh wow, that didn't make the scandal sheets. Just Stacy and Dean, then him with Ilsa."

"Kickers don't have a very high profile. Mostly, the paparazzi don't care who we date."

"I think I'm glad about that. Freckles all over," Alix continued with speculation in her voice.

How he wanted to show her right now in the palm grove, but they'd rounded the mansion. The barn and pavilion entered their view. Daddy Joe, standing by his big Samoan friend and current Sinners cornerback, Adam Malala, monitored the pit where two whole pigs roasted island style. The men waved to them. People gathered around the corral took their eyes off the male two-thirds of the Billodeaux triplets who led a brace of ponies bearing small children around the ring and looked their way. Nothing to do but go forward and join the party.

His dad had purchased horses for his youngest set of twins since the ones the elder children had ridden now grazed in that big pasture in the sky. The brown Welsh pony with a lush forelock hanging in his eyes and the stockier Shetland palomino would be around for little Beck to ride whenever he visited. Now, the blond boy, holding happily to the saddle horn, crowed, "Gid-up" and flailed with his heels as the horse meandered around the ring. Cute.

His dad's trick horse stood saddled nearby along with his old mount, Copperhead, pretty long in the tooth by now. "You ride?" he asked Alix.

"No. I'd like to learn."

"If we have the time, I'll put you up on Copperhead. He's so old he won't take off with you. Hard to believe he was once a top barrel-racing horse, but he still has some life in him."

The horse did indeed have a copper head, but also a gray muzzle. "I'm not too sure about that name. I don't know much about horses, but I've killed a few snakes over the years I've been camping." Alix approached warily. "Does he bite?"

"Only apples. Give him one, and he's your friend for the rest of his life."

They joined Teddy, moving along steadily on his crutches toward the corral. "I think I'll get a little riding in before Rascal gets too exhausted from hauling children around."

"You ride?" Alix asked, then must have realized how condescending that sounded as she added, "I don't."

"It's good for core development when you have spina bifida. Watch this." Teddy approached the trick horse, big, red Rascal, and executed a hand signal. The animal knelt before him, and Teddy climbed aboard. "Dad got him especially for me. Get up on Copperhead, and I'll show you how it's done."

"Minute," Tom said. "She'll need the stirrups longer." He made the adjustment and showed her how to mount from the left. Opening the corral gate, he gave Copperhead a swat on the rump that moved him forward. "Take good care of her, Ted. I'll be over by the pavilion with Dad and Adam." He lingered long enough to make sure she wouldn't fall off, not likely at the plod they were going. Alix felt brave enough to unclutch one hand from the horn and wave as the horses moved away. Nothing more to do right now than go over to the pavilion and check in with his mother.

As he approached the screened building, he saw the forms of three women working on the picnic preparations, two fairly hefty and one, his mom, quite petite. He recognized a familiar voice speaking her mind that he hadn't expected to hear at the ranch—Miss Krayola, his cleaning lady. Since the topic was Alix, he slowed and ducked behind a tree to listen.

"Alix, she ain't tidy like your boys, Miss Nell, clothes all over the floor most days."

"Messy, then?

"No, bathroom is always clean like she scrubs it herself. I know the girl cooks, but never leaves the pots in the sink for me to scrub. More like she's always in a hurry and can't make up her mind what to wear. I jus' hangs everything up again, and she writes me thank you notes. But those white rugs of hers need washin' all the time. She does track in some dirt."

His mother's lighter voice responded. "If those are her only flaws, she seems rather nice. Do you think they are intimate?"

"I'd say no, and I washes both sets of sheets. If I were that young woman, I'd be on Mr. Tom like a tick on a red-eared hound dog. To my mind, he's a catch, but being a football player and all maybe she's cheering for the other team, you know what I mean."

"Yes," his mom replied. "That would be too bad because Joe thinks Tom is already badly infatuated."

"If you mean hung up on, pro'bly," Krayola answered. "I come in on them more than once. She's always dressed. Mr. Tom, he's wearing a robe and showing his chest like one of them orangutans trying to attract a female."

"Better than a baboon who shows his behind," said Corazon, the Billodeaux's stout housekeeper and the third occupant of the pavilion. All of them laughed heartily and that stung a little. Maybe he was making a fool of himself, but he refused to be discussed so openly by three women, all of whom mothered him.

Tom made his entrance and shut their mouths in mid-guffaw. "Talking about me, ladies? I thought us Billodeaux kids were allowed to have our own private lives once we left home." His mother's pixie face colored across the cheekbones. Nice to have someone else blush for a change. With Krayola's black skin and Corazon's face a deep Hispanic brown, hard to tell if either one of them were embarrassed. He suspected not.

Corazon, who'd had a big hand in raising him, spoke first. "We only want to see you happy, Tommy."

"Yes, we aren't really interfering, only talking," his mother claimed.

Tom set his eyes on Krayola. "If I'd known you were coming, I could have given you a ride along with Alix." He'd always wondered if she spied on him and Dean and reported to their mother.

"I come up early to help. You know Miss Nadine don't allow no caterers and says homemade is always better. It's a lot of work for yo' mama." As if she hadn't said a word about his sex life and his sheets, Krayola continued to slice long pineapple spears and fuzzy kiwis for a big fruit tray. Spy or not, he simply couldn't fire her. The condo wouldn't be the same without her big, white-clad frame bustling around and bobbing her head wrapped in a colorful do-rag to the tunes on her iPod.

For better or worse, all of these older women cared about him. He moved forward and gave each one a big hug.

\*\*\*\*

To the clop of her mount, Alix thought, "Here I am at Lorena Ranch. Here I am at Lorena Ranch."

The horses moved so slowly she could take in the view as they moved around the ring. Along with a horde of dark-haired, dark-eyed Billodeaux relatives of all ages, the rails were lined with big men who played with the Sinners, now or in the past, several hall-of-famers among them. She recognized handsome Connor Riley with is fair hair going from blond to white and worn much shorter now than in *Morfar*'s photo album. In complete contrast, Curse 'em and Crush 'em Calvin Armitage, huge, dark and forbidding but not so handsome, leaned on the top rail beside him. Calvin's hair, always shorn close to the scalp in pictures, had gone to tight gray knots. The nearly as famous Billodeaux British butler, wearing Bermuda shorts, long white socks stuffed into his sandals, and an incongruously loud Hawaiian shirt, served them cold drinks from a silver tray. Gawking, she was nearly unseated when Copperhead broke into a slow trot following Teddy's horse around the ring.

Teddy made a tight circle and pulled up beside her. "Get your hands off the horn and use the reins. If you want him to go slower, pull back—faster, a kick of the heels and a loosening of the reins. Lean in the direction you want him to go and let him feel the pressure of the reins on his neck. It's easy, really."

Shamed by a man wearing braces on his legs, Alix

did her best but called it quits after a few circuits of the arena. "The way I'm slapping against this saddle when he trots, my backside will be too sore to do any kicking." Gratefully, she slid off the animal at the gate and turned him over to two children, a sturdy boy and a petite girl, the younger set of Billodeaux twins.

She looked for Tom, always easy to locate with his blazing red hair. He was her roomie, her best bud, her security in the world of the Sinners and sadly nothing more. Maybe if she wore something more provocative to make breakfast than jeans and a tee—like only an apron since she lacked any sexy negligees, but she didn't own an apron either. Hard to be good at something when you lacked the proper equipment, exactly like playing sports.

Alix headed for the barbecue pavilion intending to search the interior for Tom, but she found Vince Barbaro instead. Just inside the screen door, he loitered with a beer in his hand and his eyes appraising the side dishes three women placed on the long tables covered by red-checkered tablecloths. "Nice spread," he said to Alix as if he weren't referring to the array of coleslaw, potato salad, platters of hamburger and hot dog fixings, fresh fruit, a tray of veggies and dip, not to mention the baked beans bubbling in a cast iron pot on the indoor grill.

"What goes on the empty plates?" he asked a heavy Mexican woman with gray-streaked hair, her body encased in a scarlet bib apron edged with dark blue rickrack, and sporting a star-shaped pocket on one cushiony breast.

*Maybe that's the kind of apron I should get*, Alix thought as the older lady answered.

"For the corn on the cob and the sweet potatoes and plantains from the *umu* oven."

Vince snagged two long-necks from the silver tray as the butler passed with refills and plunked down his dead soldier. "Here you go, old man." He tried for a British accent and failed in a way Tom never would. The butler stiffened but continued out the door without a word. The Mexican cook's round, black eyes went hooded. She turned her back on Vince and continued a conversation she'd been having with a small, perky brunette woman who had been obscured by her size and surprisingly, Miss Krayola in the flesh. Alix waved hi to her and the cleaning lady, her hands busy, nodded in acknowledgment.

"So I say, you not coming home for the big picnic, Junior? My own son, he says, nope, going to Florida with his college friends. I tell his Papi, and Knox tells me a boy got to grow up and go his own way. I say why can't that way be through his mama's kitchen, no?" She gave the bean pot an extra hard stir for emphasis.

"I know, I know, it's hard to gather them in again once they leave home. He'll return when he gets older, never fear." That sage advice offered, Nell Billodeaux laid slices of purple onion in a row next to the lettuce leaves.

Vince held out a bottle toward Alix. "Here, I got you a cold one, babe."

She grabbed it in passing and went right by the man straight toward the Mexican. "I know you are Corazon Polk, the woman who saved Tom from being kidnapped as a baby. Thank you for that. He's such a great guy." She shook Corazon's only free hand even though it was the left one.

"Sure, my *Rojito,* my Little Red, is a good boy, a second son, one who comes home on holidays."

In the background, Vince snickered. Nell Billodeaux tossed a suggestion his way. "Why don't you go outside and mingle with the men? I'm sure they will need your strength to lift the pigs from the oven, Vince."

Vince puffed up a bit, flexed his biceps slightly. He'd dressed not unlike Prince Dobbs in a tight sleeveless shirt that flattered his muscles. The American flag pattern covering his hairy chest rippled a little. Alix had to admit he possessed beautifully muscular calves and heavy thighs, a feature she always noticed in men, but his were covered in dark hair that also scattered across his exposed toes clad in heavy-duty flip-flops. He'd slicked his black hair straight back from his swarthy face, and the ends rested on his shoulders, a perfect extra for a gym scene in a *Rocky* movie.

"Want to watch me lift those pigs, Alix?" he asked with another small jump of his pecs.

"Maybe later, Vince. I need to say hello to our hostess first."

"Fine by me. I'll hang out with *Rojito.*" He punctuated that statement with a snorty chuckle. "This is kind of a family affair, kids and dogs and horses running around everywhere. Most of the unmarried guys don't come. You need masculine company, keep me in mind."

"I'll do that." She turned toward Nell as Vince shoved off and rolled her blue eyes. "I hope Dr. Funk teaches me how to get rid of guys like that as slickly as you just did, Mrs. Billodeaux. I'm Alix Lindstrom, the Sinners' punter. I room with Tom. Anything I can do to help?"

Nell held out both hands and squeezed hers. Her big, dark brown eyes crinkled in the corners, but she seemed very youthful for a woman sliding toward fifty as agilely as a base runner diving into home plate. Her trim little figure and short, pixie-cut hair contributed to that impression.

"I've been so anxious to meet Tom's roommate. Getting rid of young men might not be as easy for you as it is for me. I'm an old married woman with a degree in psychology and an air of authority despite my size. I can only tell you that giving a man a task that flatters his ego usually works when they are underfoot."

"I'll remember that."

Joe Billodeaux entered the pavilion with a slam of the screen door. He let in three dogs, one large and black, two small, white and fluffy. All three went to sit hopefully at Corazon's feet as if they knew the easiest mark when it came to treats. She took a hot dog striped from the grill, broke it into three pieces and tossed each a tidbit.

"Good to see you again, Alix. You've met Nell, I guess. Adam says the pigs will be done in a half hour." Joe made his way to the bean pot and sampled the contents with a small spoon. "Needs a few dashes of hot sauce, Corazon."

"There will be hot sauce on the table for anyone who wants it, Joe's Special Reserve brand. Would you mind telling your mother to warm the rest of the hot dishes? You're the only one she listens to, dearest. Please take the dogs out with you," Nell requested.

"You got it, sugar." Joe snatched a hamburger from a mound being kept warm on a metal platter. He held it high as he backed toward the door. Three pairs of canine eyes tracked him. "Oh, if you're looking for Tom, I sent him to get his sister lifeguarding at the pool. We'll close it down for the picnic, but I hope you brought a bathing suit."

"I'm wearing it under my clothes," Alix said.

"Good thinking. You're bound to get wet one way or the other." Joe broke up the hamburger and tossed it outside. The dogs stampeded for the meat, and he followed.

"Maybe you could help carry the hot dishes over from the kitchen, Alix. I would appreciate it, dear."

"I'd be glad to do that." In a second, Alix found herself trotting behind Joe to the kitchen of the big house and wondering if she'd been manipulated into leaving Nell, Corazon, and Krayola alone so they could complete their preparations in peace. Maybe, maybe not. Not only did she walk among the rich and famous, who seemed awfully like her own relatives in many respects, but she'd gotten a free psychology lesson from Nell Billodeaux herself. She simply loved this place, this family, and maybe she could love Tom if only she could figure out how to get him to take an interest.

Chapter Eleven

According to Adam Malala, a heavy feast called for a long nap afterwards Samoan-style, and more than one person dozed on blankets under the oaks. Even the dogs rested in the heat of the day and gnawed a pig's ear each in the shade. Alix made her contribution by toting endless dishes from the kitchen, holding them with big barbecue mitts on her hands: among the offerings a pan of rice dressing, mac and cheese, and the crock of sauerkraut which she strategically placed between the hotdogs and the planks that would hold the roasted pigs. When she'd reached for the bread pudding, its peaks of meringue now nicely browned, Mawmaw Nadine slapped her mitts away.

"We put the desserts out later, *cher*, but I got to say you a helpful girl, not like some who think they're queen of the Mardi Gras ball."

Alix assumed that referred to Ilsa, who had sailed through the kitchen without stopping on her way to the buffet line already forming up. Nadine caught Prince sniffing behind the German woman like a dog after a bitch in heat and thrust a basket of warm garlic bread into his paws.

"Dean says you got good hands. Put 'em to use." No one refused Mawmaw Nadine.

Now Alix lolled on a big, worn quilt under the boughs of a spectacular live oak with low-hanging limbs and a curtain of Spanish moss. It would have been a rather private place with Tom stretched out beside her, one arm behind his head and the other sprawled wide open as if he wanted to invite her to lay her head on his chest, but Vince found them, parted the veil of moss, and invited himself to sit down.

"Looks like you have room enough for three." He positioned himself on Alix's other side.

Between the heat the two men generated along with a blazing Louisiana sun, she hoped Nell soon gave permission to reopen the pool. That wouldn't happen immediately as Joe Billodeaux banged on an iron triangle loud enough to wake the soundest sleepers.

He used the voice he'd once saved for audibles to reach his audience. "Hate to interrupt your naps, but we have a special event to celebrate, the birthday of our first grandchild. Thanks to all of you who brought gifts. We'll be saving most of them for later since Granny Nell says they are too overwhelming for such a small child, so we'll just trot out one big present from me to Beck and get on with the cake and ice cream and the rest of the desserts. I highly recommend my mama's bread pudding." Joe made a come hither gesture toward the barn and the biggest of his triplets, Mack, who had reached man size and then some, led out a paint pony beautifully mottled with black and brown patches.

"Horsey!" screamed Beck who sat wearing a paper crown at a small table just right for his size.

"Pony," his grandfather corrected. "Might as well get your terms right, boy."

"Po-nee!" Beck repeated and scooted across the grass to hug the animal around the neck.

"Look at the way that child can run already.

Walked at nine months, a natural athlete," Joe said, inflated with pride.

Nell stuck a pin in his balloon. "Did we really need another pony? Edie and T-Rex have nearly outgrown theirs."

"Sugar, I think we're going to have more than one grandchild, don't you?" His little wife couldn't argue with that. Having twelve children, there were bound to be lots of third generation offspring.

Mack set the little boy on the pony's bare back and as Beck clutched the mane, led both to the table that now held a small chocolate cake with one big wax candle aflame in its center. "Cake!" Beck squirmed off his birthday gift and buried his face in the icing before the candle went out. Nell pinched the wick before the boy singed himself. His audience laughed as he raised his frosting-smeared face and tried to wipe it on Ilsa's white shorts. She stood behind her child along with Prince, giving those not interested in the antics of little children a fine view of her long legs, bare midriff, and spectacular breasts.

"No, no! You take that dirty face to *Oma*." She gave the boy a slight shove in Nell's direction. "Also, we have a very special present for Beck. In December, we will give him a baby sister. *Wunderbar, nein*?"

The lawn of Lorena Ranch had filled up as Tom predicted. Over one hundred pairs of eyes swiveled toward Dean who stood off to one side with Stacy. Alix thought Stacy had gone white, but hard to tell with her pale complexion. Dean placed a steadying arm around his wife's waist and shook his head. "Not my gift—I got my son a football."

He drew a full-sized football quartered in Sinners

red and black from behind his back. Beck shouted, "Ball!" and careened off his grandmother to seize it with still sticky hands. "I think he likes it," Dean said as calmly as if he were at a press conference. Stacy murmured something in his ear, and he simply nodded.

"Way to go, bro," Tom whispered from his place beside Alix.

Ilsa immediately drew the attention back to herself. "Ach, we are so over. My baby daddy…" She checked to see if she'd gotten the right word with Prince who seemed stuck tight to her side by sweat and lust. "My baby daddy says we are going to call her Princess, and when I get my shape back, we will have a big wedding, grander than Stacy's, and all of you are invited."

Ilsa nudged Prince who delved into one of the many pockets of the cargo pants that rode low on his narrow hips and came up to a ring. He slipped it on one of Ilsa's long, scarlet-nailed fingers. "Red, my favorite color. It is a ruby, a very large ruby *mit* diamonds all around." Ilsa flashed it for the crowd and received the acknowledgement she craved in a round of tepid applause.

Nell, such a tiny person compared to the people surrounding her, stepped forward into the breach of etiquette, the making of Beck's birthday all about his mother. "We are very happy for you and Prince and hope the baby will be healthy and as wonderful as Beck. Now, dessert for everyone in the pavilion, a choice of cakes, pies, bread pudding, and ice cream to top them."

"I-cream?" said Beck and dropped his football.

"Yes, buddy." Dean picked up his son with one arm, never letting go of Stacy's hand, and took all three of them to the pavilion.

Women gathered around Ilsa to see the ring. Team members offered Prince their congratulations with a handshake or pat on the back before moving toward dessert. Neither Tom nor Alix moved. Vince got to his feet and batted the Spanish moss out of his way.

"Looks like Ilsa really is off the market now. What about your twin sisters, Tom? I heard they're nurses and were once cheerleaders, twin nurse-cheerleaders. You can't beat that, huh, not in your best dreams?"

"They're in grad school studying to be nurse practitioners. They take their work very seriously, so I'd be careful what you say to them. They may be short, but both can still do those high kicks—right to the crotch, Vince. Fantasize about that," Tom said with a chill in his voice that put the frost on a very hot day.

Vince shrugged, undaunted. "Just saying. I'm going to get some dessert. You coming, Alix?"

"In a little while."

"Suit yourself." Vince hulked off to pig out on cake and ice cream, though how he had room for it Alix didn't know.

"How you can stand that guy? He's from Philly and thinks he's a real Italian stallion, totally irresistible to women," Tom said.

"I think it's wise to be cordial to my personal protector. I can't say I admire your taste in women if Ilsa is any example," Alix answered a little more sharply than she intended. She had no right to be jealous. She, too, was a tall blonde, though not nearly as voluptuous as Ilsa and Stacy—but at least her breasts were real and not silicon or saltwater. Not that Tom took notice of them. Heck, they weren't even dating.

"Ilsa has her ways of making a guy forget she isn't a very nice person."

"With sex, you mean?" She should have let it go.

He let that punted question sail into the end zone unanswered. "Say, if you want something sweet, now's the time to get it before the dragon boat races start."

A kiss would be sweet here behind the veil of Spanish moss. Should she snuggle closer, lean in? No, if she did either and he didn't respond, the drive home would be awfully long. Tom stood up and, grinning, pulled the quilt out from under her.

"Better hurry or Mawmaw's bread pudding will be gone."

"Yes, I wouldn't want to miss that." Tom gave her a hand up, and they parted the moss together.

\*\*\*\*

In a place where the brown bayou ran straight and narrow past Lorena Ranch, Tom organized his team for the dragon boat races. The smaller children, always in a boat captained by his dad, finished their competition— and lost to Adam Malala's crew of kids. He strongly suspected Adam's family hadn't spent all their time in Samoa lounging on the beach and eating taro. Even his pretty green-eyed daughter and the younger boy—built very much like a childhood version of the cornerback— were formidable paddlers. Adam's wife, lean as always, had shown some muscle as the drummer. One thing he could say for Adam, the man made sure not to embarrass anyone by holding back his team a little and winning usually by a dragon's head instead of a full and humiliating boat length.

Tom explained the finer points of rowing to Alix as a newcomer to the sport, like the importance of keeping to the beat of the drum and never trying to out-row anyone, but to work as a team. He'd pared her with his lifeguard sister, Lorena, who resembled Alix in height and build but contrasted nicely with her long, black hair and very Billodeaux brown eyes. He noticed Vince's gaze crawling all over the striking pair and wanted to deck the guy for whatever prurient fantasies went surging through the personal protector's brain. Hell, Lorena was barely legal, and Alix didn't belong to the guy.

Tom turned away to control his temper and when he turned back, both girls had stripped out of their shorts and tops and stood there in bikinis. His first thought was to tell his sister to put her clothes back on and his second that Alix took a great tan for a Swede. He pressed his chin with a finger to make sure his jaw hadn't dropped open when he looked at his roommate. Good, it had stayed shut, but he needed to swallow the drool pooling in his mouth. Neither bikini was particularly brief, but the duo resembled a two-woman Olympic volleyball team—trim, athletic, and beautifully attractive. Vince whistled. Lori smiled his way, and Alix nodded in acknowledgement. Before Tom could make an utter fool of himself by demanding they both dress again, his dad moved in with two life vests big enough to make Mae West proud and covered the most provocative parts of the female scenery.

"Everyone wears a vest, no exceptions," he announced. He moved to cover the twins whose bikinis really were too brief though only Jude sported a thong. Joe buckled his daughters in and spoke a word or two in their perfectly dainty, shell-shaped, and now burning ears. Both pulled on their discarded short shorts again.

The boats loaded. Tom helped Teddy into the drummer's seat and took over the tiller. In the opposing boat, Dean positioned Trinity—smallest of the triplets, big on brains, short on muscle—as his drummer. Tom had signed on the twins since Jude could only be described as fiercely competitive and Annie would keep up with her. He'd taken on Xochi, too, though in his opinion her well-developed breasts got in the way of her being a really good rower, but paired with one of the many lithe Billodeaux second cousins, she'd do okay. He'd gone for light and fast with his crew.

Dean had strong and heavy on his side since he'd signed up all those whom Tom turned down by saying his boat was full. He'd accepted his full-bodied but still slightly uncoordinated teenaged brother, Mack. Vince Barbaro sat side by side with Prince Dobbs in the center, their combined weight making the boat ride low in the water. Ilsa lounged on the grassy bank with Beck sitting on her crossed legs. "Wave to your daddies," she ordered, and Beck flapped his small hand. Teeth gritted, Dean waved back, and Prince raised a paddle causing the boat to rock. With Dean irked, Tom figured he had the psychological advantage, too. He rarely beat his brother at anything but had the urge to impress Alix going for him.

His dad collected Beck and helped him pull the string on the miniature cannon that started the race. The drummers set the pace. The paddlers dug into the brown water churning up a cappuccino-colored foam. Spectators lining the bank cheered for their favorite team or in some cases, for both teams at once. Tom called on Teddy to increase the pace. His rowers responded to put them a dragon head in the lead.

Slightly past Dean at the tiller, he didn't see the disaster coming when Vince and Prince, the terrible twosome, took over the other boat by rowing deep and out of sync causing the long, inflexible craft to veer left suddenly. He heard a splash and glanced back to see Dean overboard and the red tongue and bulging eyes of the dragon on the prow of his boat heading into their lane. It hit hard amidships with a splintering of fiberglass and capsized his craft. Oars went flying. The overturned boat sailed on at an angle and came to rest between the knotty knees of a giant cypress firmly entrenched in the opposite bank.

Tom's first thought leaped to Alix. He had no idea how well she swam, but she did have her life jacket on and Lorena by her side. He had to search for Teddy first. His handicapped brother could swim and had developed a strong upper torso from using his crutches and the wheelchair, but his useless legs would be weighed down by his braces. Amidst the school of black Billodeaux heads bobbing in the water, he didn't spot a single blonde. Unlatching his life jacket, Tom dove under the stern of his boat sticking out into the bayou like a shining spear lodged in the cypress roots. He found Teddy hanging onto the drum as if it were a giant beach ball floating in a pocket of air.

"About time someone noticed I was missing," Ted said wryly.

"I don't think I can flip the boat. It's wedged pretty tightly among the cypress knees. We need to duck under to get out. I'm not too sure how well that will work with a life jacket trying to hold you up, but we can try."

"Take it off me. I trust you to get me to shore,

Tom."

"Okay, then." He helped Teddy remove his floatation device one arm at a time, then taking deep breaths, they cleared the overturned boat. Tom grasped his brother under the chin in fine lifeguard form and towed him slowly to shore with the current of the bayou and those leg braces fighting them all the way. A cheer he totally ignored went up as he dragged Teddy over the muddy bank and laid him in the grass where his brother immediately sat up and gave the okay sign. Alix—where was she?

He counted his crew, most of them already ashore. Billodeaux kids grew up swimming in the bayou and were as agile in the water as any catfish or cottonmouth. Speaking of mouths, a soaked Xochi, her clinging white T-shirt clearly outlining a crimson bra, cursed fluently in Spanish, words that Corazon would have washed from of her mouth at a younger age. Jude said about the same in English as she reamed out Vince and Prince for causing the accident. Half their size, she had both men hanging their heads. Annie moved among the bedraggled crew offering her nursing skills to help with any injuries. Only two not accounted for from his boat—Alix and Lorena. And Dean, his brother Dean, from the other.

"Dad!" he shouted. His father, always cool in the pocket, moved among the teams handing out towels and pats on the backs. "Dean, Alix, and Lorena are missing."

"Dean is okay. He swam out and ran downstream trying to catch up with the girls. Looked like the current got hold of them. Jesus, Mary, and Joseph, they need to be all right."

Dean appeared, sprinting around the bend in the bayou just beyond the finish line, and Tom breathed a little easier. Dean always knew what to do in a tight situation. "They're out of the water, but we need a stretcher."

Tom knew that rationally he should head for the pool house where the stretcher for Camp Love Letter emergencies was stored, but instead he took off running for that bend in the river dreading what he might find—Alix with one of her magnificent legs shattered or Lorena bent over her blonde head giving CPR. He'd just cleared the angle of the stream that blocked his view when he saw her moving along the footpath with his sister in her arms. Lorena's long black hair hung over Alix's arm and her head rested in the crook of the punter's elbow. She strode along as if the weight meant nothing—an Amazon warrior, her pale wet hair forming a helmet pressed to her cheeks, carrying a fallen comrade from the field of battle.

"Thank God," he murmured as he caught up with them. "Want me to take her?"

"No, I'm okay. A paddle hit her in the head when the boat went over, but the life jacket held her up. There's way more current in that puny stream than you'd figure. She floated away, so I went after her."

"You could have drowned, too."

"Hey, Tommy the Toe. You're not the only one who has a lifesaving badge. Besides, no sense in jostling her twice before we put her on the stretcher."

As if summoned by the word, the stretcher appeared, borne by Vince and Prince who had probably volunteered to carry it simply to get away from Jude's sharp tongue. Alix laid Tom's sister in its cradle. By the time their group reached the others, Lorena's dark eyes fluttered open like black butterflies on her pale face.

Nurse Shammy arrived in her full, old-fashioned, starchy nurse's regalia right down to her white stockings and shoes, the heat and the formerly festive atmosphere be damned. Usually, she administered to bumps, cuts, and bruises earned in the bouncy house set up for the kids and doled out medicines for Camp Love Letter kids the rest of the summer. In this case, she checked Lorena's pulse and pupils, uncovered the gash matting the black hair with blood and declared that stitches and a tetanus shot were in order as well as a precautionary X-ray. One should never take a head injury lightly. No one argued with Nurse Shammy.

By the time the stretcher-bearers reached the big house, Knox Polk had let the ambulance in the gates. It carried away Lorena, Nurse Shammy, and Nell Billodeaux. "Keep things going, Joe," she told her husband. "I hope we'll all be back for the fireworks."

Joe delegated dinner to his mother who soon had Krayola and Corazon shredding leftover pork into two tubs to be doused with either Joe's Hot and Spicy or Connor Riley's Mild and Sweet Barbecue Sauce. Plenty of fruit, vegetables, and desserts left for after. She negotiated a spat between Calvin Armitage's big, dewberry dark wife and Miss Krayola over who got the pig heads and feet to make hog's head cheese by splitting the remains down the middle, one head and four trotters each. Both women swore they'd come back with samples and let her decide who made it better.

The men took care of stowing the dragon boats and fishing the paddles from the bayou. Then a bunch of them drove over to the other side of the river in Joe's silver truck, its bed filled to the brim with fireworks that they laid out along the cane road edging the fields his daddy once plowed. But, before the feasting and the skyrockets, Adam Malala solemnly crowned the winners of the dragon boat races with circlets of tropical leaves and red feathers he'd had flown in from Samoa along with floral leis for the women.

"By foul and default, I proclaim Tom Billodeaux's team winner of the last race." He laid the wreath atop Tom's curls gone to wild red corkscrews after getting wet. Tom beckoned Alix from his group being bedecked with leis by Adam's children. He removed his crown and placed it on her fair, straight hair. "For saving my sister." He followed that up with kisses that warmed both her cool cheeks. The applause beat considerably louder than it had for Ilsa and Prince's earlier announcement.

She wore the crown for the rest of the evening until the sun finally sank behind the half-grown sugar cane crop across the bayou around nine p.m., and the men went to light the fireworks for the delight of the many children already wound up and running about with sparklers in their hands. Tom returned to Alix smelling of gunpowder from the smoke and cinders in the air.

"It's a privilege to be allowed to help set off the sky rockets. Notice, they didn't ask Prince or Vince to help. Dean isn't allowed to do it since he has to protect his hands. When Dad still played, my uncles took care of the chore. But man, I love blowing those things up."

"Vince left before they started. He said he'd see me at training camp and sorry about the dunk in the bayou. Kind of embarrassed, I think. Someone told me today if I tasted bayou water I'd want to stay here. To be honest, it has the flavor of mud, but now I've gone and done it. Guess I'll have to live in Louisiana forever."

"I think that would be great," Tom said, but his mind thought, *Good, no Vince to get in the way*. He decided to make a move, just a small one. Giving Alix's shoulders a tight hug, he repeated, "For saving my sister," again, but let his arm linger there because that really wasn't what he wanted to say at all. Alix didn't shrug him off. She let his arm remain as they walked back to the SUV crammed full of leftovers and siblings ready to leave the ranch.

"I could stay here forever," she said as he helped her into the car. Not that she needed his hand clasped in hers to manage it.

"You didn't mind all the typical Billodeaux drama?"

"No. If Lorena hadn't been injured, even the boat wreck would have been exciting. You know, I really don't deserve this crown. The life jacket held her face out of the water. Anyone could have towed your sister to shore." She made an attempt to reseat the circlet of leaves on Tom's unruly curls.

"No, you keep it, a souvenir of how we celebrate the Fourth at Lorena Ranch."

"Tom, are you ever going to start the engine?" Jude groused from the backseat.

"I think his engine is already revving," Teddy chipped in making Annie laugh softly, but not in a mean way.

Tom ignored them and put the SUV in gear. He knew Alix was modest about her kicking skills and her looks. Today, he'd added courage to the list of qualities he loved about Alix Lindstrom.

## Chapter Twelve

Digging into the omelet Alix had stuffed with sautéed vegetables from yesterday's leftovers Tom sat fully dressed at the dining room table. He remembered Krayola's orangutan comment all too well, took it to heart, and covered his chest hair with a green T-shirt, thinking he might already have turned Alix off by wearing his robe to breakfast. Maybe he should consider waxing like Brian Lightfoot.

After he dropped off his jabbering sisters last night, he'd hoped to sling a casual arm around Alix's shoulders, but she'd gone to sleep slumped against the window on the far side of the car. Waking her in the parking garage for the walk across the street, he believed she truly was too groggy for any other kind of activity. He'd spent the night dreaming of her in that bikini minus the life jacket, at one point carrying him held close to her chest as she had Lorena, only his head wasn't lolling on her elbow. He rested his cheek on one warm breast. Maybe embarrassing that he didn't carry her, but the fantasy still worked for him.

"Try these. They're an experiment. I washed off most of the spicy barbecue sauce and added green pepper and onion, a little egg and flour to hold them together. I'm calling them pulled pork patties." Alix slid two disks of pan-browned meat onto his plate beside the half-eaten omelet. She seated herself at the place he'd set for her with coffee and juice waiting alongside a stack of whole wheat toast he'd made as his contribution.

Alex added milk liberally to her coffee and tried one of her patties. "Whoa, your dad's sauce still packs a wallop." Alix fanned her mouth.

"Yeah, it gets way down deep in the meat fibers. Using Dad's hot sauce is a Billodeaux test of manhood. I can handle it. Besides, the sales of his sauces support Camp Love Letter. We can do good and show how tough we are all at the same time."

Alix gifted him with her wide, wonderful smile and slid her meat patty onto his plate. She'd barely started to eat when Tom's cell phone rang. He wiggled it from the pocket of his jeans and checked the number before answering. "Home," he said.

"Is Lorena worse?" Alix asked.

Tom held up a finger. He nodded a few times in response, though no one but Alix could see him. "Do I need to pick up anyone? Oh, not good. Can I bring Alix? Okay. I'll be there by noon." He disconnected. "Team meeting at the ranch."

"When do we leave?" Alix shoveled up more of her breakfast and took a big swallow of juice. "Does the team usually have meetings at your dad's place?"

"Not the Sinners. That's just what my father calls a family conference where serious decisions are made and punishments are meted out. Sorry, I can't take you along."

"Sure, I understand. I'm not family. How is Lorena?"

Tom wasn't entirely certain she did understand considering her crestfallen countenance. She appeared to be taking an unusual interest in the tower of toast as she glanced down.

"Believe me, you don't want to be there. Lorena is still in the hospital under observation, but they think she'll be fine. She's complaining about the headache, having stitches in her hair, and whining over missing the fireworks. More seriously, Teddy is running a fever and checked into the same hospital. He has all these shunts and things in his body because of the spina bifida. An infection contracted by that dunk in the bayou could be serious, so better safe than sorry."

"I like Teddy and hope he's better soon. So who is being punished, for what, and how?" Alix inquired, revealing her keen perpetual interest in all things Billodeaux.

"If they were family members, I'd say Vince and Prince, but more likely, they won't be allowed to participate in the dragon boat races again. When we were kids, the punishments usually consisted of mucking out stalls and clearing brush or having privileges taken away like driving or being allowed to use our laptops after we finished our homework. Whatever we hated most. Boy, did Stacy ever despise shoveling shit, or manure, as my mom would insist. Since Teddy couldn't do a lot of the manual chores, he'd lose computer time and that hit him right where it hurt. He's been trying to write fantasy novels since he turned ten."

"I guess there's always pencil and paper."

"He did exactly that, stayed up writing hard copy to be put on the computer when the ban lifted. No idea what's going on this time. Dad didn't say. Look, I have to shower and get moving. It is three hours up and three back, and I'll be expected to stay for dinner. See you around nine or ten. Will you be okay?"

Tom watched her face change from avid to disgruntled. "Do you think I need a babysitter? I can go for a long run, do some shopping, walk over to Mariah's Place tonight if I want company. I am a big girl, a very big girl."

Tom backed off immediately. "All that sounds great. Only promise you won't walk alone in the Quarter. Call a cab."

Relenting, Alix nodded. "You want to take some of the pork patties for your dad?"

"He'll love them, guaranteed."

****

All things considered, the family meeting at the ranch went very well. Puzzled at first that honorary family members, Knox and Corazon Polk and the Brinsleys, had been included, he soon learned why. A debate ensued about continuing the dragon boat races in the future. He and Dean spoke up, saying they'd never had an accident before, and the fun shouldn't be stopped because of two jerks who could easily be banned from participating.

"Yeah, his mama and *papi* are so embarrassed about how Prince acts, they do not come to the barbecue this year," Corazon said with her arms crossed under her ample chest.

"Yes, I missed them, but I'm glad they were spared witnessing their son's latest act of arrogance." Nell shook her head over a child ill-raised and spoiled. Not on her watch. She eyed each and every one of the kids she'd brought up as if searching for weak spots and flaws, then smiled having found none.

Of course, Mom, Corazon, and Nurse Shammy voted against further racing. They were outvoted by the men and children. Democracy at its best.

Stacy took the floor next standing in the center of the circle of elders on the long leather sofa and recliner chairs and the children, even grown ones, sitting on the floor. Dean stood beside her, but let his wife do the talking. "We are also pregnant. When we first got to Germany, I thought the strange food and water made me ill. As it turned out I had morning sickness of Duchess of Cambridge proportions. It's fading now. Regardless, the baby is due in January and appears to be a girl—whom we will *not* be naming Princess."

That drew laughter from the ring of relatives, both the elated and those concerned for her health. Dean spoke up. "We wanted to tell just the family last night after the fireworks but with all the hoopla about Prince and Ilsa and then the boating accident, we decided to wait until today. Sorry you had to make the drive to the ranch twice, Tom."

"It's not like we didn't have to come back, too," Jude said, but she received a rare poke in the ribs from Annie.

"Stop complaining. It's a baby, Jude, another Billodeaux girl."

"Fine. I'm happy about that."

"You gonna call Mawmaw Nadine now?" Corazon asked.

"Um, no. I'm not up to the battle over what Stacy should be eating or whether we'll raise the child Catholic yet. We aren't announcing to the press right now either. So, let's keep this at the ranch, okay." Solemn nods all around.

Corazon threw out another question. "Who's ready for baked potatoes stuffed with pulled pork?" Despite a few groans, especially from the children who would be dining on pig the rest of the week, they all sat at the large dining room table and ate without complaint because that's what it meant to be a Billodeaux. Despite being wealthy, you ate leftovers, never hired a caterer as long as Mawmaw lived, and carpooled whenever you could.

Tom dropped off the twins in Baton Rouge with Jude still complaining that all this business could have be done by phone or email. Sometimes, he thought she didn't get how important family should be, and he was the adopted one. As he drove along the side street to the garage, he glanced up at Alix's bedroom window. No lights shone. Possibly, she was dancing in Vince Barbaro's arms at Mariah's right now. Maybe he should go over there and cut in, but no, six hours on the road were enough even for a major birth announcement. He parked and headed for the condo.

As he entered his apartment the sweet whiff of baked goods loaded with butter, sugar, and eggs tickled his pug nose. Alix sat in one of the recliners holding a blond child in footie pajamas half asleep in her arms. In the dim light, he thought he saw his future as the child's brown eyes opened wider. "Unca." He held out his toddler arms.

"What's Beck doing here?"

"Ilsa dropped him off when she found out Stacy and Dean weren't home yet. She said the nanny is ill, and she doesn't want her son to catch it. He's had some milk and a tiny piece of cake for being a good boy, and his bath. I almost had him asleep."

"Sorry. Hey Beck, you want to sleep in Unca's bed or with Auntie Alix?" Alix beamed at his bestowal of the honorary title.

"Unca."

Not the choice Tom would have made, but Beck was only a baby. "Let me tuck you in then. Did I hear we had cake?" He scooped the boy into his arms.

"I made two, a chocolate and a brown sugar bundt. Mom left me plenty of pans."

"Cut me a slice of each, and I'll fill you in on the Billodeaux team meeting. Let's go nighty-night, buddy."

After Beck settled, Tom returned to the dining area where his dessert waited along with a tall, cold glass of milk. Alix joined him with her own full plate. She hadn't brightened the lights, simply lit a pair of yellow beeswax candles placed in wooden holders and centered them on the table.

"I own candlesticks?" Tom questioned.

"No, my mother left them and the candles. Beeswax doesn't drip and make a mess on the table. She read New Orleans has plenty of thunderstorms, and I should be prepared for power outages."

Tom watched her wide blue eyes glimmering in the candlelight, the best way to appreciate flames. "We have flashlights under the sink, but I like this better."

"Me, too."

Wanting to make up for leaving her behind, he told her every detail of the team meeting.

"I'm so happy for Stacy and Dean!" she exclaimed. "More cake?

The wedges she cut had been generous, and he shook his head. "How did your day go?"

"I went for a long run, but passed up shopping. I'm really not a girly-girl and need someone along to tell me what looks good. Instead, I baked cakes, one thing I excel at doing.

"Xo or Uncle Brian would go shopping with you. I'll give you their numbers. He loves to tell people how to dress, but I warn you, Xochi likes bright colors and low cuts. Besides, you excel at lots of things, and the cakes are delicious. A man would marry you for your cooking alone."

"You think so?" Her face lit brighter than the flames of the candles.

"I know so. Sorry if you didn't get to Mariah's because of being stuck with Beck. During the football season, Dean has him Mondays and Tuesdays and during the off-season on weekends. I think Ilsa is pissed because he and Stacy were gone so long. She likes to party on Friday nights and Saturdays. It's not like she doesn't have a nanny for the boy, but even that poor woman gets some days off, so Ilsa dumps him on Stacy whenever she can. Good practice for the new baby coming, I guess, but unfair."

"I didn't mind. I'm not the best dancer and don't drink all that much. Mariah's is only a place to hang out where I know a few people. *Morfar* didn't spoil his grandchildren. We were expected to earn our spending money babysitting and also lifeguarding in my case. He did put all of us through college though."

"A good man and a great kicker. Anyhow, thanks for taking care of Beck." Tom leaned in and put his lips softly on hers. She tasted of brown sugar and chocolate, and he wanted to lick the tiny crumbs from the corners of her mouth and delve inside exploring her many tastes more deeply. Alix seemed a little stunned and unprepared. Too soon, no rush, no hurry. Take it slow.

"Ah, that was for the babysitting. I'd better get to bed. If Beck wakes and finds out I'm gone, he'll start screaming. I think he gets shifted around so much he doesn't always know where he is." Tom shoved his chair back and stood.

"I understand." Alix dabbed at the cake fragments with the tip of her finger as if only now aware of them, then put that finger in her mouth and sucked it clean. "You know, Tom. You don't need an excuse to kiss me."

"Really? That's good news." He started to lower his head, but a wail with the volume of a police siren sounded from his bedroom. "Gotta go."

Chapter Thirteen

Thoughts of Tom's kiss kept Alix awake that night. How soft and gentle it had been as if she were tiny and precious and easily broken, not some big, sturdy girl whose past sexual encounters had always been athletic romps, enjoyable but soon over. She knew she didn't read men very well. Her mother warned most of them only wanted sex, and that seemed to be true. Women could want just sex, too. Something her mother never mentioned. She liked intercourse, only not the stuff leading up to it. She didn't flirt well, and obviously her attempt to tell Tom he had a green light fell flat as he hadn't attempted to sneak away from Beck and be with her. Maybe he really had been thanking her for babysitting.

In the morning, she woke to the cry of the toddler, soon quieted, but she got up and dressed to see how she could help, maybe by making pancakes for all of them. As she clattered the pan and bowl from the cupboards, Tom appeared with Beck wearing only a sagging, bulging diaper and snuggling sleepy-eyed against his bare chest in the nest of rusty curls. How confidently and lovingly he held the boy. What a great father Tom Billodeaux would make—and between them, they might create a child who looked very much like this one, only in her fantasies, she favored red hair for her offspring. If Tom could read her mind, he'd probably thrust the kid into her arms and run like most men at the mention of children.

"Say, did Ilsa think to leave any clothes and diapers? He probably has some at Dean's house, but I am clean out of nappies, and he is really, really soggy. So are his jammies and my sheets. Sorry about the partial nudity. I couldn't see getting baby pee all over a clean T-shirt." He shifted the child's squishy bottom as if to cover more of himself.

"I'm sure I'll see worse in the Sinners locker room. There's a small bag by the sofa. Do you want me to change him?"

"Hey, I'm the second of twelve kids. A male Billodeaux in my family who can't handle a diaper change is not considered a man." Tom moved to retrieve the diaper bag with Beck now clinging to his chest hair like a little pet monkey and his big brown eyes peering over his shoulder at Alix.

She wiggled her fingers at him, but Beck didn't release his grip to return the greeting. "I thought I could make pancakes."

"No, as soon as I get both us cleaned up, we'll go to the coffee shop. They actually make cups of oatmeal with chopped fruit for kids, I guess for anybody, and Stacy approves of that. We can have whatever we want." Tom pried a few of his nephew's fingers from their clutch. "That hurts some, buddy. I don't know how orangutans do it."

"Orangutans?" Alix questioned.

"Never mind. Let's get you all nice and dry, Beck, and don't you dare piss all over me."

"Piss," the boy said, savoring a new word. He did wave a bye-bye to Alix as they moved down the hall to

Tom's bedroom.

Alix put away her utensils and not long after, Tom appeared fully dressed and smelling sweetly of baby wipes. Beck wore tiny cargo pants, a bitty Sinners tee, and very small sneakers.

Tom held Beck's hand as they all moved downward in the elevator after the child pushed the button. Once on the street, he mounted his nephew on his shoulders. "He likes it and can't get away," Tom said. Now the monkey clutch applied itself to his curly hair. "I think I need to get it cut before training camp."

"Oh, I kind of like it long," Alix said.

"I think I'll be saving on barbershop visits then."

They rounded the corner onto Canal Street. Passersby took them for a happy family and offered up benign smiles. Alix returned them as she strode along only realizing Tom and Beck had fallen behind when she reached the door of the shop. Her companions stood in front of the news and tobacco shop staring into the window. Beck poked a finger against the grimy glass and uttered, "Dat." Exposing his little milk teeth, he looked at Alix and grinned.

"That's Who Dat, little man," Tom corrected, but he seemed to have gone a bit white under his freckles. "Let Auntie Alix hold you for a minute." He deposited the boy into her arms. "Go ahead and order some oatmeal for him."

Beck stuck out his lower lip. "Cookie!" he demanded.

"After the oatmeal. I'll be with you in a minute."

Alix held onto Beck while she ordered the hot cereal, two grande coffees, and a large plate of mixed croissants: two almond, two chocolate, two plain.

Fortunately, Tom appeared before she had to juggle all that to a table with a toddler in tow. He carried a bundle of magazines still in their strapping tape and a loose issue under his arm. Choosing a table deep within the shop, he set his burden on the floor and placed the last paper face down on top. He moved a wooden highchair in place and deposited his nephew.

Alix placated the boy with a half a chocolate croissant while Tom waited for the hot items to come up. Idly, she turned over the tabloid, and there she stood with Lorena draped over her arm like a dying black swan. The headline proclaimed, *Sinners Amazon Saves a Sister*.

"Oh, no!" she whispered to herself and glanced at Tom pouring almond milk over the oatmeal and mushing it around in the cup. She skimmed the article. The account sounded remarkably like the description she'd given her sisters when she'd talked to them while the bundt cakes baked yesterday. Okay, she'd been bragging, not about saving Lorena, anyone would have done that, but about being invited to the Billodeaux ranch and meeting all the famous people there. She wasn't a big talker and never chattered like Tille and Rika, but she'd had something fabulous to share for once and hadn't stinted on the details from the two roast pigs to the dragon boat collision.

*Noting that Lorena Billodeaux had been rendered unconscious by an oar to the head and drifted downstream in her life jacket, the Sinners new female punter, Alix Lindstrom, courageously swam after her and rescued the young woman, towing her to shore. Mighty Alix carried her burden singlehandedly over a mile to a place where first aid could be applied and an ambulance called.*

Alix doubted if the distance had been even a quarter mile, but what disturbed her the most was being called an Amazon. She always imagined them to be big, muscular women who hated men. What did Tom think of her now, especially when she'd refused his help in carrying Lorena?

He set down the three containers. "I fixed your coffee with lots of milk the way you like," he said just before noticing the stricken look that must have covered her face like the chocolate streaks coating Beck as he reached for more croissants. Tom moved the plate out of reach and began shoveling oatmeal into the open maw of his nephew. "Damned vultures. Only two days, and they've already got the story. If my dad finds out who took and sold that picture, they will never be invited back to the ranch. I bought all the copies next door and the one in the window so we can at least have breakfast in peace before being recognized. Not that it isn't a great picture."

"Damn vullers," Beck repeated with oatmeal oozing out both sides of his mouth.

Tom scooped up the dribbles and shoved them back between the toddler's lips. He glanced back at Alix. "No need to be so upset. At least, they painted you as a heroine. Could be far, far worse. You should've seen what they did to Dean last year."

Alix nodded. She had saved the clippings as she did all things Billodeaux. "Oh, Tom, this might be my fault. I-I told my sisters about the barbecue yesterday on the phone. I told them everything, and I wouldn't put it above Tille not to sell the story. I simply didn't think before opening my mouth. Now, your family will hate me." She bent her head over her coffee cup so deeply it might have held consecrated wine. The wings of her pale, blonde hair swept forward hiding her face. Her shoulders shook though she tried to hold them still.

"Boo-boo?" Beck asked.

Tom raised her chin with the fingers not engaged in shoveling oatmeal and caught a few tears that hung there. "Hey, hey, Sinners do not cry, not about garbage like this. First of all, you certainly didn't take your own picture and send it to anyone. I'd suspect Prince Dobbs of doing that, but that's only because I don't like him and he's a publicity hound. Jude was chewing out him and Vince when this happened. They're off the hook. My guess is one of my many Billodeaux cousins. You know my dad would, and has, put a bunch of them through college and trade school, but every family tree bears a few rotten apples.

"But they called me an Amazon. I'm not. I mean I know I'm big, but I do like men, to be with men." She knew she blubbered and couldn't seem to stop. A few people glanced their way, probably suspecting a public breakup scene, but Tom had chosen their table in the shady depths of the shop well for some privacy.

"Once I tried the other way with a coach I admired, and she knew exactly what to do. It felt good, but not right to me." Alix ducked her head again, not able to meet his warm, brown eyes. "Only one time, Tom, I swear."

"That's how I thought of you when I saw you carrying Lorena, an Amazon, strong and beautiful like Wonder Woman. As for the rest, glad to know it, but your life is your life, Alix. You do what you want with it. I don't judge. After all, I slept with Ilsa. Major lapse in taste. At least, you admired the woman." He handed Alix a few paper napkins.

She tried to blow her nose like a lady, but the honk came out louder than intended and made Beck laugh. He buzzed his lips at her and blew oatmeal across the table. She managed a little smile as she cleaned up both her face and the bits of cereal.

"We good now? Okay, just remember what happens at the ranch stays at the ranch. But, if you go to Vegas, the paparazzi will find out everything you do." Tom shoved more oatmeal at his nephew.

Beck clamped his mouth tight. "Cookie!" He pointed at the croissants.

Tom checked the contents of the cup. "Okay, kiddo, you've had enough healthy food. Here you go." He turned over the second half of the pastry and watched the child lick out the chocolate filling. "I think I'll have the other one unless you want it."

"No, go right ahead." Alix broke open a plain croissant and stuffed it with butter and a pat of jelly. She could still feel the warmth of Tom's fingertips against her chin. Her appetite returned.

Tom finished his breakfast in big bites, one chocolate and an almond down the hatch, leaving half of a plain and one almond for Alix to finish. Then, he sat back and phoned Dean. "Where you at, bro?…Good, because I've got your kid, and I'm low on diapers…Yeah, Ilsa dumped him on Alix last night. Says the nanny is sick, but I think what she really means is, you missed four weekends with Beck while you were in Germany. She's a piece of work, that woman. Anyhow, I fed him breakfast." Tom leaned back and snapped a photo of the chocolate and crumb-covered boy. "I heard that gasp. Tell Stacy he had oatmeal first. Yeah, see you soon."

Alix cleaned up the small, happy, besmirched face turning it into frowns. "Finish eating," Tom directed her. "I'll take care of the crevices. Dean and Stacy are about an hour out returning from the ranch. They'll stop off here."

"Oh, good, we can play with the baby some more."

Beck scrunched his face, turned red, and grunted. "You might not say that when we get back to the condo. It's your turn to change the diaper, and it'll be nasty. Nothing cleans this boy's pipes out up quicker than chocolate. We'd better go before management notices the stench isn't coming from the homeless guy by the front door."

"I'm ready."

"Take Beck, would you? I have these tabloids to carry to the incinerator."

The vagrant near the door turned out to be Big Lou, her shape disguised by a black knit Sinners hat and many sweltering layers despite a morning soaring into the high eighties. Before she could make any lewd offers, Tom shoved a twenty into her extended empty soda cup and kept on walking, though she shouted some filthy suggestions his way.

"That's how it's done. You just keep moving," he coached Alix.

Alix kept up with him step for step. It was her life, he'd said so, and she wanted Tom Billodeaux more than ever.

## Chapter Fourteen

Summer training camp opened with a team meeting not likely to make Alix any more popular with the guys. Didn't help that Dr. Funk, team psychologist, decided to call it Sexual Sensitivity Training. Only Alix was exempt from this awkward start to the upcoming football season. General Manager Michener sat at the head table with the shrink along with wiry, wizened Marty Buck, but right from the start, Dr. Funk ran the meeting.

He began with the obvious. They now had a woman on the team. He expected a change in demeanor. A hand went up. "Let's call that a change in attitude or 'tude instead," the doctor said, anticipating the question. The hand went down. "Let's begin with the number one word we should never use."

He did not say it, simply wrote c-u-n-t on an oversized tablet mounted on an easel. "Can you suggest any other words that should go on this list?"

Ah, group participation. Some of the younger players really got into it a tad too joyfully. Disgusted, Tom kept his mouth shut. Dr. Funk, the red in his face continuing across his completely bald head, flipped to a second sheet and kept on writing until he finally said, "Enough. You get the idea."

Vince Barbaro, sitting right up front, raised his brawny arm. "Going back to bitch, can we still say 'that was a bitch' so long as it doesn't apply to Alix?"

"I suppose so, but I'd rather you didn't. I'd like to see a big cut back on use of the F-word, too." Snickers broke out over his delicacy. "Yes, yes, I know some of you call me Dr. Mind Fuck. That does not concern me. I've developed a tough hide over the years since Dean's father dubbed me that. Please try to restrain yourself in front of the young lady."

Dr. Funk pushed his bifocals back up his sweating nose. "Moving on to a happier topic, our new punter is very competent at what she does. Should you wish to express your approval of her performance, no hands below the waist! A gentle shoulder pat or friendly knock of the helmet will do."

Vince shot his hand up again. "High fives, fist bumps?"

"Certainly, if not overly vigorous. You don't need to prove how manly you are. Next on the agenda—Locker Room Etiquette."

The groans nearly drowned out the team psychologist. He ignored them. "We, meaning the management and myself, have decided the easiest way to handle this situation and create a comfortable atmosphere for everyone is to allow Alix to lead the team off the field at the end of the game. She will proceed directly through the locker room to her private shower area and when she has finished cleaning up, she will exit from there through a second door into a vacant corridor. In that way, you need not change your usual state of undress or be worried about being caught out."

"Like I'd care if she saw me naked," someone sneered. Tom thought the voice belonged to Beef Bolivar, who sat in the back.

"Hell, I'd like it and the other way around, too," Vince added.

"That is exactly what I am talking about, Mr. Barbaro. Keep those sorts of thoughts to yourself, and I know you and some others on the team will have them. In fact, I'd like any of you to express what reservations you might possess about a woman on our team at this time. Speak freely. No one will be fined at this meeting."

Beef Bolivar lumbered to his feet. "Women don't belong in the NFL. Let 'em work in those lingerie leagues if they gotta play. Alix should be sent back to the soccer team or other girly sports."

"Beach volleyball," some wit suggested. Dr. Funk appeared to take special notice of the man and wrote something in his notebook. "Special appointments for the two of you. Anyone else?"

Tom stood. He could tell no one, including Dr. Funk, expected this. "I have a problem with how Beef is snapping the ball to Alix really hard, way harder than he ever did to Brian Lightfoot."

"Alix is more masculine than Lightfoot. I figured she could handle it." Beef folded his arms across his chest as if he dared Tom to cross the room and take him on.

Tom pointed a finger instead. "You're trying to make her fumble and look bad so she'll be cut, but she's too good to mess up. If you do that during the game and cost us points…"

"What are you going to do about it, Lightfoot's lady?" Beef searched the room for support and found surprisingly little. Tom, their light-hearted jester, owned a popularity on the team that the heavy-handed

Bolivar never would.

Tom started for the aisle. Dean, right next to him, forced him back into his chair by grasping his belt. Instead, Dr. Funk, five-six, middle-aged, and lightly built except for a small paunch, walked the distance and pressed a finger against Bolivar's vast chest. "Sit down! See me at nine tomorrow."

Bolivar obeyed. The crunching of antacids by Mitch Michener could be heard throughout the room, though the manager remained impassive. Coach Buck had given Bolivar one of his meanest, squinty stares reminiscent of an elderly Popeye. Perhaps that helped, but tension remained in the air.

Laconically, massive Adam Malala said, "Say, does Alix get bubble bath in her private stall? Because if she does, then we should all get bubble bath. That's only fair."

Usually, Tom was the one who broke up tense situations with a funny quip, but not this time. Laughter cut through the tension. Dr. Funk appeared to be the only one without a sense of humor. He simply answered the question. "No, she does not. However, at Tom's suggestion we have provided a selection of scented bath gels and shampoos. We would be happy to allow the rest of you the same."

"Oooh, Tommy the Toe has a feminine side," said one of Beef's better special team buddies.

Dean answered. "Tommy the Toe isn't the one with an appointment in the morning to straighten out his head. Better add Beef's bro to your book, Dr. Funk.

"I shall. Anyone else with something to say before we close?"

Tom stood up again despite a grab at his belt by

Dean. "You know how we mess with the rookies a little, play small tricks, give them nicknames like we did with Beef." For the benefit of the newbies, he explained, "Beef used to drive cattle to the slaughter house before he walked on with the team. I went up to the ranch and brought back a livestock trailer. We dared him to tow it the length of the field. He did. That earned him a lot of respect and the name Beef. I think if we exclude Alix from any hazing at all, she won't feel like a real part of the team."

"Hazing, not allowed." Mitch Michener put a hand to his flat stomach.

"I don't mean anything bad or physical. I thought we might put on a little song and dance for her. You know, dress up like cheerleaders. I think a good nickname would be Legs…Legs Lindstrom. Legs aren't on the list of forbidden words—yet."

Dr. Funk pondered. "I suppose that might be a good idea, an official welcome and sign of acceptance, a rite of passage so to speak."

"Great! Since Teddy's the writer in the family, I'll ask him to whip up a little ditty. Who's with me in the chorus line?" Tom scanned the audience for raised hands and noticed none.

He reached out to Dean, widening his eyes to make a small plea, little brother to the big brother he'd idolized. When they were at Ste. Jeanne's Parochial together, the nuns said Julius Caesar possessed gravitas when they studied that play in English class. Dean had gravitas on the football field and in real life. He never played the fool for a laugh. That had been Tom's role. Now, he begged Dean mentally to come through for him, him and Alix.

"Okay, I'll do it," his brother said.

"Me, too," Adam Malala agreed. "Even if the folks back home think I've turned into a *fa'afafine*." No one asked what the Samoan word meant. They got the general idea and knew Adam did a mean war dance before most games. No one messed with him.

"I'm in." Tom stared in wonderment at Prince Dobbs who'd sat in silence, his head hung as if in meditation throughout the meeting. Only last year, he'd been an example of sexual harassment toward women. "Admit it. I have the best legs on the team."

That sounded more like Prince. Tom nodded. "Okay, I need one more to make this work."

Vince Barbaro put up a hand. "I'll do it, but I got hairy legs, and I ain't waxing 'em."

"Hairy is funnier in a case like this. Great. I'll get some costumes together. Maybe Brian will help if he's free. Thanks, guys. No team I'd rather play with than the Sinners."

"This meeting is adjourned," Dr. Funk pronounced.

Coach Buck stood. "Now get your insensitive asses out on the field. Stretches first, then bleacher runs. Move it, move it, move it!"

\*\*\*\*

Alix arrived late at practice. She drew more than one resentful stare. Most of the team lay on the ground doing push-ups. Tom at the end of one row got up to greet her. No one seemed to care if he opted out.

"Where have you been?"

"I had a session with Dr. Funk on how to deal with the guys."

Tom cupped his hands and shouted to get everyone's attention. "She had to meet with Dr. Funk about putting up with you jerks." That got a few grins.

Alix imitated him by making a loudspeaker with her big hands, too. "Yeah, we made up a list of words. I can't call any of you a d-i-c-k." She earned her own laughs. "He asked what I would do if any of you came on to me in a vulgar way. I said kick you in the nuts with my large foot." A few of the men lost their rhythm and collapsed on the ground. "Just so you know."

Tom took her aside. "Well-handled. Did you really say that to Dr. Funk?"

"No. I sat there and listened to him tell me to ignore any lewd remarks directed at me personally and to report the perpetrator. Now that's going to make me really popular with the team. Female jocks can be pretty foul-mouthed, too. We aren't shy violets to be crushed beneath your feet."

"I never thought you were. You're more like a steel violet, or maybe that should be magnolia, but you aren't from the South. I'll have to work on it."

"Don't dig yourself in any deeper, Billodeaux. What did I miss?"

"Just stretches and bleacher runs. We don't have to do any of the heavy training."

"I'm glad Coach didn't make me work out in full pads again." She wore a short-sleeved Sinners jersey untucked that covered most of her torso and Spandex pants that came to her knees. When she went into her stretches, a few eyes shifted her way again as if measuring her long, long legs. They seemed to particularly admire some of her yoga poses.

She took Dr. Funk's advice and ignored the glances, but Tom shouted, "Eyes straight ahead, rookies!"

"You don't need to do that. I can cope on my own. Dr. Funk also said to be firm and not to put up with any B.S. He actually used the initials. What I said back there was me being firm. Now, how many times up and down the bleachers would impress them, but not wipe me out the rest of the day?"

Tom gave her a number, but thoughts of being firm stayed in his brain, which translated it to firm breasts, backsides, and erections. He joined the squad in doing squats vigorously while she finished her runs. Back in control again, he took her to a vacant area of the field to practice doing onside kicks of just ten yards low to the ground. "As a soccer player, these should be easy for you." They were.

"Nice work. Usually I do them, but if I should be injured, you'll have to take over for me the rest of the game. The Sinners have only one kicker, one punter, and one long snapper. They put their money into getting a variety of receivers for Dean to target. If either of us is out for any length of time, they'll call in one of the retired guys or find a free agent who wasn't signed. Oh, by the way, I lodged a complaint about how hard Bolivar is snapping the ball to you."

Alix placed a hand on Tom's shoulder. "I only bobbled it once that first day before I got him figured out. Some guys just are d-i-c-k-s, pardon my language. But please, let me handle it. I need to earn the team's respect by myself."

"Your kicks will do that for you. I can't wait to see our opponents' faces the first time they get a left-footed punt. Snow cone time."

"Yeah, I'm up for that."

"What do you have on your wrist? It wasn't there

this morning." Tom pointed to a rather masculine-looking watch.

"It's waterproof. I'm supposed to enter the locker room here at the training field one half hour before the rest of the team at the end of the day. Management doesn't want me to lose track of time in the shower. I need to be out of there before the rest of you enter. Nice they gave me an extra fifteen minutes this time."

"I guess they figure girls need more time in the bathroom. With my sisters, that's pretty much been the case."

Her light blow to his shoulder caught Tom off-guard. "Did you just call me a girl and compare me to a sister?"

"Sorry?"

Others watched. A deep voice hollered, "Hey, no brutalizing the kicker or touching in inappropriate ways, Lindstrom!" His Italian stallion black mane slick with sweat, his impressive biceps exposed by a sleeveless exercise jersey, Vince Barbaro grinned toothily their way. The chuckles he drew were good-natured and aimed mostly at Tom.

"Who knew Vince had a sense of humor," Tom muttered. "It's a whole new world."

"Tell me about it," said Alix.

Chapter Fifteen

Tom felt as if he were cheating on Alix as he turned down her suggestions on where to go for dinner or how about hanging out at Mariah's tonight. Every time he offered an excuse saying he had other plans and being very vague about them, he had to endure the look of disappointment in her big, blue eyes. He needed to make up reasons to sneak off for chorus line practice and get the costumes fitted just right. In the end, she'd love it and understand.

Getting pom-poms—no problem. He borrowed them from the team's cheerleaders. Finding red sports bras that would span chests the size of Vince and Adam went harder. What to stuff those bras with required some experimentation. Balloons floated out when they did their routine. Vince declared oranges too small. If he had to dress up like a girl, he wanted bigger tits. Adam suggested coconuts, but they turned out to be uncomfortable with their hairy husks and hazardous to the toes if they fell. After much trial and error, grapefruits won out since the bras couldn't contain melons, which made a terrible mess in Dean's recreation room when they slipped out the bottom and smashed to the floor.

All agreed on black sneakers for footwear. None felt secure enough to dance in heels and feared off-field injuries even if they could find the appropriate sizes.

Short, pleated skirts remained a problem. Brian Lightfoot stepped in to measure their waists and take the list to a shop favored by transvestites of which New Orleans had many. Only he wasn't afraid to be seen in such a place, not that his tastes ran that way, but he did have friends who practiced dressing as sexy ladies and knew where to go for such goods.

Brian returned with five red skirts piped in black and possessing comfortable stretchy waistbands. "You know, you could have gotten the whole outfit there complete with padded bras. Turns out dressing as a Sinners' cheerleader is fairly popular."

"Thanks, but we'll stick with what we have," Tom said. "We aren't likely to use them again."

"Grapefruits—really?" Brian lifted his nicely shaped dark brows.

"If one slips out, it will be funny," Tom claimed, not wanting to send Brian back for the tops.

For his service, Brian demanded to sit in on the rehearsal. Stacy joined him on the sofa pushed back against the wall to give the chorus line lots of space. She laughed so hard at her husband in drag that Dean questioned if excessive hilarity was good for the baby. He'd let their secret slip!

Adam shook his quarterback's hand. "That's great, man!"

Vince thumped his back. "Way to go. Boy or girl?"

"A girl, we think."

"Freakin' fantastic. She'll be able to play with our Princess," Prince said of his expected daughter, always turning the conversation toward himself when an opportunity came along.

"Better luck next time," Vince added, obviously

without thinking. Seeing Stacy rise from her seat with her blue eyes narrowed, and her fists clenched, he quickly back-pedaled. "I mean girls are great, too. I'm still working on being more sexually sensitive."

That not only pacified Stacy, but made her laugh some more. She sank back into the cushions with tears running down her cheeks as the men attempted to coordinate their movements to words of Teddy's hastily written jingle. All of them had good footwork as might be expected from football players. Dean, Adam, and Prince actually possessed a sense of rhythm, and Vince thought he did. Tom acknowledged that he did not. As for singing, he and Dean couldn't carry a tune in a Sinners helmet, but Adam and Prince turned out to be fairly good. The big surprise came when Vince sang the opening line in a strong, deep, and on-key baritone. His teammates stared.

"What? So I used to be a choirboy at St. Cecilia's back in Philly. Had to give it up when my voice changed, and by that time I was into football. Always thought I'd like to cut an album some day."

"Me, too," Prince said. "We need to talk later."

"I'd suggest Vince sing the opening line and last line solo," Brian said. "Then, Adam and Prince join in while Dean and Tom chant along in an undertone until the end. I'd start with you lined up behind Vince, all shaking your pom-poms in front of your chests. Fan out on either side of Vince. Cross step left, then right. Proceed to high kicks with your arms around each other's shoulders, left, right, and the grand finale, Dean, Prince, Tom, and Adam kneel shaking pom-poms while Vince stands behind to deliver the final words."

"Say, I only asked you to get the skirts, not do

choreography," Tom grumbled.

"When you've got it, you must share it. Let's do a run through. A one and a two and a three." Brian snapped his fingers and attached himself to the end of the chorus line to show them how to go about it. "Good, but it could use a little more oomph."

Tom lofted an idea. "We could paint our fingernails red and put on lipstick."

"She'd notice the nail polish and know something was going on," Stacy said, still enjoying the view of the big men acting like fools in order to make Alix feel part of the team. Dean mouthed her a "thank you."

The vote went against Tom when it came to wearing lipstick. Or as Vince put it, "Some of that stuff don't come off, especially the red. Ever tried to get it out of a shirt collar?"

"No, no, I meant something to add pizzazz to the finale." Brian paced, waving a finger like a metronome and humming the song. "I think you're all too tall to do a successful pyramid. We'd need a little guy for the top, and none of you fill the bill even if Tom is lighter than the rest. Can anyone do a split?"

Heads shook. Tom, eyes sliding sideways away from the group, said, "I think I could."

"Don't think it. If you pull a groin muscle, Alix will have to be both punter and kicker for all the pre-season games," Dean admonished.

Still not looking directly at the guys and knowing the red was creeping up his neck, Tom confessed. "I've been practicing some yoga with Alix at home. Really stretches out the hamstrings." Slowly, carefully, he lowered himself to the floor and raised his arms over his head shaking the pom-poms.

"I'd prefer if you could speed it up. Work on it, Tommy. Vince, don't sing the last words until he's down. From the top, ending with the split!"

By the time Brian released them from a punishing but perfecting practice, Tom hoped he wouldn't be too sore to kick at camp the next day. Eager to get it over with, the guys elected to perform the song and dance in two days' time and get it out of their minds forever.

"I cannot miss this! I'll come to the training field under the guise of imparting all my punting wisdom to Alix," Brian said.

"Do film it for me," Stacy asked with a slight smile on her lips.

"I will. Copies for everyone!" Brian promised.

As the men packed their costumes and grapefruits into black Sinners gym bags, Vince sidled up to Tom. "So you and Alix practice yoga together. You doing anything else? I mean you doin' it? That's what I really need to know."

"No." Tom wanted to say they would be doing it soon, but had no reason to claim that. After they put on the show, he planned to have his chest waxed. Maybe his legs, too. Prince already did that. Adam came by a bare, bronze chest and legs naturally. Dean was lucky enough to have just a patch of dark hair between the pecs that arrowed neatly toward his jewels. Fur as curly and russet as a teddy bear's coat covered his own chest and belly, but he considered himself way better off than Vince who had a heavy Neanderthal pelt that extended to his back. The Virgin Mary tattooed on one of his biceps appeared to have a beard. For the skit, that would be funny, but surely if Alix were attracted to Vince's thick, glossy black hair and the nearly permanent dark stubble on his jutting jaw, she'd be turned off by seeing him partly naked in drag. Yeah, he'd bravely schedule that waxing.

Vince leaned even closer to his ear. Tom inhaled the garlic smell of the punt protector's dinner. "She's not a lesbo, huh? I know you can't change 'em. I tried once."

"She told me she wasn't." Oh, how he wanted to lie and spread the rumor to keep the team away from his Amazon, but if Alix found out, he'd never have a chance with her.

"Great. You two are just roommates then, kinda like girlfriends if she tells you that sort of stuff and teaches you yoga and cooks with you."

"We're not like girlfriends! We talk, we eat, we on occasion do yoga."

"Okay, okay. I know you're straight in spite of hanging out with Brian. Beef said that shit about being his lady to get your goat. Nobody believes him. We all know you were with Ilsa first. Too bad she's off the market again. I would have liked a piece of her schnitzel." Vince glanced around to make sure the other men who'd slept with Ilsa didn't hear. Only Adam wasn't a member of that club.

"Thanks for the vote of confidence, Vince. I have to get going."

"Me, too."

The chorus line departed through the rear courtyard of Dean's Garden District home, past a fountain with gargoyles spouting water, and out through a gate in a wall well-camouflaged by banana trees heavy with pink blooms and tree-sized cerise crepe myrtles. Stacy buzzed them out, and each headed for their cars that lined the street like a display of luxury vehicles. Without warning, Big Lou stepped from the shadow of a live oak and exposed her pendulous breasts.

"See anything you like, boys?"

"Jesus, no! Get away from me, you hag." Vince pushed her out of his way.

"Not what I'm looking for," Brian replied mildly, crossing the street.

Adam Malala pressed a few bills into her grimy hands. "We should be kind to the insane."

"Who you saying is crazy?" Big Lou opened her hand as if to toss the money into the humid air, but thought better of it and stuffed it in her pants.

Tom made his getaway, saying, "Just gave you twenty not too long ago."

In the safety of his SUV, he drove around the first corner before making a call to Dean. "Big Lou is hiding out near your rear gate. You might want to call the police and have her moved back across Canal Street. She seems obsessed with the Billodeauxs."

"Good idea. I don't want her upsetting Stacy."

Tom drove on hoping Alix was waiting for him at home. She wasn't there.

****

Alix waltzed in around nine-thirty as the summer dusk turned to true darkness. Tom sat in one of the recliners, legs raised, and clicked through the channels, obviously unhappy with his current selection. He glared her way. "Do you know what time it is? Where were you?"

Taken aback, Alix answered. "Add a missy to that and you'd sound exactly like my mom and dad when I broke curfew. I might ask the same of you."

"I only went over to Dean's for a guy's night and got home before dark. You know, poker and snacks. Nothing special. We broke it up early because of practice tomorrow. Summer training doesn't leave much energy for carousing. I hope you had the sense to take a cab back from wherever." Tom turned off the TV with a savage click and ratcheted the footrest of the recliner down with a thud.

"Wherever was across the street. I had a late dinner with Xochi at the Palace. We sat at an outdoor table, had some wine, splurged on dessert and coffee, talked like women do, a nice change after being at camp all day with football players. Then, I crossed Canal Street and came home." She frowned, not recognizing or particularly liking the sullen version of Tom.

"You could have been followed!"

"I wasn't! If you are so concerned about me, you could have invited me to Dean's place. I am a good poker player. There isn't much else to do nights at a hunting camp or waiting in an ice fishing hut for something to bite. If the boys didn't want me in their game, I could have visited with Stacy." She almost added, "So, there!" but didn't want to sound childish.

Tom took a breath that made his chest heave as if he dove deep searching for patience. "Maybe next time you can come along."

"Well, thank you. I might add you're the one who's been out every night this week without explanation while I sit here alone. I don't know that many people in the city yet. I even called Brian Lightfoot to see if he wanted to visit and talk about punting or fashion or whatever, but I couldn't reach him."

"He was at Dean's, too. He said he'd stop by camp

day after tomorrow and give you some pointers." He didn't meet her eyes when he said that.

Although the thought made her throat hurt, Alix took a turn at being generous and understanding. After all, he'd taken her under his freckled wing and escorted her everywhere. Maybe, he needed some time and space on his own, some privacy to pursue someone he really wanted without her in the way like an annoying kid sister.

"Look, Tom, if you're seeing someone, you should feel free to bring her around. Don't mind me. I can stay in my rooms out of the way or make some nice canapés for the two of you to have with wine."

She'd revealed a personal dream. Tom coming home to a tray of tempting tidbits she'd made for him. He'd open and pour the wine. They'd talk about their day, their thoughts. Maybe delay dinner for a timeout in the bedroom. She shouldn't have made the offer since she wouldn't be able to bring it off. If he brought a date back to the condo, she'd slip across the street and stay overnight with Xochi. Maybe Tom had felt this way when Dean brought Ilsa into their home, like he wanted to run and hide.

"Believe me, there isn't anyone else. I swear."

Did he sound like a guilty husband? Alix dismissed the thought. "You don't have to answer to me."

"Let's forget all about this. Saturday night we'll go out and do something special together. I promise. So, what did you and Xochi talk about?"

"Ah, girl stuff." Once she'd worked the conversation around to Xo's brother, he'd become the major topic, but she knew how to evade his curiosity. If Dad or *Morfar* pried too deeply into her life, all she had to do was ask them to stop at a drug store for feminine hygiene products and return with a big bag full, previous conversation guaranteed to be forgotten in the meantime. "Um, what kind of birth control we use and which tampons are the most comfortable and absorbent. Things like that."

Although Tom pinked up a trifle, he stared directly at her now. "Really? That's all? Not a word mentioned about me?"

"Some. Only good stuff. Well, I think you're right. We need to get to bed early. Practice tomorrow. Good night, Tom." She swung down the hallway to her bedroom as fast as she could go, shut the door, and leaned against it, heart thudding. Surely, Xochi wouldn't tattle on her.

After her third and final glass of red wine, she'd plaintively asked Tom's sister, "Does your brother like me?" as if she were an insecure seventh-grader with a bad crush. Come to think of it, that is exactly how she felt.

Xochi tipped back her head and laughed with a sound so rich and warm it could have coalesced into hot chocolate. "Yes, I think he does, but I refuse to call him and say, 'Alix likes you. Do you like her back?' Since trying to get Dean and Stacy together, I have given up matchmaking. It's far too dangerous no matter what I see."

"See?"

Xochi had searched the tables nearby for people who might be taking too much interest in their conversation. Everyone appeared to be chatting with friends, enjoying a mellow evening and fine food. She looked across Canal Street, squinting into dark doorways.

"What are you doing?" Alix asked.

"Checking for paparazzi, cameras, and directional microphones. Dean is their main target, but they stalk Tom, too, because both are Sinners. The Billodeaux girls aren't of quite as much interest, though I am sure if we acted out, the vultures of the press would be right on top of our bodies. What I tell you is a family secret. Do you understand?"

"What happens at the ranch, stays at the ranch," Alix breathed.

Xochi smiled and laughed again, a sound so alluring, heads did turn. She waited for them to look away before saying, "That sounds like something Tom would say." Xo hesitated another moment before revealing her secret. "Since I reached adolescence, I've seen auras. The local *traiteur* who treated me for my fears said I possess a gift for healing and this is part of the gift. So far, I can only say it has prevented me from going out with questionable men whose glow is muddied or dark or flaming with the red of violence."

"Neat power to have." Not sure if she wanted to know, Alix finally asked, "What is my aura like?"

"A very lovely blue that brightens when Tom is nearby."

"That's a relief. I thought you might say orange. I hate orange."

Xochi shrugged. "Orange can be good or bad depending."

"What about Tom?"

"You know, he's never asked me about himself, but he has a bright yellow nimbus. Along with that red hair, he glows like a candle on fire."

Eagerly, Alix leaned forward. "That's good, right?"

"Yes, he is intelligent and creative. Once, his creative mind saved our lives."

"I know about that, hiding out in the big urns, but does he glow brighter when I'm around?" Alix tried to take a sip from her empty wine glass and settled for ice water, probably a better choice anyhow.

"Since you've been around, he rarely comes to see me, so hard to tell. Actually, his aura couldn't get much brighter regardless."

"So you don't know if he really, really likes me."

"I think you should find out for yourself."

They were tying up the table with their conversation, but the ever so polite waiter merely stopped by to inquire if they wanted anything else. They ordered coffee and cheesecake and waited for him to leave.

"I think he does. Tom kissed me a couple of times, but always makes it seems like he's thanking me for something."

"He's going slow, I'd say. Dean and Stacy moved too fast, and we ended up with a disaster. My fault since I suggested Stacy try to get his attention by dating inappropriate men knowing Dean would come to the rescue, but that almost got Prince Dobbs killed. It was awful." Xochi accepted the cup of coffee as gratefully as if the balmy night were freezing.

"I read about it. In the end, they lived happily ever after." Alix lifted her cup and blew across the surface to cool it. She dumped in several little pots of cream, knowing how strong it would be.

"No one really knows that until they're dead," Xochi said.

That sent a shiver up Alix's spine. "If I throw myself at Tom, and he doesn't feel the same way, I'll have to move out. We won't be able to be friends any more."

"I have a spare room if you need it."

"Does that mean it won't work out?" Alix probed.

Xochi's brown eyes crinkled in the corners as she smiled. "I don't see the future, Alix, only a bunch of colors."

"So, no hints, huh? I'm on my own. But jealousy worked with Dean."

"Highly not recommended! Let me tell you some stories about Tom as a kid, ones that didn't make the tabloids."

Xochi regaled her with tales of nuns and whoopee cushions, of the truck he and Dean shared locked up in chains when they'd done a bout of drunk driving in their teens, of Tom slathered in so much zinc oxide at the family pool, he'd been mistaken for an albino by the nearly blind mother of one of the Camp Love Letter kids. "The woman said, 'It must be hard to live with your condition. I am sure people stare.' And Tom says, 'You mean red hair and freckles?'"

Alix's laugh wasn't smooth and sexy. It blared out loud and honest. People did stare but grinned along with her. The lights in the condo came on across the way. "Tom's home! I should go."

Xochi pressed her back into her seat. "Let him have some time to miss you."

Alix stayed another half hour but every five minutes checked that ugly, unfeminine waterproof watch she kept forgetting to take off. Finally, they split the tab and walked to the corner together, putting Xochi within a few yards of her apartment. She raced home to Tom only to find this grumpy version of him ready to chew her out like Coach Buck on a bad day. Miffed that she wasn't there waiting for him? She'd give that some thought.

## Chapter Sixteen

Alix checked the waterproof watch. She still had ten minutes and could blow-dry her hair if she wanted, but outside the locker room at the practice field, she heard the shifting of large bodies, hot and sweating and ready for a shower at the end of their series of two-a-days. Considering their probable state of exhaustion, deep chuckles found their way under the sill. Alix decided to simply slick her wet hair behind her ears and let them in early. She'd had a great day, spent mostly conferring with Brian Lightfoot, who was not only knowledgeable but very entertaining, and generous to all.

Alix opened the door to find herself confronted by a line of five burly cheerleaders with Vince Barbaro, hairy as a highland gorilla, in the lead. He burst into song, surprisingly tuneful as he drew out the notes.

*Alix Lindstrom, Alix Lindstrom!*

The other manly cheerleaders fanned out shaking their pom-poms with vigor.

*We don't care about your T's or your A...*
*And we have only one thing to say, today!*

The chorus line swayed in one direction, then the other.

*We only care about your legs, your legs,*
*Your wonderful, miraculous legs!*

Her teammates, a very unlikely bunch of dancers,

went into high kicks. Tom, all fuzzy, kicked the highest, naturally. Vince dropped back. Dean, Prince, and Adam knelt. Tom did a split in front of her. A deep voice in the arc of players surrounding the dancers said, "That ain't natural in a man."

Vince glared at Beef Bolivar, but didn't let the comment ruin the finale. He sang out sweetly—

*Legs Lindstrom, Legs Lindstrom!*

"Got it recorded," Brian declared. "Copies for everyone on the team."

"Leave me out. It's revolting, guys dressing up that way." Bolivar pushed through to the showers, stepping over Tom still on the ground.

Brian shook his head sadly. "There's always one in the bunch."

Everyone else stayed to enjoy the moment. Vince got to Alix first and patted her on the shoulder. "What did you think?"

"That was outrageously funny. What a good voice you have."

"Um, thanks. Just remember, I always got your back, babe. Ah, I mean babe in the way I mean dude when I talk to a guy. Maybe I should have said dude instead."

"I'd prefer just Alix or Lindstrom."

"I think we're supposed to call you Legs now, but Alix, that would be great. Say…"

On the ground, Tom held out a desperate hand to Dean. "I can't get up. Help me before…"

"You want to go out tomorrow night, Alix? I know this great Italian place on the other side of the bridge. Mafia dons used to eat there. Best place outside of Philly, I tell ya."

Alex watched Tom struggle to his feet and hoped he hadn't done any permanent damage. His brown eyes looked a little wild like those of a shying red stallion. She answered Vince. "Sure, I'd like that. What time?"

"Seven. I know where Tom lives. Pick you up there." Vince stepped aside since Tom was breathing down his hairy nape.

"Did you like it? My brother Teddy wrote the song. I know it's not great, but he had deadlines to meet. Brian did the choreography and helped with the costumes, but the idea was mine. You know, to welcome you to the team, Legs."

"I loved it. I think everyone did but Beef."

"That just says it was great." Tom rooted in his sports bra and withdrew a grapefruit. He presented it, still warm and fragrant from his body, to Alix on an open palm as if it were a golden apple and she Helen of Troy. "You like grapefruit? I think they're still good."

"Sure, with brown sugar on top and a cherry in the middle—which makes them taste like dessert." Alix accepted his tribute.

Vince barged in again. "Here, you can have mine, too. The grapefruit was Tom's idea. He wanted to use oranges. Way too small, I said." His grapefruits smelled like sweat, but Alix took them and deposited all three in her gym bag.

Dean stalked by and put two more in her hands. "Here, get these out of my sight."

Adam Malala clapped his quarterback's shoulder. "See, Dean can be fun. He's not all work and no play, right guys?" That got a sustained laugh. No one worked harder or longer on the field than Dean who rarely joked about anything. He left that to Tom.

Tom removed the rest of the citrus from his bra and took the two Dean left behind. He began to juggle the fruit. "Adam, toss your two in one at a time."

Adam did. Tom caught the first but the second went splat on Alix's sandaled feet. "Sorry, balls are easier. I learned to juggle for the Camp Love Letter kids."

"It's been a long time since I had a grapefruit pedicure." Alix kicked the split fruit aside.

"They have those?"

Before she could answer, Prince Dobbs cut in. "You can get anything you want if you pay enough, Tommy boy. Say, mind if I keep mine? My woman has a craving for sour right now, pickles, kraut, you name it." He didn't bother removing them from the sports bra, but merely ran his hands down his thoroughly waxed body and taut abs. "Say, I make a pretty fine looking woman."

"Absolutely." Alix pressed her lips together to contain a wide smile.

"Except for this." Prince lifted his skirt. "See the scar? That's where my life-blood spurted out before Dean put a tourniquet on it. Got to be grateful for that. Praise the Lord!"

"Praise the Lord," Alix echoed, happy when the man moved away.

Vince returned from what had to be the world's quickest shower. He'd put on a snug fitted red shirt and tight jeans and run his fingers through his long black hair giving him the air of an Italian gigolo hanging out on the beach. "You need a ride home, Alix?"

"I drove today, but thanks."

He cocked a finger at her and pulled the trigger.

"Saturday at seven." Vince strode away, working his gluteus maximus like a male stripper.

"Mafia dons," Tom muttered. "He's probably related to some."

"Could be. You'd better shower or else I'm driving home alone. Evidently cheerleading is hard, sweaty work." She crinkled her long nose at him.

"But you did like our skit?"

"I loved it. Thanks, Tom."

When Tom smiled broadly at her, Alix swore she could almost see his golden aura.

\*\*\*\*

On their way up to the condo, Arturo mentioned that some packages had arrived for Alix. He'd left them on the doorstep. The man wasn't jesting. Several boxes, large and small, all from Wisconsin, cluttered the foyer. Tom helped her drag them inside and got a knife to cut the numerous strands of strapping tape that surrounded the cardboard. The easiest to extricate turned out to be a nice selection of Wisconsin cheeses bearing the message, "Happy Birthday from Rika. I know you don't have cheese this good in N.O."

"It's your birthday? Why didn't you tell me?" Tom struggled with one of the larger boxes.

"I didn't want you to feel obligated to get anything. Believe me, that show you put on was gift enough. I'd planned to bake a cake tomorrow—red velvet—that we could have after our usual dinner. I still might if I have the time before my date with Vince."

Alix broke into one of the smaller packages that glugged when she set it upright and bore numerous "fragile" stamps. She withdrew a card with a leaping fish on it clearly designed for a man on his special day.

It read, "Enjoy what you love best on your birthday" and contained a sizable check with the notation, "For a fishing trip next time I visit." The contents proved to be a bottle of good, pale amber Swedish aquavit with a note around its neck. "Save some for me. Your *Morfar*."

"Original. I have to admit my folks never gave me booze and a fishing trip for a birthday gift." Tom finally penetrated the box he'd sawed upon for several minutes and opened the flaps.

"Not original for *Morfar*. Aquavit is his all-purpose gift and strapping tape, his favorite fixative. Oh, no!" Alix pressed her hands to her cheeks in complete dismay. "Mom sent my scrapbooks. Now I am embarrassed. Don't look!"

But Tom had already flipped open the first one. "These go back a long way. I still have braces on my teeth in this one with my mom and the rest of the kids at some charity event." He refrained from pointing out she'd drawn a heart in red marker around his face.

Alix snatched the album away and slammed it shut, but Tom had already delved into another one. "Wow, all of Dean's mess from last year and at least two dozen pages devoted to Stacy's nuptials from the ring to the gown to the formal pictures released to the press. How many years have you been doing this?"

"Since I turned twelve, I guess."

"Tomorrow you'll be…"

"Twenty-three tomorrow."

"Going on a dozen years. I'll bet my mother doesn't have files as complete as these. Something is missing, though. It ends with the wedding."

"I went into training to be a punter and had no time

for this nonsense any more. I've grown up." Very primly, Alix shut the cover.

"Give me a second."

Tom had that impish grin on his freckled face that always preceded mischief. He'd worn that expression at yesterday's practice nearly all day. She should have known something was up before she opened the locker room door to be serenaded by hirsute cheerleaders. He returned with pieces of newsprint waving in his hands, grabbed the last album, and turned it to the last unused page. Lifting a flap, he inserted the picture and article about her rescue of Lorena from the tabloid and smoothed the plastic top sheet over it.

"There. Your first official encounter with the entire Billodeaux family. I sort of wish the paparazzi had been following us around so there could be more. I hope there will be—in a good way. Here's a few extras to send to your family. They should be making scrapbooks about you!"

"You saved these. You're so sweet." She dared to touch his cheek. It turned red under her fingertips.

"But not sweet like Brian Lightfoot," Tom hastened to add. "Hey, it's a great picture of you. Everyone should have a copy."

"Now I am sorry I won't be celebrating my birthday with you. Maybe we could do something together in the afternoon." Staying home in bed with him had crossed her mind and disappeared swiftly running on red sneakers into the distance as Tom answered.

"Uh, I have an appointment tomorrow that's going to take a while."

"Nothing serious, I hope." Her hand returned to its

proper place in her lap.

"Nope, just time consuming. You do realize I only left you alone here all week in order to prepare the skit. You'd think football players would be quick studies, but not so much when it comes to singing and dancing at the same time."

"That's okay, Tom. I know my family asked you to look out for me, but it needn't be every second of every day. We train and live together. I get you need some space."

"Not very much space, just tomorrow afternoon."

Not meeting his eyes, Alix fished out a couple of greeting cards from the side of the box. One had a floral design and the sentimental phrase, "For a Beloved Daughter on her Birthday." It contained a gift certificate from her mom and dad for a spa day in New Orleans. The second had a half-naked, hunky guy on the cover and the message: "Don't do anything I wouldn't do on your birthday—so anything goes!" Tille enclosed a gift card from the same spa for a pedicure and added a note. "Got to take care of those million dollar toes. Give Dean, Tom, and Vince a kiss for me."

She showed them to Tom. "Looks like I'll be spending my afternoon at a spa."

"Which spa?" He snatched the cards and handed them back again. "Good place. I think Stacy goes there."

"I guess we both know what we'll be doing tomorrow. Would you help me drag these boxes to my closet? No need to open any more of them." Alix lifted one herself. Tom took the other two stacked under his chin.

"Just put them way in the back." Alix nudged on

the light in the deep walk-in.

He complied, but did a double take as he noticed his own face peeping out from a gap in the hangers full of clothes—that photo from *Sports Illustrated* taken after his longest, game-saving field goal ever last season while Alix trained to be a punter. She threw down her box and moved in front of it too late to save her dignity. Hands on hips, she said defiantly, "So what. Mia Hamm is on the other wall. Both of you are great at your sport. Besides, that's a good picture of you, also."

"One of my best," he agreed. He seemed entirely too happy to have caught her crushing on him.

"Out! I need to decide which dress to wear on my date with Vince tomorrow." That should put a damper on his vanity in case he thought he was her only option, and she'd simply sit around waiting for him to make a move. It succeeded. His expectant grin faded. Tom left her closet and her bedroom, tripping only twice on a stupid white throw rug and a pair of running shoes tossed on the floor.

Chapter Seventeen

Tom paced the floor like an expectant father in a Fifties movie. Dads didn't do that any more. They waded right into the blood and gore of the delivery room. Dean had filled him in on those gruesome details. Blood and gore. He wished he hadn't thought of that. Vince planned to take Alix across the Huey P. Long Bridge from the Eastbank to the Wank or Westbank. Once a steep, terrifyingly narrow, two lane structure that vibrated when the trains sharing the bridge rumbled across it, the structure had been widened and modernized making it no longer a thrill ride, but still the fog might come up off the river and turn the trip into a hazard.

Vince arrived early, all spiffed up in a charcoal suit with a wide gray silk tie and a matching shirt, his black hair combed straight back, raising those mafia connections in Tom's mind again. As if he were Nels Lindstrom, he told the man to take good care of Alix and to drive safely. Vince nodded solemnly, presuming Tom had the right to tell him what to do with his roommate instead of getting belligerent. They waited together as uncomfortable as a father with his daughter's prom date for Alix to appear.

"There's no rule about dating a teammate, is there?" Vince asked, ending the silence.

"Not yet." Tom wished there were, but then he'd

be forbidden to see Alix, too.

Rosy and polished from her day at the spa, she swirled into the living room. Her little black dress came to mid-thigh and swung about her fabulous legs, flirty and light, not at all tight, but short, very short in Tom's opinion. The scoop of the neckline showed her breasts, pushed together by one of those magical bras with which he had some experience. When taken off, the contents often disappointed, but he knew that would not be the case if Alix disrobed. She'd be perfect. She wore her hair in her usual white-blonde bob, but sported a headband with a black velvet rose on one side. She hadn't bothered with any jewelry. Vince stood. So did Tom. Neither spoke, though Tom wanted to suggest she wear a jacket despite it being in the nineties all day and not much cooler now.

Made uncertain by their stares, she blurted, "I wore black in case I spill on my dress. Tom can tell you I'm a messy eater."

"I like a woman who enjoys her food. You look great, really great, Alix." Vince had a naturally deep voice, but Tom swore it dropped another notch as the male hormones rose to the personal protector's throat. "Shall we go?" Vince gallantly held out an arm.

"Don't be late," Tom heard himself burble. "I mean we still have lots of training camp left and should get rest when we can. Me, I'm resting tonight."

"Like kickers need to rest," Vince said.

Alix squeezed his arm, actually his bulging bicep. "Hey, don't forget I'm a kicker, too."

"If all kickers looked like you, I'd love that a lot."

Off they went to enjoy Italian food on the other side of the Mississippi as if there weren't any good places in the city. Tom filled his evening setting up a surprise for Alix, a delicate table of white and gold that the antiques dealer said had cabriole legs and a checkerboard inlay of onyx and ivory, probably at one time serving for games of chess or draughts kept in the little drawers inset in the sides—late seventeenth century, French, Louis Quatorze. Whatever the hell it was, the thing cost a pretty penny. On his way out, he spied a teapot and matching cup the exact shade of blue as Alix's eyes. He held the cup up to the light and could see his hand on the other side it was that thin. Both pieces of porcelain were tricked out with plenty of gilding and sprays of dainty flowers.

The salesman glided up beside him. "What exquisite taste you have, sir. Also French, very old, Limoges."

"Yeah, I thought so," Tom bluffed. He picked up the teapot, examined the bottom as if he were one of the guys on Antiques Roadshow. He liked when they did sports memorabilia. "It's really faded, but I think this says 'museum reproduction'."

The antiques dealer reddened to the edge of a stiffly styled toupee that didn't quite match his remaining hair and tidily trimmed mustache. "Perhaps only the cup is Limoges. Allow me to include both as a gift from Royal's of Royal Street. I'll have them delivered with the table."

"Nice of you, Mr…"

"Randy, Randy Royal, proprietor. Please consider shopping here again." The last seemed almost a plea to Tom, the heck if he knew why.

"Just make sure to ask Arturo to keep them for me behind the desk, okay?"

"I've already written the particulars on the delivery slip."

"Good, see you around." Tom left doubting he would.

That out of the way, he kept his appointment for a chest waxing at a salon recommended by Brian Lightfoot, not the same place Alix would be spending her afternoon. This establishment seemed to have mostly male attendants. He hoped that didn't apply to hers. After he stripped and lay on a linen-swathed table sheeted in a layer of plastic, his genitals modestly covered by a thick towel, Steve, who warmed the wax strips, suggested he might want to sign up for the whole package—chest, legs, and pubic area. For the last, a number of designs were available. He handed Tom a binder with suggestions to peruse while Steve proceeded with the chest waxing. Evidently, a penis could be adorned with a pouf like a poodle or surrounded with close and imaginative razor work or go completely bald. Tom didn't think he'd like a razor so close to his goodies. One slip and…

Steve ripped off the first strip with gusto. Tom arched off the table but stifled an unmanly scream. Braced for the rest, he simply dug his fingers into the edges of the table and hung on until the pain ceased.

"First time, honey?" Steve asked.

"Probably the last, too. I think I'll pass on the full package. The things we do for love, huh?"

Steve tossed his artfully tousled and streaked hair. "You don't need to tell me about that. Let me rub some lotion on to take away the sting."

"That's okay. I'll take a tube of that stuff home. I might need more later."

"Excellent. I'll put it in one of our signature bags and add it to your tab while you dress." Steve took his black-clad and very buff body from the room.

Tom dressed in a hurry but picked up the tube Steve indicated and slathered himself with the cream before putting on his white T-shirt with the discreet Sinners logo available to all at the Sinners gift shop. It stuck to his chest. Jesus, his pit hair had been pulled out by the roots, too, and smarted like the devil's torment for the damned.

Steve returned. "My, that shirt really shows off your physique." He held out the little black bag with Deke's Body Works emblazoned across the chest of the golden figure of a well-built man. "Come again and ask for me."

"I wouldn't let anyone else wax me," Tom said. What he meant was never again! He shoved the suggested gratuity into a little brown envelope on his way out, wondering why a guy had to tip after being tortured, and headed home.

On the way, he detoured to Gambino's Bakery and purchased a half-and-half doberge cake, six moist layers, half with lemon filling, half with chocolate and the top decorated the same way. He thought it matched the little chess table in a way. Besides, no one should have to bake their own birthday cake, and with Alix at the spa, she had no time anyhow.

By the time he got back to the condo and stashed the cake in his room, his chest ceased to throb and the red burn faded from his skin. Checking in the bathroom mirror, Tom thought his muscles looked sleek, but damn if a whole mass of freckles he'd forgotten about since late adolescence hadn't reappeared on his pale skin. He certainly hoped Alix liked freckles more than body hair because he had plenty to offer.

Well, he needn't have hidden the cake in his closet because Alix buzzed in at six and with no more than a wave of the hand and a "Hi, gotta get ready" and disappeared into her bedroom until Vince arrived to make off with her. Tom hoped that didn't lead to making out with her as he retrieved the antique table and porcelain from Arturo and set it up in her room beside the slipper chair. True, the view was still of a parking garage, but now Alix had an elegant little area to sit, have tea or coffee, and read magazines, not that he'd ever seen her thumb any but copies of his *Sports Illustrated*.

Putting the cake in the refrigerator to make sure it didn't slough frosting, he sat to wait and wait and wait. Around ten, he placed the cake resting on its frilly doily and cardboard base on the small French table in the belief that Alix would be home soon. He waited. Midnight arrived before the elevator door slid open and footsteps sounded in the foyer: the thud of Vince's wingtips, the tap of the heels worn by Alix. Muted conversation ensued too low for him to hear. Tom in his stocking feet crept closer to the door until he could put his eye to the peephole. The back of Alix's head blocked the view as if she leaned heavily against it. He could see only the strands of her blonde hair through the glass. Was Vince pressing her other side? They weren't saying a word now. Tom put his ear to the door convinced he'd hear sounds of struggle. Nothing.

His hand shot for the latch, giving it a hard, sudden turn. Alix fell into him and both hit the hardwood floor with Vince plummeting down on them, making her the center of a man sandwich. Luckily, Vince caught some of his substantial weight on his hands and rolled aside. The first to regain his footing, he offered Alix a hand, sneaking only a rapid glance at the pair of black lace panties exposed when her skirt flew up in the collision. From the bottom of the pile looking over Alix's shoulder, Tom glared at him.

Sitting and leaning on his elbows, he said, "I didn't expect that. Thought I'd invite you both in for cake and coffee since it is Alix's birthday. Glad I broke your fall, Legs. Everyone okay?"

They had no time to reply before the security system on the door beeped like a bomb about to explode. Tom got off his duff and hurried to reset it. "So," he said, "anyone for cake?" Beneath his shirt, he felt fairly certain those newly exposed freckles had disappeared beneath a sheen of red.

"I couldn't possibly eat another morsel," Alix said, a little huffy.

"Yeah, four courses and a dessert. More than even I could put away." Vince gestured to a scattering of takeout boxes, some oozing red sauce like blood onto the hardwood. "We bought you some leftovers. That's the spaghetti and meatballs and chicken cacciatore."

Alix raved over her meal. "I think the herbed chicken was even better, not to mention those oysters. They served them breaded in a skillet and topped with parmesan cheese. I'm afraid I ate all the marinated crab salad. I didn't know there would be so much more to come."

"Yeah, I go there lots and know to pace myself. There's still some spaghetti bordelaise left, though. The old folks who run the place kept bringing out dishes for

Alix to try. Me, I'm nothing, but she's a real celebrity, ya know," Vince said modestly as he scooped a couple of weighty boxes from the floor and took them to the fridge.

"It was the quaintest place, old-fashioned with checkered oilcloth on the tables and Chianti bottles holding candles that must have been there forever with all the wax dripped down the sides. They brought me tiramisu with a sparkler stuck in it for my birthday. Vince got up and sang for me. Then, some of waiters did opera pieces. We ended up with corny Dean Martin songs, everyone joining in. I had so much fun!" Oh, how her eyes sparkled for Vince, his voice, and his choice of restaurants.

Tom retrieved the rest of the leftovers, stowed them away, and returned to mop the floor with a paper towel. "You were at the restaurant all this time?"

"Sure, long drive out and back, all that eating, then the sing-along. Where else would we be?" Alix stared down at her flirty black skirt. "I didn't spill a thing on myself until you opened the door. Now my dress smells like garlic."

"I'll pay for the dry cleaning. Glad you had a good time." He tried very hard to mean that second part. "Coffee?"

"No," Vince answered. "We had espresso at the restaurant. Guess I'd better get going. See you Monday. Or maybe tomorrow, we could…"

"She needs her rest, Vince. So do you since you work out harder than either of us. Better get going."

"Monday, then, and next Saturday." Vince cocked that finger pistol at Alix and pulled the trigger, surely his most annoying habit.

"I'll look forward to it."

"Let me show you out. I have to reset the alarm." Tom led the personal protector to the foyer and snapped the door shut behind him.

Alix stretched, and Tom followed the length of her body with his eyes as the dress rode up. To think, his hand had rested on one side of the pair of black lace panties she wore under it for a few seconds.

"Guess I'll turn in." Alix walked down the hallway to her suite.

"Me, too." But Tom lingered waiting for her cry of surprise.

It didn't sound exactly the way he'd heard it in his mind. "Thomas Cassidy Billodeaux, are you responsible for all this?" came out more like a reprimand. Tom moved down the hall and lounged in her doorway waiting for a reward for his thoughtfulness and patience. "Guilty," he said.

Alix raised the fragile cup in her large hands. "Tom, do I strike you as the kind of woman who sits at tiny tables and drinks tea out of delicate vessels like this? One stumble on those ridiculous throw rugs my mother made me buy, and I could wipe out the whole setting because I'm a big, husky girl. That table is spindly, beautiful, and most likely very expensive. It probably survived the French Revolution, but doesn't stand a chance with Alix Lindstrom in the room. You should take it back before I destroy it accidently."

Alix waved the teacup in the air by its gilded handle. "I'm a white coffee mug kind of person. I can't drink out of this and feel comfortable. It might snap in my hands."

Tom went hot, then cold, as if his body couldn't

decide whether to be embarrassed or afraid. "Your mother said you needed a sitting area. It's a birthday gift from me. You don't need to be afraid to use the teapot. That's only a replica."

Alix set the teacup gently on top of the dresser, safely out of the way. "My mother doesn't understand me and evidently neither do you."

"Yeah, well, you aren't husky or outsized. I don't know why you see yourself that way. When you kick a punt, you are more graceful than Brian Lightfoot. I could watch you all afternoon. You are beautiful as a whooping crane. But if you keep going out to dinner with Vince at all those Italian places you'll have to watch out for husky."

That stopped her tirade dead in its athletic cleats. Alix tipped her head back and let loose with one of her booming, unfettered laughs. Tom failed to see what was so very funny.

"If you'd compared me to a swan, I would have called that a complete pile of B.S. But a whooping crane, yes!" Alix flapped her long arms, hit the edge of the chess table, and set it to wobbling dangerously. She steadied the teapot and caught the cake before it smashed to the floor. "You did get the cake right. I dote on doberge. I wish I weren't too full to eat some tonight. Let's put it in the fridge and have it for a decadent breakfast."

"It has both chocolate and lemon layers." Tom felt grateful he'd gotten one thing right. But no, he wasn't giving up on changing how Alix thought of herself. "Would you simply sit in the chair and sort of get the feel of the table. You can play chess or checkers on the top, too. The pieces go into those drawers underneath."

Clearly humoring him, Alix shook her head and took a seat in her blue slipper chair with her long legs stretched out to one side. Her skirt rode up to mini-dress length. Her toenails polished in red peeped out of her black pumps. Tom's mouth filled with saliva that had nothing to do with the doberge torte sitting before him.

"Well?" she asked. "I have to admit I don't know how to play chess, but I'm a killer at checkers after playing with my dad and *Morfar* all those years at the hunting camps." Alix touched the surface of the table, and it trembled again. "See, it knows it's in danger."

Tom swallowed before he spoke. "I can teach you chess, but just stay there for a minute."

First, he rolled up the white throw rug nearest the sitting area and shoved it under her bed. Then, he left the room and searched the drawers in the kitchen until he found a box with a cardboard flap he could rip away. Folding the piece in half, he returned to jam it under the unstable leg of the Louis Quatorze table. He prided himself on not trying to get a glimpse of those black lace panties while he knelt before her. "Touch the table."

It remained stable even when Alix drummed her fingers on the onyx and ivory inlay. She smiled in a way that warmed his heart. "With the throw rug hazard out of the way, this table should survive another century." Tom forced himself to get up and stand beside her.

Alix rose to full height. "You are so dear. Thank you for my presents, Tom."

She cupped his face with her long, cool fingers. The kiss wasn't lady-like no matter how soft and hot her lips. They fit perfectly atop his. Her tongue delved, and he tasted the coffee liqueur of the tiramisu and the warmth of garlic beneath it. Had she kissed Vince like this out in the hall before he opened the door? He needed to stop wondering and wrap his arms around her to show he could do it better. Before he did so, Alix stepped back.

"You'd better put the cake in the refrigerator. Can't wait to have some in the morning," she said.

Still stunned, Tom lifted the doberge from the table. "Good night, I guess."

"Yes, good night."

Hands shaking, he wondered how he ever got that cake of many layers back to the kitchen and himself to his bedroom and a cold shower.

****

Alix stripped out of her dress and flung it over the slipper chair. Too bad no one had gotten to see much of her skimpy underwear tonight. Way too soon to show it to Vince and just not the right time to expose herself to Tom who definitely displayed signs of jealousy. Tom treated her so delicately and respectfully, she pondered if he would ever make a move. But two could play at saying thank you and following it up with a more than thankful kiss.

Alix shed that wonder of a bra and the sexy panties and shrugged into the oversized tee she used as a sleep shirt though it barely covered her bottom. Lying under the blue and lace comforter, she put her hands behind her head unable to sleep. She swore she'd been a little in love with Tom Billodeaux since she'd started her scrapbooks. Sexy Joe and stunning Dean didn't attract her, but Tom, always burning bright in those family pictures amid the brunettes and the blondes and smiling with his leprechaun's grin, stood out, different, like her. She'd mooned over him as if he were some adolescent rock star. Now, he slept on the other side of the condo.

If only she weren't stuffed full as a woodchuck storing up fat for winter tonight, all Vince's fault. To be honest, she'd seen him as a guy who could get under Tom's skin, but then, he'd turned out to be so much unexpected fun. He didn't treat her as if she might break, and his aggressive kiss at the door hadn't led to any unwanted groping, though it might have if Tom hadn't turned the knob. She'd found herself saying yes to a second date with Vince, exploring where that might go, not counting Tom out, but not wanting to pin her whole life on an infatuation that might not be returned.

Distantly, she heard Tom's shower running. He rarely bathed at night. Not her concern. Both men had left her hot and bothered and unable to sleep. She reached beneath her covers and took care of her needs by herself.

Chapter Eighteen

Wearing his robe and loose plaid pajama bottoms, Tom sat by Alix as they scarfed down two large hunks of doberge for breakfast, or maybe brunch, since both had slept in late. The air conditioner cycled on and made his depilated chest feel kind of chilly. He shivered.

"You okay? You aren't getting sick or anything?" Alix polished off her slice of lemon doberge and started in on the chocolate, saving the best for last, she'd said.

Tom made a mental note that she preferred chocolate. "No, I'm sitting under an air vent."

"Good, but there is something different about you today." She scanned his face and failed to look at the V of naked chest.

He had to say one thing for being hairless. The crumbs from the cake slid all the way down those slick muscles and sifted like sand into his crotch. Not very comfortable, but he refrained from shaking them loose. Should he do the big reveal now or save it for a special occasion like the aftermath of the moonlight cruise he planned for them?

Both had downed large glasses of milk. Alix got up to move on to coffee. "You want some?"

"Sure." He'd save the surprise if she didn't notice on her own.

Alix's cell phone rang. It wasn't early, but her

folks rarely called on a Sunday before one. As she punctured the pod in the coffeemaker and lounged against the counter waiting for the brew to drip, she answered. "Oh, hi, Vince. Yes, I had a great time, too. Nope, not too tired no matter what Tom said. We both slept late. Okay, meet you there at one."

Damn Vince Barbaro for being sensitive enough to call her the day after a date. "What was that all about?" Tom stood to take his milk glass to the dishwasher and rid himself of some of the crumbs as they filtered onto the floor.

"Vince asked if I wanted to walk in City Park this afternoon. We're going to run up the steps of the art museum like Sylvester Stallone in *Rocky*."

"It will be hot as Hades. You should stay out of the sun as much as you can. You aren't used to this climate."

"Don't mother hen me, Tom. Vince said the steps aren't nearly as steep as the ones in Philly. Besides, we are going inside to cool off and see an art exhibit." Alix took her cup from the machine and doctored the contents with more milk.

"You're an art connoisseur?" Tom slammed a pod of dark roast into the machine with far more force than needed.

"Hardly, but who knows? I might develop a taste for it."

And for Vince. The water sputtered through the pod and sizzled onto the spot where a cup should have been. Tom grabbed for a mug like the ones Alix felt comfortable using to catch the boiling water. "I thought I might teach you to play chess this afternoon rather than run around in the heat."

"We'll do that later. Time for both. I should shower now and wash my hair." Alix bolted her last few bites of cake.

"Say, I thought next Saturday we could go on a moonlight Mississippi cruise. It's nice after dark on the water."

"Sorry, I promised Vince I'd go out with him. He says he has special plans." Alix took her mug and started for her room.

"Alix, can I ask why you're going out with Vince so often? Are you attracted to him?"

"I'm going because he asked, and no one else has. I wasn't all that taken with him, but Vince sort of grows on you."

Like jock itch. "Okay, I understand. Enjoy your afternoon." Considering the cold shower he'd taken last night, he hardly needed to bathe this morning. He heard the water drum in Alix's bathroom. She did like long showers when an entire football team wasn't waiting for her to finish. Tom went into his bedroom and found his phone. "Hey, Xo. Wassup?"

His sister spoke over the noise of bypassing traffic. "Unlike you, I went to Mass at old St. Louis. Now, I am enjoying a reward of hot beignets with lots of powdered sugar on top at Café du Monde. Do you and Alix want to join me?"

"No, we had birthday cake for breakfast."

"Sounds healthy."

"About the same as beignets. You interested in going to an art exhibit this afternoon at NOMA?"

"I have no other plans, so sure. Have you been there before?"

"Ah, no."

"Is Alix interested in art?"

"Not much." How did Xochi always see through the most simple of statements and punch a hole to the other side so fast? "But she's going there with Vince Barbaro today."

"Aaaah—we're chaperoning."

"You've got it all wrong. We might run into them, but we aren't going with them."

"Whatever you say. What time?" She had to shout as a saxophone player started playing near her table.

"One-thirty. I'll pick you up. Thanks, Xo."

\*\*\*\*

Tom and Xochi wandered through the Robert Rauschenberg special exhibit without catching sight of Alix and Vince. Standing in front of a large, blank white canvas, he had to admit he didn't get it, but he'd done his homework before arrival and was as prepared as he would be for a trick play.

"Incoming, three o'clock," Xochi teased, hiding her full, red lips behind a program as if she were a coach relaying a secret call for that exact play.

Wearing the exact sundress she'd put on for their walk along Bourbon Street and the identical pair of flats, Alix strolled along fanning herself with the same program, Vince at her side. They'd had such a good time together her first night in the French Quarter. How could she choose the same outfit to step out with Vince? Didn't she share the same fond memories? Trying to keep it casual, Tom headed their way, not noticing that Xo struggled to keep up with his long strides.

"Hey, guys. When you said you were headed this way I recalled I hadn't seen the new Rauschenberg exhibit. Xo wanted to go, so here we are. Vince, you know my sister."

"Only from afar since Tom never introduced us at the picnic. Might I say you are more beautiful close up than in the stands, Miss Xochi. Maybe Tom can explain why anyone would pay millions for what looks like faded wallpaper glued to a canvas." Vince flirted with his sister, expressed an artistic opinion, and issued a challenge in only a few sentences. The guy did have balls.

"Rauschenberg is considered a precursor to the pop artists, a Neo Dadaist really. He made art from found objects picked up off the street." Tom grinned. Gotcha, Vince. Xochi's narrow black brows shot up.

Perplexed, Alix stared at another piece. "Looks like old cardboard pressed into the paint."

"It is. Good eye." Tom nodded sagely.

"This one here. It's blank." Vince stood before the piece that had mystified Tom only moments ago.

He recalled what the Wikipedia article said. "Not really. There are tiny inclusions, maybe a little bubble in the paint, an accumulation of dust that changes the painting from day to day. It's pure and very profound."

"I think it's crap. How about you, Alix?"

"I admit I don't understand it either. I think I could do that with a paint roller and a gallon of Sherwin Williams, and I'm no artist."

"What we saw downstairs in the permanent collection, that's classical art. Did you notice how many of the artists were Italian? We got it in the blood. The Sistine Chapel, the statue of David, the Mona Lisa, that's genius," Vince opined.

"Do you paint?" Xochi asked with great curiosity

in her voice.

Vince's beefy shoulders shrugged. "I dabble, but I can't come close to that masterpiece of Judith holding up the severed head of Holofernes in the other room."

"Pretty gruesome," Alix said.

"Yeah, it hits you right in the gut. That's what art should do." Vince moved through the rest of the exhibit, not pausing for Tom to show off his newly acquired knowledge.

Soon enough, they found themselves on the balcony overlooking the duck pond. "What did you like best, Alix? The Rauschenbergs or the classical art?" Tom pursued, hoping she'd take his side and go modern whether she understood it or not.

"Honestly, the run up the stairs even if Vince did get to the top first. Next time, I'll wear my running shoes. Look, swans. Two pair." She pointed out the birds gliding serenely on the glassy surface of the water, doubling their beautiful image.

"Dad asked Mom to have his babies right over there. She said she felt like she wasn't a swan either, more like a little brown night heron in the reeds, but he didn't want a swan, only her." Tom tried to make a point.

Xochi sighed. "I love that story."

"So, Vince, which do you prefer—swans or night herons or whooping cranes?" Tom waited tensely hoping his rival would give the wrong answer.

Vince wrinkled his broad forehead. "I'm not much of a birder. Nice pair of black swans on the pond, too. Not sure what a night heron is. Whooping cranes are great, big...ya know. Say, anyone in the mood for gelato? There's a great place on Toulouse Street. You can follow us over there."

"I've never had gelato!" Alix said, as excited about Italian ice cream as she had been about last night's restaurant.

"Oh, it's way better than American ice cream, so rich and smooth. You like it, Xochi?"

"I do," she answered Vince.

"Let's get going." Vince marched off with Alix as if he were Caesar about to conquer Gall.

"He dodged that question about the birds, but of course, he knows the best place for gelato," Tom grumbled, bringing up the rear. "You could have said you didn't care for any, Xo."

"But I do. Perfect on a scalding day like this."

They hiked the concourse in front of the museum to where Tom's SUV sat parked under the shade of an oak. Sweat ran down their backs before the air-conditioning kicked in on their way to Little Vic's. The sweltering interior didn't do much to cool Tom's temper. Damn, it *was* a great day for gelato.

"Vince is a thug, a big Italian thug. What does she see in him?" he fumed.

"Did you ask Alix? Better calm down. You're giving off little red sparks," said his very perceptive sister.

"She said he asked her out, and no one else had. They had a nice evening. I take her out all the time. I don't get it—like that white Rauschenberg painting no matter what I said."

"You certainly did your homework on modern art, maybe not so much on women. You take Alix around like you are still helping her learn about New Orleans as a good buddy. Try asking her what she'd prefer to do on a real date."

"I was going to this coming weekend, but Vince cut me out by telling her he had something wonderful planned for her. Then, he squeezes in this Sunday afternoon visit. He's going to count Saturday as their third date, and you know what that means."

Xochi quirked her lips at Tom. "Do tell me."

"He's going to hit on her, get her in bed because he's waited long enough and she owes him after a big evening." Tom cut off a smaller car in traffic trying to keep up with Vince who drove an agile red Corvette with Alix in it, but he laid on the horn as if it were the other's driver's fault for getting in his way.

"Tom, I'd like to get gelato, not into an accident. Third date could mean a breakup." She placed a calming hand on his arm, and her brother relaxed beneath her fingertips. "You know there are no set rules on when a woman will sleep with a man."

"Not in the female mind, but it exists in the brain of a sleaze like Vince, believe you me."

"Actually, Vince surprised me. He's genuinely interested in art. You said he was the vocal hit of the performance you put on for Alix. He comes on a little heavy with the everything Italian is the best, but he's not what I expected." Xochi gazed thoughtfully at the parade of heat-exhausted tourists dragging through the French Quarter.

"*Et tu*, Xochi? Vince is even slicker than I thought."

Tom found a pay lot not too far from the gelateria. Vince had squeezed his Corvette into a small parking space. He and Alix waited for them inside. They placed their orders: dark chocolate for Alix, coconut for Vince, pistachio for Tom, and blood orange for Xo. They took their treats into the courtyard, eating fast as the heat threatened to reduce the gelato to puddles. Lingering in the shade near the fountain, they stayed long enough to order Sicilian pizza for an early dinner.

Vince stretched, fortunately wearing a knit shirt with sleeves so none of them were treated to a view of his very hairy armpits. "This is the life. Dessert first, then great pizza. Hate to break up the party, but we do have training camp again tomorrow. Alix, I'll drive you back to the museum to pick up your car. It's been a pleasure, Miss Xochi."

"Call me Xo."

Damn if the Italian gigolo didn't kiss her fingers in parting. Tom wondered how often he'd touched his lips to Alix's knuckles, and why she didn't mind if he came on to another woman right in front of her. Something to chew on at home besides leftover pizza.

He stayed quiet as he returned Xochi to her apartment, but his sister talked. "Hmmm, you might have some real competition in Vince. He does have a rather slick sort of charm."

"Tell me what you see when you look at him. I bet Vince oozes black and orange like Prince or maybe an ugly brown like dog crap."

With an amused glance sent his way, his sister said, "Pink."

"Pink? You think Vince is secretly gay—because that would be great."

"Don't make assumptions." Xo wagged a finger at him. "Vince exudes a love of life and the ability to bounce back from disappointment, two very attractive traits in a man."

"Go slow. Everyone tells me to go slow, and now I'm breathing his fumes." Tom braked abruptly in front of the cul-de-sac housing Xochi's apartment.

"Big brother, I'd say you better pick up some speed."

Chapter Nineteen

Alix had to admit Vince produced a magical night after a week of sweating at training camp with coaches whipping the rookies into shape and culling the injured and those who couldn't make the grade. Prince Dobbs raced around straining to show how fit he was and praising the Lord with every other panting breath. She and Tom did the warm-up exercises and kicked and kicked and kicked. To be honest, an event that didn't stink of perspiration and testosterone held great appeal.

She adorned herself in the peach chiffon gown of many layers and a handkerchief hem, added glittery heels, matched her lipstick to her dress, and laid on the eye makeup, giving some gloss to her lids, too. When Tom's eyes widened as she asked his opinion, she was glad she'd gone all out.

He stammered a little. "M-maybe you should tone it down a little. This is your third date with Vince, and here you are looking like a gift box anyone would want to open."

Alix treated him to an eye roll. "You really don't believe that third date thing, do you?"

"To be honest, most girls who want to sleep with football players don't wait that long, but you aren't most girls. You *are* a football player. I don't know how that works."

"No one does. I guess I get to set my own rules."

Truthfully, she didn't know what her new rules were either. She had toyed with Tom a bit on Sunday by not returning in her car immediately from the museum. When Vince dropped her off, they'd sat for a while in her roomier, more private vehicle with the a/c running and made out. After several of his aggressive kisses, she'd let Vince get to second base. His big, rough hands found their way inside her sundress top with few impediments. His touch felt good against her flesh, making her nipples peak and her breasts swell with sensitivity—but she'd hardly go any farther in a car sitting in a public park. Yes, Vince pushed all the right pleasure buttons, but still it wasn't right, and that puzzled her.

Unsettled, she'd returned to the condo to find Tom in full daddy mode. "What took you so long? Did you get lost? That tie around your neck doesn't look right." He raised a flush on her cheeks.

Alix guessed she had a jock mentality concerning sex. If it felt good, do it. When the attraction wore off on either side, you moved on without tears or excuses. The sex was nice while it lasted, and then it was done. This need for something more had never entered into simple enjoyment in the past.

Oh well, they'd had a lovely evening with an early dinner at a fine uptown restaurant not too far from the theater, then a performance of *Phantom of the Opera* at the grand, refurbished Saenger Theater with its ceiling of twinkling stars. Pressing through the après-theater traffic, Vince delivered them to the Café du Monde for beignets and coffee and a discussion of the play. Alix admitted the music didn't grab her—too much like opera, but she'd been awed by the special effects, the river of lights, the crashing chandelier. Vince briskly defended true opera. He had season tickets as it turned out.

Alix held up her hand. "Don't ask me to go. Opera sounds like screaming in a foreign language to me. I'm more a *Sound of Music, Oklahoma* kind of gal."

"Yeah, I'm beginning to see that," he said as he wiped the powdered sugar from the five o'clock shadow covering his heavy jaw.

Alix blew the sugar from the bodice of the filmy peach-colored dress and considered. She and Vince weren't right for each other. Better to end it tonight. With the condo not a far walk for two athletes, even one in high heels, Vince left his car in the pay lot and escorted her home through a night as warm and sticky as hot maple syrup. At the entry, Alix invited him in praying he wouldn't interpret that in the wrong way, but she knew Tom would be home, waiting like an anxious father for his teenage daughter. Punching in the entrance code, she flung back the door and narrowly avoided giving her roommate a black eye as he leaped backwards.

Regaining his balance, Tom said, "Have a nice evening?"

"Great. Magical in fact." Alix tossed him the small, greasy bag she'd carried from the café. "Brought you some beignets."

Tom caught it with a puff of white powder escaping from the top. "Vince, you want something to drink?" he asked as the punt protector made himself at home on the couch.

"No, thanks."

"Ah, Tom. Could we have some privacy, please?"

Alix requested.

"Sure. I'll eat these in the kitchen. Glad you thought of me while you were on the dream date."

Alix detected a hint of sarcasm in his statement, but he left the living room to them.

"Vince, I need to…"

"Alix, I want to… Ladies, first," Vince said, minding his manners.

Alix took a deep breath and noted Vince watched her bosom heave. "I need to say I've had a wonderful time these last couple of weekends. You spent a lot of money on me and I appreciate that, but I think we aren't very compatible." She waited for a burst of anger, accusations of leading him on and delivering nothing, but Vince only sat there studying his hairy knuckles.

"Yeah, I think you're right. I'm Verdi and Wagner. You're Rodgers and Hammerstein. I appreciate good food, and you gobble it down. I enjoy fine art, but the highlight of your day was running up the museum steps and getting gelato. I want to say you are a great gal, but just too much of a jock for me. I need a more girly girl. To give myself some credit, I think we both liked making out."

"You do that well, too."

In the kitchen, glass shattered. "I'm okay! Just a mug. I'm cleaning it up," Tom shouted loud enough that he seemed to be nearly in the same room.

"So no hard feelings, babe. I mean Alix. How about a goodbye kiss?"

"I think a handshake or buddy pat might be a better idea."

They stood and Vince engulfed her in a huge hug. As they walked to door, he asked, "You think your sister, Tille, would be interested in going out next time she's in town, or maybe you could set me up with Xochi."

With a dustpan still full of broken glass in one hand and a broom in the other, Tom burst from the kitchen. "Never a good idea to date a teammate's sister."

"Yeah, I guess so. Most people think I got this scar playing football." Vince pointed to a break in one heavy eyebrow. "Veronica Mennoti's brother gave me that when we played ball in high school. Ronnie and me got a little too intimate for him. See you at practice, Alix. I still got your back." Vince aimed a finger at her and pulled the trigger, a gesture that seemed to fit all occasions.

"You're a good guy, Vince, and I think my sister will hate me if I don't put the two of you in touch. I'll let her know you're interested. She played in the chorus of *Cats* in college. Big Andrew Lloyd Webber fan."

The glitter entered Vince's deep, dark eyes again. "No kidding. I wonder what kind of cat she portrayed. Does she still have the costume?"

"No idea. She'd love if you asked her."

"I'll do that!" Vince pulled his imaginary trigger again and sauntered away.

Alix shut the door behind her personal protector. That had ended well. She turned to Tom. "I'll bet you heard every word."

"Only the important part—that you aren't dating him any more. If you're free next weekend, may I invite you to go on the Moonlight Mississippi cruise?" He made the offer so formally with the dustpan and broom still in hand as if he'd been ready to sweep Vince away and a ring of white sugar around his mouth from the beignets that Alix's big laugh exploded into the high corners of the living room.

"Is that a yes, no, or a don't be ridiculous, I wouldn't go out with you on a real date in a million years?"

She offered her wide smile. "It's a yes, but you've got powered sugar all around your mouth."

"Oh, sorry." He juggled the broom and dustpan trying to get them into one hand in order to free an arm for a quick swipe across his lips. A large white shard slid to the carpet.

Alix picked it up and placed it back in the pan. "We wouldn't want anyone to get hurt. Let me take care of the problem."

She placed her hands on his shoulders and affixed her lips to his. Her tongue licked the sugar from his light growth of ginger-colored weekend beard and slipped inside his mouth. Sweet, very sweet. Maybe Tom wanted to wait for a special occasion, but she didn't. Alix's hands strayed from his shoulders down his sides, caressing each rib she passed, circling round to his buttocks when she arrived at his waist. Oh, how she loved watching that well-developed backside in motion every time he kicked, so firm beneath her fingers now. She drew him close right into the V of her legs where they fit so perfectly. Through the layers of peach chiffon and a very small pair of matching panties, she felt his desire grow. Glass tinkled to the floor as the dustpan tilted.

Alix stepped back and poked Tom's chest with one strong finger. "Don't say thanks. Clean that up, and meet me in the bedroom."

"Yours or mine?" Simple question, stunned expression.

"Mine." Sometimes, a woman or a football player had to take charge, and she was both.

Alix left Tom picking shards from the area rug. She strode into her bedroom feeling powerful and free of doubt. Kicking off those beautiful heels that were killing her feet, she maneuvered out of the chiffon dress, flung it over the slipper chair, and stretched out full length on her blue and white embroidered bedspread. She'd invested in this fancy underwear, and by damn, someone should appreciate it.

Tom most certainly did. A low whistle escaped his lips as he took in the scene. Little stood between him and Alix except a scrap of peach lace and a front-clasp bra. He toed out of his sneakers. Strangely, he chose to shuck his somewhat baggy Saturday jeans first. Alix enjoyed watching them drop to reveal those lengthy muscular legs with their light coating of russet hair. Long and strong, his erection strained against a pair of red boxer briefs. Pausing for a moment, he opened the three buttons of his dark green polo shirt and slowly drew it over his head.

She loved this slow striptease, but couldn't hold in a gasp at the end. "You're naked—I mean hairless—and freckled all over."

"Yep, all over, everywhere." Tom shed his briefs as if to make his point. "I had my chest waxed for you—because I sure wouldn't go through that for anyone else."

"I've had bikini waxes. I appreciate what you suffered for me, but I'm glad you left the fuzz on your balls."

"I'm not that brave."

Alix cupped her large hand. "I want them right here, right now."

"I'm eager to please." He straddled her body at the waist and gave her maximum exposure. While she fondled, Tom opened her bra and did the same to her breasts. His touch was light and firm, not heavy like Vince. He played with her nipples, thumbing them, as she stroked his shaft.

"Been dreaming of this," he murmured, eyes closed.

"Me, too."

His warm brown eyes opened. "I knew we'd like the same things, but give me a minute."

"Awww!"

He slid down the length of her body, hooked the lace panties on the way, and took them with him. Finding a condom in the pocket of his jeans, he held it up. "Gotta suit up."

"I'm on the pill, and I trust you."

"Famous last words. I promised my dad. Besides, if I got you pregnant, Coach would have my furry balls."

"I wouldn't want that to happen."

"Neither would I." He got the condom on none too deftly in his hurry but very snug and made his way back up her body, kissing her toes, the arch of her foot, the inside of her thighs, the apex of her sex until he seated himself in her cleft and moved slowly against her most sensitive spot. His hands possessed her breasts again and his tongue her mouth. She pressed against him and folded her long legs over his back as she felt the tension building low in her body. Urging him inside, Alix pressed hard with her heels.

"Patience," he whispered. "Let it come."

The orgasm came fast and lasted long enough for him to slip in and recreate the sensation again with swift, sure strokes going deep. The second time he joined her.

"Tom!" Alix shouted his name.

\*\*\*\*

They snuggled under the covers. Alix's fair hair fanned across the smooth expanse of his chest. Her blue eyes remained closed, but she stroked his torso. Tom marveled that she'd invited him into her bed without fine words or fancy dates. He still owed her a cruise and wouldn't renege on that, but they fit so perfectly together. He'd known they would since the moment she'd taken off her helmet on Rookie Day and revealed her sex, the ideal woman for Tom Billodeaux, kicker.

"I kind of miss it."

"Miss what—because we can do it, whatever you want."

"Your chest hair. I used to fantasize about licking *ebelskiver* crumbs from it. Not that this isn't nice." She patted one bald pec.

"Hair grows back, and if you tell me I'll never have to undergo another waxing, I'll ask you to be mine forever."

She answered immediately. "Never wax your chest or anywhere else again."

"Mine forever." Tom wrapped both arms around her.

She probably thought he was joking, Tom the jester, Tom the funny guy. But he meant those words. She'd lain herself out for him. Her breasts, not large but enough to fill his hands, that patch of pale hair between her legs, soft and inviting, her hips wider than a man's and so beautifully formed he wanted to enter from the back simply to fondle her cheeks as he did with her urging him on. Alix, Alix, Alix. He hadn't shouted her name. Now he whispered it and realized she'd drifted to sleep with complete trust in his arms. He wouldn't have to call her in the morning because he intended to be right here when she woke.

## Chapter Twenty

Training camp took up where it left off under a blanket of steaming humidity. Tom would rather have stayed home under his own blanket with Alix by his side and the air-conditioner blasting but nothing he could do about it. He'd sent her for ice from the snow pile, teasing that as senior kicker he got to tell her what to do. "We'll see about that tonight," she whispered as she went on her way.

Dean paused for a break and sidled up next to his brother. "You and Alix did the deed, right?"

"How did you know?" Tom watched Alix bend from the waist to fill the cups. So did a few of the other players.

"Your freckles give you away. When you came back from Ilsa's place they were a deeper orange. Now they practically glow red."

"Huh?" Tom grabbed the nearest shiny surface, a black Sinners helmet, and tried to catch his reflection in it.

Dean elbowed him. "Gotcha. And they say I don't have a sense of humor."

"Never believed it for a minute." Tom tossed the helmet to the ground.

"You wearing your rubber raincoats?"

"I am. I promised Dad—which is why Ilsa had your baby and not mine. Besides, I don't want to get in the record books for being the first guy to impregnate an NFL football player."

The humor of the second statement took the sting out of the first. Dean smiled ruefully, admitting the truth of both. "That would definitely be a new one."

"I thought Vince might have said something about us. I don't want Alix's name spread all over the locker room." Tom squinted hard at Vince still out on the field. He received a friendly wave in return.

"No, Vince was quite the gentleman. He said he thought you two might get together because neither one of you can sing, dance, or knows shit about art. No hard feeling on his part."

"Pink," Tom said.

"Huh?"

"Resilient, able to bounce back."

"That's Vince for you. Oooh, did you see that hit he took when he stopped to wave to you just now? He's getting up, shaking it off."

Alix arrived with three paper cups full of ice chips. Tom poured a bottle of blue sports drink over them. She held out a snow cone to Dean. "I thought you might like one, too."

"Thanks. I never turn one down." Dean grinned at the couple and raised the cup in a toast. "To the future, yours and the Sinners."

"He knows," Tom told Alix.

"But how? We've been careful to keep it quiet." She'd pinked up, but not from the extreme heat.

"Because I've never seen any two kickers touching fingertips when handing the other a ball from the pile or gazing into each other's eyes. Just don't let it get in the way of the game, okay?"

"We won't," they both swore.

Having done his duty as team captain, Dean returned to the field and the grueling exercises that would get the team ready for the first pre-season game not all that far away.

"I don't know why he's worried," Alix said.

"Sure, we'll be fine, sweetheart." Tom let the endearment slip and glanced around to see if anyone heard. Nope, grunts and groans from their fellow players drowned it out.

\*\*\*\*

The pre-season games came up fast. Dean played a quarter or two, then let his backup take the field while the rookies strained to prove themselves and avoid last minute cuts from the team. Prince Dobbs ran like he had the devil on his tail, caught balls as if they were live grenades he couldn't let hit the ground, danced and gave credit to dreadlocked Jesus in the end zone. He was super-hot with the constant threat of a trade to the cold of Cleveland always hanging over his head. Tom and Alix, being the only kickers, played in every game, good experience for her, easy-peasy for him.

Life at the condo couldn't be better. Tom took her on that moonlight cruise, free of paparazzi on the water. Alix wore the lacy white dress because he'd asked her to. They danced close in the lounge as a band played slow, moody jazz. Tom sprang for a bottle of champagne and cracked crab, but he had the feeling Alix would have been just as happy with a cold beer and a platter of chicken wings at Mariah's. Seeking out a dark corner, they made out so hard, both prayed for the boat to return to the dock where they could make a dash for home and the bedroom.

Dutifully, they hung out with the team, mostly sitting with Dean and Stacy who imbibed only ginger ale. They did what Dean still called their whooping crane dance, but Alix went out on the floor with other guys as they'd agreed to keep a low profile about their relationship, not that Tom liked it much. He sometimes steered Stacy around, but he didn't hold her close enough to feel her little baby bump because that would be weird. He had no desire for anyone else but Alix.

One morning, Alix greeted him wearing a brand new full-length apron and a wide grin. When she turned back to the stove to pour the pancake batter, Tom noticed she wore only a pair of tiny, black bikini panties beneath it. He came close behind her, his robe parting over his erection, and found her breasts naked under the bib. As he massaged, he said in her ear, "I'm testing your ability to overcome distraction and concentrate on getting the job done."

"Which job?" she answered, as he slid down the scrap of panties, and she stepped out of them.

"Cooking breakfast, of course." The crinkle of the condom wrapper being opened betrayed his true intent.

He slid his penis between her thighs and worked it back and forth as Alix flipped the pancakes and moved with him. With Tom's hands on her breasts and his lips nibbling down her neck, she removed the flapjacks from the plates and poured two more. She let them sizzle as he entered her, pressed her hard against the stove, and worked up a rhythm that had her buckling over the burner in record time. Breathing hard, she turned the pancakes to keep them from blackening. As Tom shuddered against her rear, she lifted their breakfast to the plates, turned off the heat, and said,

"Now!"

He moved his fingers between her legs to provide an assist and bring her over the top. Alix finished with a great spasm and slid bonelessly to the floor. Lying against the cool tile, she gazed up at Tom with shining blue eyes. "Did I pass the test?"

"Absolutely. And what's this?" He examined the plates and found each one topped with a heart-shaped pancake. "Honey, I think you are more than ready for your first real NFL game."

Chapter Twenty-One

The League liked to start the season off with a bang, the Sinners against their arch division rivals in Atlanta. Alix found she enjoyed doing the same in Tom's bed just before they left for the game. The sex released her tension and helped her relax. Not so much for Tom who appeared to be nervous for her. No worries with her first punt of the season to be delivered in a domed stadium without wind and foul weather to send it astray, and no blazing heat and high humidity either—a real blessing.

Tom with his mild jitters on her behalf didn't execute his best kickoff. Instead of going into the end zone or even better, landing on the ten-yard line, it came down shorter than usual around the twenty and was run back for another ten yards. Not a big deal in the end as their opponents failed to keep the ball very long, but Alix could tell his performance bothered Tom. She gave him a back pat he didn't get from other team members and subtly slid her hand down his side to squeeze his fingers before she went back to keeping her leg warm for a punt.

With Dean being a Super Bowl winning quarterback, he generally needed only three or four punts per game rather than the usual six or more. Alix's skills weren't called upon until midway through the second quarter. With the Sinners up by fourteen points, not a lot of weight rode on her shoulders. As she walked onto the field, the Georgia fans roared to unnerve her while the announcer hyped the fact that the first woman punter in the NFL, Alix Lindstrom, was about to make her inaugural regular season kick. From patches of red and black in the stands denoting Sinners fans a chant of "Legs, Legs, Legs" started. She acknowledged their support with a slight wave as she swung her foot a few times, and Beef Bolivar readied for the snap. The ball sped into her hands, hard but accurate. Alix dropped it into the air and booted the pigskin to the ten-yard line where the length and accuracy of her kick slanting to the right seemed to catch the return team off guard. Hitting a potential receiver square in the chest, it bounced hard away from him. Free ball! "It's a muff," the announcer declared. Chaos ensued for possession as Alix jogged a few yards forward sure to stay behind her personal protector as other Sinners scrambled to regain the football. Her team did around the thirty-yard line setting them up for another easy touchdown.

She'd done her job and done it well. Beaming, Alix trotted off the field to where Tom stood waiting to congratulate her. Beef Bolivar, newly released from his part in the dog pile, stood nearby, hands on hips. "I guess it takes a muff to kick a muff," the long snapper said with a strange mixture of admiration and belligerence in his heavy voice.

Tom's face flamed. "You can't say that to her! Muff is on the list of forbidden words—at least used that way."

Dean strode by on his way to back to the field. "I heard it, too. Thousand dollar fine, Beef." He paused to point a finger at Bolivar. "I wouldn't make it worse by adding on the F-word either."

Their quarterback didn't stick around to find out what would come out of Beef's mouth next, but Tom glanced a blow off the long snapper's shoulder that didn't cause the man to move an inch. "Apologize to her."

Beef folded his hefty arms across a chest twice the size of the lanky kicker's. "I said what I said. I'll pay the *fricking* fine, but I ain't taking it back. So what you gonna do about it, Tommy boy?"

Alix squeezed between them. "He isn't going to do anything. Believe it or not, my ears aren't all that delicate. I'll ask Dean to forgo the fine since I believe you meant that as a compliment, Barton, but try to call me Alix in the future."

"Huh?" Bolivar's dark, hostile gaze shifted downward in his broad, ox-like face. He studied his cleats for a moment. "You'd do that?"

"Sure, for a teammate. I know you're on my side."

"Maybe—I mean yes."

"Just make sure your snaps are good, and we're even."

"Yeah, sure." As if stunned by a cattle prod, Beef moved to drop on the bench.

"You shouldn't let him off. He won't respect you," Tom fumed. "And what's all this Barton stuff like he's your brother."

"Maybe I'm a little more sensitive than your average Sinner. Can't you tell he hates being called Beef like he's a side of meat?" Alix removed her helmet and shook out her blonde hair.

"It's a fun tradition to give a newbie a nickname.

He's tough enough to handle it." Tom wrinkled his freckled forehead. "Do you hate being called Legs?"

"No, because I've got great ones."

"You sure do."

The majority of the crowd groaned as Dean threw a short pass into the end zone for a third touchdown. "I think they need you for the PAT, Tom," Alix said as he didn't seem to be paying attention to the game.

"Right." He snapped on his helmet and loped toward the end zone. Alix did the same, following to hold the ball for him. In training, she'd learned exactly what angle he preferred. In the bedroom, she knew his preferences as well.

\*\*\*\*

Tom sighted the way the ball should go by extending his arm toward the goalposts. He took a few practice swings of the leg, gave the indication he was ready, and sent the ball soaring between the uprights, another point scored for the Sinners. His last view before his foot hit the pigskin was of Alix's tender nape as she knelt before him. Then, his eyes followed the trajectory of his kick to its destination. He rarely missed, but perhaps he didn't understand Alix as well as he did field goal kicking. Offering her a hand up, she didn't allow her fingers to linger in his grip. Other team members gave him the usual pat on the back and helmet bumps for a job nicely done, and he returned to the sidelines until his services were needed again.

In the second half, Alix executed three more punts since the Sinners tired. All of them stretched for more than fifty yards, slightly over sixty on the last, but the game had become a little chippy toward the end, tempers high, egos bruised with the Atlanta team taking a drubbing. Alix let that last ball sail, but the Sinners line broke down, and one tackle charged her. Vince hit him square in the shoulder, but instead of going down, the guy toppled over on Alix, setting her down hard on her backside. Penalty flags flew like yellow birds loose in the stadium.

"Roughing the punter, five yards."

That pushed their opponents to the one-yard line. Alix rose limping slightly. Vince offered her an arm back to the sidelines. "Sorry, Legs, I didn't think he'd fall that way," he said.

Tom, heart in his throat, rushed to meet her. "You should be taking better care of her, Barbaro," he snapped.

Alix brushed away the apology and Tom's statement. "I'll be fine." She pushed away both of their arms. "Let me walk it off. I probably have more natural padding on my behind than anyone else on the team."

"You're great, Alix, just like working with a dude." Vince let her be, but Tom lingered.

"Yeah, keep moving. Don't let yourself stiffen up. Remember, you aren't playing with girls any more."

"Some of those *girls* knocked me around pretty good, too."

"Big difference between a *woman* shoving you out of the way and a three-hundred pound tackle coming down on top of you."

"I know, I know, I know. Leave me alone, Tom." Alix shifted her shoulders, much broader with their pads, in irritation.

The trainers snared her next and led her away for a quick checkup. Tom paced near the locker room entrance like an anxious father-to-be and missed the scoring of a safety by his team as the opposing quarterback was sacked in the end zone, ball still in hand. The Sinners didn't need the points. Alix might have been hurt for nothing. She returned to the game with her right ankle taped and no sign of the limp. "Just a precaution." She wasn't called for another punt for the rest of the game, which ended with a zero score for Atlanta and a stunning opening victory for the Sinners.

Because of the afternoon scheduling and the close proximity of Atlanta by air, the team flew back to New Orleans that night. As usual, the biggest lineman claimed the seats in first class. Dean sat behind them with the mid-weight guys, and Tom moved to the back where he'd usually paired with Brian Lightfoot. He waited for Alix to join him, but she slipped into the seat next to Beef Bolivar, which Vince Barbaro usually occupied. Vince simply shrugged and moved back a row. Tom sat alone until Dean worked his way to the rear doing his usual pats on the shoulders for good work on the field, issuing compliments here and there, before he reached his brother and took the seat beside him.

"Good thing everyone else is turned the other way or they might notice that sucking-lemons expression on your face."

Tom kept his voice low, real low. "Why is Alix sitting with Beef? What did I do to deserve this? Last night, it's okay to slip out of the room I share with you and walk to hers cradling an ice bucket so I have an excuse to be wandering around if anyone sees. Alix welcomes me. We have a great time—more than once. Now, she's taken up with Bolivar."

Dean shook his head. "Evidently kickers have lots of excess energy to work off before a game, while the rest of us have to save our strength. Don't expect me to pity you. Besides, I wouldn't say she's taken with Beef. They were looking at pictures of his little girl on his phone when I passed so show some maturity, huh?"

"Sweet, I guess. I forgot he has a wife and kid." A weighty load of jealousy lifted from Tom's shoulders like a large raptor taking flight.

"Had a wife. Got divorced last year. Don't you remember?"

"I guess I didn't." The talons of the green-eyed eagle or condor or whatever creature it was came to roost again, digging into Tom's flesh. "Is the daughter cute?"

"Adorable. Must take after her mother in looks."

"Alix wants children. If she had a step-child, she could nurture and keep on punting."

"I guess. Or the two of you could babysit for me and Stacy—and of course, Ilsa."

Tom failed to see the humor. "I mean, why did she abandon me for Bolivar?"

"I don't think she has. If Alix were a regular football player, she'd tell you straight out, but she's a woman, too, so she'll probably make you sweat and get it all wrong. You might just ask her, but if I had to guess, I'd say you are a tad too over-protective and possessive, maybe a trifle clingy."

"Clingy. Me?" Tom shook his head in a red-haired frenzy of denial. "I don't cling. I just protect my turf."

"See, there you go. Aren't you the one who told me women can't be passed back and forth like footballs? She's not turf. Seatbelt signs are coming on. I'd better get back where I belong."

"Yeah. In front," Tom said sulky as a two-year-old

denied candy before dinner.

Dean leveled a finger at his best bud and brother. "Don't take this out on me, bro. Work on it. I tell you this as both a friend and team captain."

The landing was a little rough, and the plane bounced a time or two. Tom wondered if Alix felt that in the seat of her pants. He didn't try to push through to her as the team deplaned, and he brought up the rear as usual when they walked the concourse to the bus. Clingy, not him!

Alix dropped back and fell into step with Tom. She made no excuses about her choice of seat partners, none at all.

"So, have a nice chat with Beef?" Tom tried to keep the sarcasm out of his voice but it slipped out between his gritted teeth.

"Yes. He has a beautiful little girl he's very proud of, but says his ex is a bitch."

"Good thing Dean didn't hear him, or he'd get another fine. Even if all is forgiven between you and Bolivar, Dean won't let it go. Rules are rules. He believes in respecting your fellow players—mostly. Prince Dobbs still gets on his nerves, but Dean holds it in."

"Barton wasn't talking about me, and his ex does sound bitchy."

"Barton, now is it?" Tom caught a glimpse of himself in the plate glass window of a bookstore and attempted to smooth out a scowl that would have terrified his tiny nephew.

"It's what his mother calls him. I'm trying to get to know Bolivar better."

"If that's what you want to call it."

"I call it knowing my teammates so I can depend on their protection and their best efforts on my behalf."

Tom studied Alix's face. She wasn't playing games or making him guess, just told him right out what she was doing and why. He owed her the same. "I suppose I was a little jealous."

"Of Beef? I mean Barton."

"Sure. I just assume every man on this team wants you, and I'm not the biggest or most handsome or the best paid or famous." He hung his head as he clumped along in step with her.

They'd fallen way back of the pack. Suddenly, Alix bumped him hard with her hip into the alcove leading to the restrooms. She caged him against the tile with her arms. "Idiot. You've been famous since you were born and adopted by the Billodeauxs. You are the best kicker in the league and darned cute if not handsome. Besides which I don't need your money. I've got my own." She laid a kiss on him that drew giggles from a pack of teenage girls exiting the ladies room and a "Way to go!" from a college guy leaving the men's. Tom was the one to blush.

"We're still on then—for tonight?" he asked.

"I call dibs for the top position. My backside is bruised, remember?"

"I'll kiss each cheek before we get started. We better catch up, or Coach will blow a fuse and have that stroke we keep anticipating."

"I'll claim a bathroom emergency. He'll be too embarrassed to say anything."

"Oh, I like the way you think." As for his own thoughts, all the way home he couldn't keep them from imagining being ridden by his own personal Valkyrie.

Chapter Twenty-Two

The season progressed well with the Sinners already looking like a sure thing playoff team. They'd lost a squeaker to the Seahawks, but only that one game. Alix "Legs" Lindstrom averaged fifty-four yards on her kicks and was probably the only punter in the league most fans knew by name. Announcers still made much of her sex. Naysayers who felt having a female player violated the sanctity of the game waited for her to break down in some way. She didn't. Chants of Legs, Legs, Legs followed her onto the field. She knew she'd taken some of Tom's shine, but he hadn't mentioned it over *ebelskivers* or in bed.

Regardless, excitement filled Alix as the Green Bay game approached. Her family planned to attend no matter what the weather. *Morfar* would have it no other way. *Ja*, sure, he'd wear however many sweaters his daughter insisted upon, and a cap with earflaps just to see his granddaughter punt. The foam cheese head would stay at home this time around, he told her over the phone. Her anticipation grew.

So did the weather—into a lousy, sleet-filled rain. Dean muttered as he always did, "Why the hell don't they build an enclosed stadium?" Coach Buck answered, "Because the climate is always on their side, no matter what the fuck it is."

Only Alix seemed to thrive on the conditions. Her

cheeks burned a rosy red, and the stadium lights gleamed in her blue eyes. She paced and swung her leg, getting ready for the first punt. It wasn't long in coming.

Dean fumbled the snap on the second possession, regained it, but went down hard, sacked on the frozen tundra. They turned the ball over without a score when Prince Dobbs dropped a pass that simply slipped through his fingers like an elusive ice cube dropped to the floor. Alix came out and made their opponents start from the ten-yard line. Her grandfather stood, applauded with his mittened hands, and hooted to make up for the lack of sound. Green Bay fans asked him to sit down. A couple of less impressive but still good punts later, the Packers did score.

Dean answered them just before the first half ended with a touchdown accomplished by short, sharp passes and the running game, the only way to play in the wind and slippery field conditions. They'd kept a ball warm for Tom's PAT, but as usual the other team called a timeout to freeze him, and there was some truth to the term. It wasn't that Alix didn't hold the ball right as she knelt in the slush or that he shanked it too badly, but a gust of Lake Michigan wind plowed down the field like a three hundred pound lineman and forced it to the left of the goal post.

Tom returned to huddle on the bench under his parka without the signs of appreciation that usually came his way. "Jesus, by the time I kicked that pigskin, it had gotten hard as that crystal Sugar Bowl trophy shaped like a football and just as unwieldy," he told Alix. Because of his failure, they went into the locker room to thaw behind 7-6.

Warmed up, the Sinners scored early in the third quarter with Tom making adjustments for the direction of the wind before he kicked the successful extra point. By the end of the quarter, their opponents had pulled ahead again by one point. Deep into the fourth, the Sinners lost the ball again with two minutes to play. Green Bay would dawdle that time away and maybe go for a field goal at the very last second to win by four points.

Alix rose to punt the ball as far away as she could when Coach Buck drew her aside. They'd go for the onside kick to get the football back into their possession, no surprise there to either team. Alix nodded. She'd practiced these low, ten-yard kicks often with Tom but never executed one in a game. That deed usually fell to him. In fact, Tom had thrown off his parka and begun warming his leg for the crucial kick. She started for the bench, but Marty Buck called her back. "Lindstrom, I want you to do it."

"No!" Tom protested. "It can get dangerous out there, especially in conditions like this. Besides, it's always been my job."

"Not today. Look at her. She's used to this weather. She's all bright-eyed and bushy-tailed like some kind of goddamned snow bunny while you're all huddled up like you wish someone would give you a locker room pass to use the hot tub."

"Just because I missed that first PAT—"

"Got nothing to do with it. Hell, I wish this game were over so I could soak my old bones in a Jacuzzi, too. Lindstrom, you're on." Coach Buck gave Alix an encouraging push toward the field.

She took her place fifteen yards behind Beef and

knew she had to add another ten yards to that to make the onside kick legal. Her friend, Barton, delivered the ball to her right on target. She dropped it cold and hard as an ice-packed snowball into the air and gave it a good nudge, but not the full force of her leg. The football came down and took a bounce right into the hands of a Green Bay player. She'd failed—until the wet pigskin squirted from his grasp and took another hard bounce back in her direction. Somewhere out there, Beef and Vince were in pursuit of the ball, but it returned to her like a favorite pet to its owner making one more little hop before it jumped into her arms.

They were coming for her, all the big men, determined to rip away the prize. She saw no openings for a run and knew what had to be done. Alix fell on the ball, tucking it between her breasts just below her shoulder pads. Wasn't but a few seconds before the first heavy opponent threw his weight on top of her, crushing, squeezing, trying to free the prize. Hands groped her, seeking not a cheap feel but a football.

The dog pile built above her, adding to the pressure man by man. Through a bit of daylight between someone's elbow, Alix could see Tom on the very edge of the sideline with Dean right next to him, an arm thrown around his brother, his fingers digging in to hold the other kicker back. At last, the whistles sounded and man by man, the pressure lifted off her body. The refs sorted out the mess. With great relief, she heard, "Sinners' ball" and one of them tapped her to get up. She'd kept that football safe as a mother hen sitting on an egg and just as proud of it.

Vince and Beef, standing nearby, came first to congratulate her with helmet bumps and back slaps and a triumphant procession to the sidelines. "You're the real deal, Alix, a football player, not a girl," Beef told her with deep sincerity just before Tom shoved him aside.

"You all right? Any injuries?" He swept his hands over her.

She pushed him away. "I am fine! Let me enjoy the moment, okay?"

"Jeez, I was just concerned. You on the rag or something?"

Vince and Beef stepped back with horror on their normally brutal faces. "I can't believe you spoke to her like that," the long snapper said, echoing Tom's own words about the muff.

"Yeah, show some sensitivity, Tommy." Vince backed toward the bench.

Alix's hands went to her hips clearly delineated by the wet uniform. He was ruining her moment, not in the sun, but in the sleet, with his smothering over-protectiveness. "Well, you would know, wouldn't you? There are lots of other reasons I can be bitchy, like putting up with your jealousy. You can't accept I'm a real football player now."

The announcer mimicked her words to the entire ice bound stadium. "Alix Lindstrom in her first onside kick has just proved that punters can be real football players, too." A cheer went up from both sides. She was after all a native Wisconsinite even if she played for the opponent.

As the roar died down, Tom sputtered, "I'm not jealous, I…"

"Break it up." Dean moved between them, leading the offense back onto the field.

Alix turned her back and moved away. Tom called out, "I'm sorry. I didn't mean it," but she gave no indication that she heard. The trainers cornered her and drew her inside to check her over as she accepted fist bumps, high fives, and back slaps all the way to the locker room. Alix watched the last minutes of the game on a monitor. Dean moved the team downfield in small increments. He got them within field goal range with ten seconds to play. The camera panned to Tom on the sidelines swinging his famous leg maybe harder than usual, getting ready to win the game for the Sinners. In the end, he wasn't needed. Dean lobbed a short pass into the end zone. Game over, a Sinners' victory by five points and no necessity or time to kick the extra point. Tom walked alone to the locker room.

Chapter Twenty-Three

Among the last of the stragglers, Tom entered a post-game locker room more chaotic than usual. In a corner, Dean and Coach Buck did the expected victory interview out of the pissy weather. Waiting his turn, another reporter glommed onto a feature story and held his mic to the cold, ruddy faces of Alix Lindstrom and Ancient Andy Mortenson standing fair cheek to grizzled jowl. Of course, the legendary kicker had been allowed into the locker room. "*Ja*, sure, my granddaughter is a great kicker. How could she not be? I trained her myself," Tom caught as he pushed through the crowd surrounding them and sat to untie his shoes. Usually, Alix had disappeared by now into a rented car that whisked her back to the hotel for bathing as most stadiums didn't have the facilities she enjoyed at the Dome.

Over the noise of players shedding shoulder pads, steam rising from their chilled bodies in the warmer air, he heard a summoning. "Tommy, Tommy the Toe, get over here. We call this picture Three Fine Kickers." The command came with a Swedish accent attached. Ancient Andy hadn't forgotten him even if Alix had. He joined their group, and Andy immediately crushed him to his other side. The old man had put on some weight and gained strength since their last meeting now that he'd recovered from chemo. He'd shed his furry cap and revealed a scalp covered with thin white strands of hair.

"See, one, two, three." Andy poked a thumb at his own chest on the count of one and squeezed Alix's shoulders at two, then Tom's, leaving no doubt where his loyalty lay. Flashes went off from professional cameras and cell phones. In seconds, his teammates shoved in for selfies.

Tom slipped away and had the showers mostly to himself. When he emerged, the players were heading unwashed to the bus. "Hey, Tommy, we're all going back to the hotel to clean up, then heading to a place called the Weingarten. Andy reserved a room for us. Coach says we can use the bus to go back and forth because he doesn't want any of his goddamned, idiot players crashing on these slick roads. That guy is all heart. With this ice, we ain't flying nowhere until tomorrow afternoon," Beef Bolivar said. "You coming?"

"I don't know."

Alix still stood in her cubicle stripped down to a black sports bra, the one he'd dreamed of once upon a time. She lowered a long-sleeved jersey over her head. Before it fell to her thighs, Tom noted the bruises blossoming on her back. Already without her cleats and stockings, Alix dropped her uniform pants. Tom knew if she bent over, he'd catch a glimpse of her Jockey for Women underwear, but she didn't flex, simply sat on a bench and put on athletic pants and her sneakers.

She'd developed this routine to get out of the locker room and practiced it without shame in front of the guys who continued to speculate privately what sort of panties she wore. Only Tom had the answer to that and told no one. She saved her finer stuff for him, at least until now. From the thin line of her lips and the narrowing of her fjord blue eyes he could tell she was truly pissed with him.

"Tonight belongs to my grandfather, not me, not you. Be there, Billodeaux," she said with a snarl he'd never heard in all the months they'd been together. There'd been purrs and giggles and shrieks and moans, but nothing like this.

"I guess you're coming if the pussy says so," Bolivar remarked. "And I mean that in a cat-like way, not the other kind," he quickly added.

Tom got into some sweats almost as discreetly as Alix. He pulled a black knit Sinners cap low over his wet, red curls. "Yeah, I'll be there."

He didn't know if Alix heard because she'd gone. Now, he'd have to sit with Bolivar on the bus and take his needling like a man.

****

The proprietor of the Weingarten welcomed the Sinners profusely even though all things Packers—jerseys, posters, photos, enshrined helmets—cluttered the walls and obscured a motif of painted grapevines. Jolly as a German with a large beer belly could be, he should have been wearing lederhosen and an alpine hat like the band who oompahed away in the main dining room. Diplomatically, he shunted the team into a large private room without passing through the bar where melancholy Green Bay fans drowned their sorrows over the loss.

Long lines of tables covered in red cloths waited with complimentary dishes of pickled herring and baskets of soft pretzels spaced out along their length. At intervals, chilled bottles of aquavit like small amber towers rose amid the shot glasses set at every place. Andy Mortenson already sat at the head table anchored by his entire family, a seat saved by his side for Alix who moved to the front of the line as the team deferred to her.

She wore high white boots with short heels, a pale blue dress of fine wool with long sleeves and a flared skirt that met their tops, a high back covering her bruises, and her modest seed-pearl necklace showing in a notch of the neckline. With her white-blonde hair longer than it used to be, she reigned like the queen of ice and snow over the beer hall.

Tille, garbed tight and sexy in red, waved to Vince and summoned him to a seat on her left. Mrs. Lindstrom beckoned Tom to sit beside her husband while fitting Dean in beside her stocky son-in-law who already wore that star-struck glaze beneath his glasses. The rest of the Sinners piled in settling in groups with their buddies, offense with offense, defense with defense. They'd pulled off a close one and were ready to celebrate with crispy schnitzel, mounds of fries, red cabbage, thick wedges of Black Forest cake, and steins of dark beer.

But first came the aquavit toasts. Andy Mortenson stood with tears clouding his faded blue eyes. "For my Alix who became a true football player today." Though meant to be sipped, everyone tossed back their shots like whiskey, Alix included.

She rose and took a turn. "To my *Morfar* who taught me everything I know about kicking and living life."

Tom thought he could take some credit there, too,

but she failed to include him. The amber liquid slid easily down her long throat. The beer arrived, and some used it as a chaser, but the bottles remained on the tables throughout the evening, thoroughly drained by its end.

The Sinners gorged, drank in excess, and celebrated by dancing improvised polkas with women coaxed from their dinners by the chance to be seen with a pro football player. Vince already knew the dance and showed off with Tille in his arms. "Lotsa Germans in Philly," he said in passing.

Alix bounced and hopped with the best of them, her own footwork evading any serious injury by the drunk and inexperienced. Often, she led. Tom asked her to show him the steps, and she froze him out saying, "You know you can't dance."

True enough, but they'd been good together. Now she let Beef stumble around the floor with her, graceless and clumsy as a bear on a chain. That was the trouble when a guy stuck to a single stein of beer while everyone else got shit-faced. You saw and heard things you'd remember while they would not. He had to admit her rejection hurt. Were they no longer mating whooping cranes?

Once Rika and Mrs. Lindstrom had their toes crushed often enough by overly large feet, their husbands gathered them up and departed for their hotel. Rika's husband bore with him a stack of autographed napkins with Dean's name encircled by a devil's tail heart, the same emblem the quarterback had engraved on his butt. At that point, Tom knew they'd better head out. Evidently, his brother had matched his dinner companion shot for shot until they'd emptied the aquavit bottle because Dean ordinarily hated to be reminded of the night he'd gotten that tattoo. He had no doubt Dean could have out-polka danced everyone if he still possessed the ability to stand up. Now, the quarterback sat on the sidelines, seemingly mesmerized by the swirl of the dancers.

"I think it's time to leave. You need some help, bro."

"Let me shit…sit for a while, then get me out of here with some dignity, okay? Don't let me pick up a girl or get another tat." Dean stared glassy-eyed at the rotund tuba player and the guy on the accordion giving it his all with sweat running down his jowls.

"I'm still your wingman. Wish you could be mine tonight."

"Any other time, you got it."

Andy Mortenson boomed out a good-bye to the team. "Wunnerful evening, like old times in New Orleans," and walked out using his daughter as a crutch while Rika supported her husband. Mr. Lindstrom, walking very stiffly, kissed his daughter good-bye. He'd polished off most of the aquavit when Tom stopped drinking, but evidently was a man who grew quieter when in his cups, and he hadn't been much of a talker to start with the last time they'd met. Tom followed them out and stowed the group in two cabs for safety.

He returned to his brother. "Ready to get on the bus now?"

"As I'll ever be." Dean stood up, steadied himself by clutching the back of the chair, and managed an about face. Tom put an arm around him in a comradely manner, just two dudes leaving the festivities.

Surprisingly, Vince shored up Dean's other side. "I'm done here for the evening. Got a better place to be, and let it never be said I let down my quarterback."

They advanced arm in arm into the storm where well-padded paparazzi stood like ice-covered snowmen waiting for something hot to happen. All three men flipped them the bird. Dean safely scaled the bus steps wedged between Vince and Tom and slumped into a seat. His escort repeated the process at the hotel, got their leader to his room, and undressed enough to sleep it off in comfort.

"Thanks for the help, Vince. You weren't drinking much tonight either." Tom stood in the portal waiting to shut it in his face, but politely. Vince had turned out to be a good sport about most everything.

"No, alcohol impairs performance. See, Tille is sneaking out to meet me once her mom goes to sleep. They got the guys in one place and the women in another, so Ancient Andy won't get wind of it if the aquavit hasn't put him out. She's bringing her cat suit from the musical. I get to be Rum Tum Tugger tonight, so could you put up Beef in your room? I know you'll be with Alix." Vince leaned into whisper, his black five o'clock shadow having grown past midnight as bristly as the tomcat he planned on playing.

"Why do you think that? Maybe she'll be with Beef."

"Ah, come on. The whole team gets you two are together. That ice bucket routine isn't fooling anybody, but very considerate of you." Vince nodded with approval. "I mean no one ever saw you holding hands on the sly with Brian Lightfoot. I'm happy for you." Vince delivered a light boff to the shoulder. "What do you say?"

"Wait a while. I don't have Alix's key, and she's not back yet. We'll see how it goes."

"You should get a second key. Some of us are light sleepers, and all that discreet knocking wakes us up. We have a little time before Tille gets here. Rap on my door when you head to her room, so I can shove Beef out. I appreciate it, man." Vince trundled off.

Tom awaited the sound of the second busload of Sinners returning from the Weingarten. Eventually, they arrived—stumbling, staggering, and in a few cases, barfing into the containers of ornamental plants in the hallway. Tom cracked his door and watched Alix pass, pretty steady but very flushed from drinking, dancing, or the sobering night air. He gave her a few moments, then slipped into the hall, knocked on Vince's door once, and nearly collided with the long snapper as Beef was ejected. Tom gave the man his key and hoped Beef possessed enough sobriety to get it in the lock. No ice bucket in hand this time, Tom darted to Alix's room and prayed she'd open for him.

She made him wait, answering with the chain lock still on the door as if he might force himself inside. Alix regarded him with one blue eye. "What do you want?"

"A bed for the night. Beef is bunking with Dean because…" Did you tell a woman her sister was playing cats with a teammate?

"Yeah, Tille is meeting Vince. She couldn't resist telling me. Typical Tille."

"So are you going to let me in? Otherwise, I'll have to sleep with Dean, and we haven't done that since we were little kids."

Alix removed the chain and allowed him to get out

of the hall where any minute Tille and probably other women would be arriving to get their fill of sports. She stood there in her very practical white underwear. No goodies tonight. "You can have the other bed. I'm not in the mood because I might be on the rag."

"I really, truly regret that remark. I was completely out of line. I deserve to sleep alone." There, an abject direct apology, but Tom still hoped she might change her mind about the sleeping arrangements.

She didn't. "Tom, do you even know the last time I had a period?"

Damn, he felt heat blazing up his face. "No, but if it's now, I can go out and get you anything you need, Midol, tampons. I think I saw a drugstore on the corner, or maybe a convenience store would be open."

"No need because I haven't had one since we've been together." She had her hands on those very feminine hips spanned only by her low-slung Jockey briefs, but his eyes went straight to her very flat belly.

His high color drained, leaving only the freckles behind. "You're pregnant! My God, Alix, you could have lost the baby in that crush today. I mean I'll marry you right away."

Her thin lips softened just a little. "No need. I'm not pregnant. I've been taking my birth control pills back to back so I wouldn't have to worry about cramps or anything else hurting my game."

"Is that safe?"

"I've done it before during soccer season. We have a bye week coming up. I'm stopping them, and you'll get to experience how tetchy I can be. Fair warning, I require chocolate and potato chips in abundance."

"You got it. So, are we good now? Can I…"

Alix shook her head. "I need to sort out some things in my head."

"Sure. I understand." No, he didn't. He ticked off the list of all he'd said: apology, offer to get feminine hygiene products, fairly decent reaction to a possible pregnancy, which he would have been fine with anyhow. A tiny strawberry blonde toddled through his mind and vanished. What else could he do?

Alix pointed to the other queen-sized bed. "Sleep tight." She slid under her covers and turned her back to him.

He shucked out of his clothes and got between the sheets naked. Alix might change her mind, but no. With her palate softened by aquavit and beer, she snored more than usual and slept soundly. Tom stayed awake sorting all the things in *his* mind.

Chapter Twenty-Four

The trip home was bumpy in more ways than one. Alix evicted Tom early even though he offered to gently wash her back in the shower. Since he, Vince, and Alix had been the only ones to remain unsnockered, Tom spared no worries about exiting her room and trudging to his own. He shook Beef awake and put him outside like last night's empties. Beef pounded on Vince's door demanding his bed. A few minutes later, someone slinked down the hall on stealthy cat feet shadowed by clicking heels and summoned the elevator, which arrived with a sharp ping. Everyone else remained comatose. No rush. With all the weather snarls, the flight hadn't a chance of getting off the ground until late afternoon.

Tom showered. Dean slept on like a dead Swede embalmed with aquavit. Tom took his toes down to the breakfast buffet where a chef made Swedish pancakes from scratch. He topped his with whipped cream and lingonberries. About two cups of coffee into his meal, Alix appeared wearing a ski sweater with a snowflake motif and trim gray wool slacks. It must be part of her former Wisconsin wardrobe because Tom never noticed that outfit before, and New Orleans stores stocked very little like it. She condescended to sit with him, not a big victory since no other Sinners graced the dining area with their hulking presence.

"Yours are better." Tom held up a forkful of pancakes dripping lingonberries like small, bloody clots.

"You're just saying that." Alix accepted orange juice from the waitress and helped herself from the carafe of coffee placed on the table.

"No, I don't lie to you, Alix."

"So you really would have gone out for feminine hygiene products last night."

"You betcha." And married her in a New Orleans minute if a baby had been on the way. He didn't throw that into the conversation, but it had been one of his long, long thoughts last night. Not a hard decision to make though he wondered how both the team and management would react to a punter who had to go on maternity leave halfway through the season. How much would they blame him because certainly she couldn't take the chance of being knocked around like yesterday in *that* condition.

"We're out of lingonberry jam. My mom is sending some more."

"Great, I've developed a taste for it."

"The problem is, where should she send it?" Alix stared at him with troubled eyes over the rim of her coffee cup.

"Huh?" It dawned on Tom this conversation had nothing to do with lingonberries.

"I think maybe I should get my own place now."

He rushed to find reasons for her to stay. "You won't find lower rent or a better place anywhere in the city."

"I know now how ridiculously little I pay for the space."

"You need to have a roommate. The Big Easy isn't the safest place to live."

"I'm aware. Tom, you've sheltered me, protected me, and coached me from the moment I joined the Sinners. I appreciate that, but I've grown up now and should take care of myself."

"If it's me, you can close the door to your suite and I won't bother you." Anything, anything to keep her from leaving.

"You were a pleasure, not a bother." She gave him that much accompanied by one of her wide smiles. "I'm going to get an omelet. You can't make an omelet without breaking eggs."

Two things he didn't like about those statements, use of the past tense in the first sentence and the word "breaking" as in break up in the third. Tom watched as Alix ordered an omelet stuffed full of ham, cheese, and all the veggies offered except jalapenos. She fed two slices of whole grain bread into a toaster and waited for them to pop.

The scrape of a chair announced the arrival of Dean who sat without invitation. He ordered a glass of tomato juice and a bottle of hot sauce.

"What—not taking the pickle juice cure?" Despite Tom's distress over Alix, an impish grin formed on his face.

Dean winced at the memory of Ilsa's hangover treatment. "I'll stick to Miss Krayola's home remedies, I think."

With one eye on Alix awaiting her toast and omelet, Tom leaned close to his brother. "Alix is talking about breaking eggs and getting a place of her own. I'm worried."

"You should be. With me, Stacy kept throwing out dog analogies. I think Titi and Macho were supposed to represent the two of us, but I never quite got her point. Breaking eggs, though, that's really bad." Dean accepted his tomato juice from the waitress and peppered it with hot sauce to a degree that opened his sinuses and made his nose run as he gulped it down. "Now for some protein." He moved toward the buffet passing Alix as she returned.

She dug in with her usual hearty appetite. Tom's stomach packed full of Swedish pancakes ached. He wanted to say, "Don't leave. I love you, have since I first saw you on Rookie Day," but the middle of a breakfast buffet hardly seemed the place to blurt that out, not with Dean returning burdened by a full plate of scrambled eggs and crisp bacon, and Prince Dobbs heading their way with the same, but heavy on the sausage.

Prince took the last remaining seat at their table. He prayed over his food, not aloud, only mouthing the words to keep them private. Tom and Dean automatically crossed themselves and said "amen" when he finished.

Vince Barbaro passed by and clapped the wide receiver on the back. "Pretty nice piece you picked up last night, Dobbs. Not as hot as Tille, though. I saw your babe when I let Beef back in our room. I think our ladies rode down in the elevator together. You sure go for those Nordic types. Sorry, Alix, didn't mean to disrespect your sister."

"Hot is all you said, and Tille would agree with you." Unconcerned, Alix scooped up some hash browns.

Prince placed a pristine white linen napkin on his lap. "I have already asked the Lord for forgiveness, and He granted it because Ilsa is big as a boa constrictor, one of them huge yellow ones, that swallowed a goat, and her temper is exactly as nasty as a giant snake right now. What's a man to do when he got needs?"

"Try back rubs and new sexual positions or you can take care of those urges yourself," Dean advised. His lips trembled with the desire to grin.

Tom caught on to his brother's sense of relief that he wasn't stuck with the German woman in the last months of pregnancy. Stacy rarely complained and bore her belly proudly under sleek clothes that showed it off in a tasteful way. Certainly, the back rubs, new sexual positions, and an unlimited wardrobe budget helped achieve that. He'd remember all three if and when his turn came to become a father. If and when. Alix avoided his glance.

Prince tossed light brown dreads growing longer each month out of the way. "I'm having second thoughts about a wedding. I mean I wanted to wait until the Temple of the Dreadlocked Jesus is finished being built over on Esplanade. Being on the road, I can't keep on those contractors. That's where I want to be married—in my own church, but maybe not to Ilsa. She's gorgeous and all, but not so fine when it comes to motherhood. I want to pass along my many talents to lots of children and suspect Princess will be the end of the line for her."

"You'd better talk that over together." Dean mastered his grin by following the tomato juice with a black coffee chaser.

"Lord Gawd no, not until she delivers and got her

shape and personality back again. Only way I'll escape alive." With that statement, Prince cut his sausage links and began to devour.

Finished, Alix stood. Tom jumped from his chair. "You going back to the room?" What better way to spend an icy day than in a warm bed?

"Nope, I'm going to visit with my family. They'll drive me to the airport. I already cleared it with Coach. See you then." Blithe and unbothered, she walked away from Tom.

In no hurry to leave now, he sank back into his seat. Vince took Alix's abandoned chair. "I really got to replenish myself this morning." That fact was obvious from his overflowing plate, half Spanish omelet, half Swedish pancakes, both crowded by bacon and sausage links. "I can tell you now that Tille owns the hot blood in her family. I mean Alix is a great punter, but I doubt she could compete with her sister in the sack."

Before Tom could prevent the words of defense from spilling out, he said, "Alix is fantastic in bed!" Dammit, he'd betrayed the woman he loved like some boasting adolescent bragging about a conquest. He'd never get things right. Dean raised his eyebrows, and Tom began to have a little more sympathy for the mess his brother had made of his relationship with Stacy. But they'd ended up together. He could hope.

Vince boomed out a laugh that drew scowls from hung over Sinners straggling into the dining room. "Got ya to admit it."

"Enough. Let's change the subject before I have to issue fines," Dean said, riding to the rescue. "We have a bye coming up, but our next opponent is…"

Tom's mind shut out the conversation. The only

person he wanted to talk about or to was Alix and how to fix this mess.

****

On the plane, Alix took her place next to Tom, but she arrived late to board and not many seats remained so that indicated nothing in his favor. As soon as the seatbelt signs went off, she roved, visiting with Vince and Barton, and a few other teammates. She gathered compliments on her covering of the ball like a bouquet of Sinners' red roses. Upon landing, Alix stayed with the pack, Tom right behind her. When the bus dropped them at the Dome to pick up their cars, she climbed into his SUV without comment since they'd shared the ride going out. Not much conversation as Alix shed her heavy sweater to reveal a white silk shell more appropriate to the climate and covered it with a pale pink cardigan she'd left in the backseat.

As they approached the garage, Tom said, "I'm going to park. You want me to drop you at the entrance?"

She shook her head sending that fine blonde hair flying. "No, after all that sitting, I wouldn't mind walking down four flights and up to our place. Your place."

"You pay your rent. It's your place, too."

She didn't answer as he rounded the ramps to his reserved spot.

He pulled in, and Alix hopped out. He popped the rear, and she unloaded her travel bag. Tom came around to do the same and ran directly into the bony body of Big Lou who'd been skulking behind the adjacent vehicle. She wore large, heart-shaped Lolita sunglasses that caused her to resemble a strange stick insect. He drew back from the squishy feel of her large breasts pressed against his chest and a dirty hand that went right for his genitals.

"How about a victory celebration, Tommy? A freebie."

Big Lou neglected to watch her rear. Alix blindsided her with a pretty good block to the shoulder and sent the vagrant sprawling into the oil stains and small puddles covering the cement floor. Big Lou howled more with outrage than pain as she pushed to her feet.

Alix shouted over her screams. "Leave Tom alone, you demented hag! Let all the Sinners alone or I'll take you down again."

"Try it, you titless girl. They want these, every one of them." Big Lou raised her shirt and waggled her pendulous breasts at Tom. "All the Sinners desire me, but their women keep getting in the way." Spit shot out from the gap in her teeth. Alix jumped aside before it hit and fell in a gob on the concrete.

"Put down your shirt, Lou." Tom peeled off two hundred-dollar bills from his wallet. "Get a place to stay before Arturo calls the cops to take you away."

Outraged, Alix had her hands on hips again. "Don't encourage her, or she'll never let you alone! Get the police to arrest her."

"Have some compassion, Alix. She's mentally ill and can't help herself. I remember when you were shocked by her not so long ago."

"Not any more! Don't mess with me or Tom again, Big Lou. You understand?"

"I hear what you say, bitch, but I don't have to obey you or anybody else. We don't have a contract."

With amazingly good posture and her runny nose lifted into the air, Big Lou retrieved her shopping cart and wheeled it away, the hundreds still in her grip wrapped around the handle.

"That's about all I can take for the day. I'm using the stairs. You?"

Tom nodded and followed. They cleared the garage before Lou made it off the ramp. Alix stopped to ask Arturo to warn the homeless woman off, tipped him, then raced up the stairs to the condo. By the time Tom caught up, Alix had gone inside and shut the door to her suite. He rapped lightly. "You okay?"

"Yes!" she shouted. "I'm going to take a nap."

"Want company?" Tom tried to keep the hope out of his voice, so hard.

"No!"

"All right then. Rest well."

They'd had a training meal on the charter flight, but he snuffled in the refrigerator for a snack. Each leftover reminded him of Alix: a pizza they'd shared—she liked mushrooms as much as he did, but not jalapenos—some sort of noodle dish made with tuna she'd topped with buttered breadcrumbs, the nearly empty jar of lingonberry jam. He settled on the pizza and TV to pass the time. After a while, he felt compelled to check on Alix again just in case.

Tom knocked vigorously on her door. "Anything I can do for you?"

"Leave me alone!"

"Jeez, Alix, you've really changed…"

She ripped the door open. Had she been more muscular, it might have come off the hinges. Wearing an old striped flannel bathrobe that looked like something her grandfather might have discarded, Alix confronted him. "Yes, I've changed! I work every day with big, aggressive men and have to toughen up to earn their respect. I can't be nice girl Alix any more if I want a career in the NFL. I must be one of the boys day in, day out, and sometimes I hate that."

"You have to leave the game on the field and be yourself off of it. That's all."

"You were born into football royalty, and besides you're a guy. What would you know about it?" Alix swiped tears from the corners of her eyes like a small child pretending not to be crying.

"Maybe you could speak to Stacy or Xo about how you feel."

"Oh, sure, they'll just say you're right like it's easy. Neither one ever played football."

"The women in my family are the first to tell any of the guys if we're behaving like jackasses. They have been around football all their lives. Stacy once said she felt every hit Dean took on the field deep in her stomach. When you ended up on the bottom of that pile, I knew what she meant. Not jealous, only afraid for you." Tom opened his arms to her.

"So you say." Alix slammed the door in his face.

Chapter Twenty-Five

Tom bent over his bowl of cereal as Miss Krayola stuffed sheets into the washing machine in laundry area at the end of the kitchen. "You want for me to make you some eggs?" she asked as she measured out the detergent.

"I'm okay. I need to get to the team meeting."

"You and Miss Alix not going together?"

"She went in early to have her back checked. Lots of bruising from the last game."

Her purple and orange do-rag bright against the white appliances, Krayola nodded. "I seen that pile wit' her squashed on the bottom."

"She hasn't been like herself since. Maybe she has internal damage." That new worry seated itself firmly in his mind. Suddenly, the red dehydrated strawberries in his breakfast held little appeal.

"Naw, she bleedin' in the regular way. I seen her panties soaking in the sink dis mornin'. Threw 'em in wit' the sheets. They a little stained, too. Give her a week. She be okay."

"Thanks for the information. Gotta go." He had to wonder if Miss Krayola would also be reporting that to his mother. Just because Dean had screwed up by getting a woman pregnant didn't mean he would, too.

Tom called for his car and figured he had time to whip around to the coffee shop and get a pastry since he didn't feel like finishing the cereal. Going into the place only reminded him of being here with Alix and Beck. He bought two chocolate croissants and went out only to meet Xochi entering. Undoubtedly on her way to work, his sister wore a variation of the Anchi Translation and Interpreting Services uniform Stacy devised, but in a deep shade of purple more flattering to her brown complexion. She'd accented it with a bright scarf in Mardi Gras colors, purple, green, and gold.

Xo quirked her black brows at him. "What, no *ebelskivers* today? Where is your Swedish chef this morning?"

"Went in early."

"But that's not all."

Damn, how did she do that? "No. I think we're breaking up, but I don't know why. Could you speak to her?"

"Sure. That's what sisters are for, at least in the Billodeaux family."

"Appreciate it. Talk her out of leaving, huh?"

"It's that serious. What did you do?" Xochi tilted her head, her big, brown eyes inquiring.

"Nothing. Nothing that I didn't apologize for profusely." His ears burned. He certainly wasn't telling Xo about his remark. Alix could do that. "Thanks, have to run."

****

Alix found herself hemmed in by Vince and Barton, her special team buddies, by the time Tom arrived for the meeting. A smear of chocolate on his freckled cheek, he skimmed in with seconds to spare and plunked down beside Dean in the front row where she couldn't read his face. Coach droned through the post-game analysis, but singled her out for a compliment toward the end. "I think Legs, here, saved our beignets by giving us another chance to possess the ball."

She received a round of applause and back pats from Vince and Barton and whoever sat behind her. Handling it like a modest man, Alix ducked her head and uttered a simple thanks when she truly wanted to leap into the air like a cheerleader and shake her pompoms. The discussion moved on to Dean's last play and why they hadn't gone for the field goal. Tom's head nodded in understanding.

As they went over the lighter training schedule for the bye week, a time to heal from sprains, strains, bumps, and bruises, she relaxed into her chair and immediately sat up again. Her back sported enough sore black spots for a plague victim, and she had a few around the front where her shoulder pads dug into her flesh as the dog pile grew. The trainers had given her some analgesic creams and meds for her menstrual cramps, a first for that they'd joked among themselves. After the meeting, she intended to do a brief workout. Exercise always helped to get rid of that bloated feeling. She'd let her aches and pains get the best of her last night in a major eruption of bitchiness. Maybe she should ask Tom to come to the gym with her, but no, he'd vanished in the first wave of men out the door. Evidently, he'd had his fill of Alix Lindstrom at her worst.

Alix took her phone from a pocket and turned it on hoping to catch him before he left the complex. Coach Buck brooked no interruptions during his meetings even if he had been cajoled into using tablet computers during games. A voice mail from Xochi appeared. "Lunch today at Johnny's, eleven thirty. Sound good to you?"

Knowing Xo wouldn't answer if she were with a client, Alix texted back. "Great. I'll see you there." At least she knew her way around the French Quarter now without Tom and could walk there from the condo.

Realizing Tom had put his sister up to it she simply didn't care. In all of New Orleans, Alix possessed no close female friends. In the past, she'd had teammates who knew all about cramps and bloating, young women she could lounge around with eating chocolate and greasy, salty foods until the urge passed. Not any more. Surrounded by men, she needed someone to talk to and didn't think Dr. Funk filled that bill no matter how sympathetic.

Alix completed her workout, showered in her private stall, hot water coursing over her bruises and puffy belly like a miracle balm, the scented soaps and shampoo making her feel womanly again. She set out to meet Xochi with time to spare.

Xo stood in the line halfway out the door of the venerable po-boy shop even at this early hour. She eagerly waved Alix to join her despite a few grumbles from people behind her. As they inched their way toward the counter, Xochi suggested they get their food to go and take advantage of a beautiful autumn day. Since the din of the lunch counter made conversation difficult, Alix nodded before placing her order for a fried shrimp po-boy, sweet potato fries, and a jumbo soft drink, not the lo-cal kind. Xo sighed and asked for a chef's salad and an unsweet iced tea.

Clutching their go-cups and bags, they cut through

Jackson Square where the banana trees bore autumn-shredded fronds, the crepe myrtles shed their small red leaves, vagrants hustled tourists, and artists displayed their wares on the wrought iron fence. They climbed the steps to the levee and found a bench in the sun to ward off the slight chill of a breezy, brilliant fall day. The Mississippi rolled by, a mighty giant tossing in its bed. Pigeons and gulls lurked expecting handouts.

Alix unwrapped her sandwich about the size of a football and ate it with fried shrimp tumbling out onto the wrapping and the dressing dribbling down her hands. "Hungry," she explained between mouthfuls. "Didn't eat much breakfast today."

"Neither did Tom." Xo picked at her salad with a plastic fork and eyed the sweet potato fries.

"He had chocolate croissants, his go-to when I don't cook." Alix took a gulp of her drink and set it down again before the wind made off with the sandwich papers. "Have some fries if you want."

Xochi pinched a couple between her fingers and closed her eyes to relish the moment. "I wish I could eat like you, but with my size and shape I'd be up to two hundred pounds in no time." She picked a piece of boiled egg out of her salad and ate it with regret.

"Work out with the Sinners every day and you don't have to worry about your weight. I guess that's one advantage. But your figure is nice, all soft and round. Men love that." Alix tossed down a handful of orange fries.

"You and Tom are so much alike."

"Because I eat like a guy?" Alix said, her back already up and ready to claw.

"No, because you both go at everything with gusto.

That's enviable. Remember when I told you I see auras?"

"Right. How am I doing?" She held out her arms and a shrimp fell from her po-boy to be snatched by a gull.

"Brilliantly blue and growing stronger. Tom, on the other hand, that candle-like glow of his is dimming. I noticed this morning." Xo crumbled the crackers that came with the salad and flung them to the pigeons. "I don't need the carbs."

"Yeah, I figured Tom put you up to this."

"He did ask me to talk with you. A pale yellow aura means jealousy, Alix."

Alix pointed a finger at Xochi and lost another shrimp to the birds. "I knew it. He's afraid that I might be a better kicker than he is. It was bound to happen, that we'd become competitors."

Xo shook her head, and the wind carried the long, dark stands of her hair over her shoulders. "No, it's not his nature to be self-centered. He's played second fiddle to Dean all his life, and with the exception of the split over Ilsa, never complained except in a joking manner. I think he's afraid that football is taking you away from him after bringing you together."

Alix contemplated her short, clean nails coated with clear polish and sucked a bit a mayo off one of them. "I've been leaning on Tom. I should man up and move out, get my own place, and prove I can make it on my own."

Xochi waited until Alix raised her eyes again. "If that is what you really want, he'll let you go, but Tom is intensely loyal. He'd wait for you as long as it took."

"The three years of my contract?"

"Certainly."

"What if I want to remain a kicker for the next ten years? I mean I did this at first to please *Morfar* and get over losing a spot on the national soccer team. Now that I know I'm good, I'm doing it for myself and maybe for other women who want to try the same thing. If I just shack up with Tom and forget about my career, won't I be letting everyone down, including myself?" Alix picked out a shrimp and tossed it into the air for a gull to catch on the wing. Despite the breeze, one of the birds succeeded in getting the offering before it hit the ground.

"Why would you have to give up your career for Tom?"

"Because he's so afraid I'll get hurt. I got a little chippy with him after I covered the ball because he mother-henned me. And then he said…" Alix pointed a limp sweet potato fry at Xochi to make her point. "He said he guessed I must be on the rag!"

Xochi smiled and shook her head again. "He knows better than to bring up that subject. He grew up with a houseful of women, and he's usually more sensitive than that. No wonder he wouldn't tell me what he said. I gather he apologized."

"Yes. I didn't really forgive him. I told him I hadn't had a period in a while. He turned white, but immediately offered to marry me, afraid the baby might have been hurt in that scrum, too."

"Awww," said Xochi. "Not your typical male reaction to news like that."

"I think he wants children way more than I do. I mean I plan to have kids someday, but not right away. Maybe not for years. Now, I really have my period, and

I guess I've been rough on him. No other outlet. I have to keep my cool with the team."

"I understand. I think he would if you explained all this to him. I've never seen two people more perfectly matched, and it would be a shame to toss that away, but you must make your own decision. I can still be your friend even if we are never sisters-in-law."

"Mean it?"

"Absolutely. I used to have Stacy to confide in, still do, but I hate to dump my concerns on her when she's pregnant, so this works both ways. Friends?"

"Damn right!" Alix offered her crossover fist bumps and a double high five, accepted by a slightly startled Xochi. The exuberance of the acceptance scattered the birds. Xo placed the remains of her greens and her cup in a nearby trashcan. Alix dunked her sandwich wrappings in the same receptacle. Sharing the last of the fries, they walked back to the World Trade Center together where Alix split off for the condo.

Chapter Twenty-Six

Alix took the condo stairs again eager to find Tom alone and talk out their rift. He'd been home for lunch. She could tell by the empty tuna-noodle casserole dish soaking in the sink with a fork leaning against one side. He hadn't bothered with a plate, a compliment to her cooking, she guessed. Other than that, no sign of Tom around.

The door to her rooms stood open. True, this had been a Miss Krayola day, but their cleaning lady generally left closed doors closed. A little twinge of anger rose from her bloated belly. One thing Tom had to learn if they were going to continue this arrangement was to stay out of her space when she told him to. She stomped into her bedroom looking for signs that he'd gone through her things or laid on the blue and white embroidered spread. No open drawers, no Tom-shaped indent in the covers, but sitting on the spindly little table by the window, Alix found a gold box of Godiva chocolates and a bag of Zapp's potato chips. She emitted a very Xochi-like, "Awww."

A hot beverage and a handful of chocolates certainly would hit the spot below the waist right now. Alix brewed a mug of strong coffee and returned to the tiny table placing it very carefully on a coaster. Before she sat down and stretched out her long legs, she retrieved a couple of her old albums from the closet. In fact, this might be a good day to start a new one. Clippings of her football career lay in the bottom drawer of the dresser. These included the one of her carrying Lorena Billodeaux from the bayou, but her favorite remained the *SI* picture of her and Tom sitting on the bench, sitting thigh to thigh, toe to toe.

Was she really going to toss away a guy who offered to fetch feminine hygiene products in the middle of the night, who left her chips and chocolates when she craved them, who truly wanted children and showed no fear of becoming a father? For what—to flaunt her independence or to become more masculine to suit the Sinners?

Alix gazed out her window on the same level as Tom's space in the parking garage. It stood empty. She wished he'd get his freckled butt home so they could talk, maybe should call him. She'd wait a bit and plan what she wanted to say. Downing a dark chocolate with a mocha center, she swigged her coffee and paged through an album.

There stood a gangling teenaged Tom with his signature wide grin in place and wearing a Speedo along with a stripe of white zinc ointment down his nose as a lifeguard for Camp Love Letter. She'd subscribed to the newsletter put out by his younger brothers and Stacy. The money went to the charity, Alix told her mom. Her sisters saw through that and teased her without mercy over what they assumed was a crush on Dean who would have been their choice. The future quarterback standing next to Tom sure had that brooding teen idol thing going for him, but no, she'd always adored Tom, the kid who stood out separately from his dark family and the two blondes.

Once that boy, feeling too keenly different she guessed, had run away from home, been kidnapped by his birth father, managed to escape and save Xochi, his Mexican half-sister. She had all the coverage of that dramatic story in one of the other albums, searched on the internet and copied long after the fact when she first took an interest in the Billodeaux family. Alix imagined Tom had finally realized his worth and the whole-hearted of love of his adoptive family following that incident. She also knew her value as a kicker now and planned to lay claim to his love as well.

A movement in the parking garage caught her eye. Tom parked the big SUV in its assigned space and got out, pausing for a moment to rummage a large bouquet of long-stemmed red roses from the backseat. She didn't need or want flowers to get over her mad. Still, a soft, girlish oooh escaped her lips, a feminine sound she'd suppressed for months beneath grunts and guy noises.

As Tom stood up, a dark shadow emerged behind him. Dammit, Big Lou panhandling and offering her dirty wares again. How much did a person have to pay a doorman to get rid of a vagrant bothering his clients? She should go over there and... No, let Tom handle it his own way. Alix settled back and poked through the box of chocolates searching for an especially good one before she closed the lid.

A small spear of sunlight pierced the usual gloom of the garage and glinted off a metallic object pressing against Tom's spine. Dear God, the bag lady had a knife, a huge, thick-bladed machete with part of the rotten haft fallen away. Tom turned slowly, smiled, and offered Lou the roses, which were accepted and shoved into her shopping cart, but she didn't put the knife down with them. They seemed to be negotiating something—Tom's life?

Deep down, fear welled in Alix's stomach, the same kind of fear Tom must have felt for her at the bottom of the dog pile—worse, a life or death fear. Alix grabbed her phone and punched in 911 as she sprinted from the condo, ran down the stairs, and crossed the street. "Assault with a knife taking place, Camp Street Parking Garage, fourth level. This is Alix Lindstrom," she shouted to the operator who told her to wait for the police. The hell she would!

Surging up the ramp of the garage to the fourth level, Alix arrived barely winded after all her training doing bleacher runs. She shot for the narrow slot between Tom's car and another SUV where he knelt on the concrete in front of Big Lou's exposed pudenda, her grubby sweatpants down around her ankles. Alix's athletic shoes slapped the cement, echoing in the space, but Lou appeared too drugged up to notice. Alix thrust the shopping cart out of the way and threw all her arm strength into a horse collar attack that bent the bag lady backwards. The machete flailed the air, cutting it to pieces.

Tom sprang from his abject posture on the ground, came in at an angle, and chopped at Lou's wrist. For all her poor condition, the woman had the strength of a maniac on meth. Alix hung onto her hold with one arm and reached for the assailant's, pulling it back hard enough to break, but the woman seemed to feel no pain. Tom wrested the haft of the machete from her grip and threw it under the SUV. Big Lou didn't surrender. Free of the weapon, she elbowed Alix in the stomach hard enough to force the air from the punter's lungs. Alix let go.

Tom pushed against Lou's spongy chest and sent her crashing to the floor. The Lolita sunglasses masking her eyes skittered across the ramp. Still, the tall woman attempted to rise. Alix mounted her naked pelvis sporting a surprisingly vigorous dirty blonde bush and banged Lou's skull against the concrete, once, twice, three times.

"Leave Tom alone! I told you to let him be. You were warned."

"Alix, honey, stop. She's passed out." Tom drew her up and into his arms.

Her voice wobbling, Alix said into his shoulder, "No one should mess with me when I'm on the rag. Remember that, Tom Billodeaux." She offered a feeble excuse that had little to do with her physical condition and everything to do with her feelings for Tom.

"I think I will." He patted her back so very gently like a father comforting a child—or a man who knew she had bruises.

"Did I kill her?" Alix refused to look at the wreck of a woman on the ground.

A low groan issuing from Lou's heavy lips and whistling out the gap in her teeth answered the question. Her eyes flickered open. Alix spun ready to go on the attack again if she must. She drew back a foot for a kick to the ribs. Tom moved to restrain her, but Alix stopped herself. "Her eyes."

"Yeah, bloodshot and dilated like any druggie."

"They're violet."

"So?"

"Remember the impersonator the night you took

me down Bourbon Street? He did a Layla Devlin impression. It's her, Layla, the woman who attacked your mother and dad years ago. I have pictures of her in my albums. She had dreads for a while, but they were blonde then, and famous violet eyes."

Tom squinted in the poor light. "You think so?"

Sirens drowned her answer as two squad cars mounted the ramp, tires screaming on the turns. They crunched over the Lolita sunglasses and slammed on the brakes before hitting Big Lou or her shopping cart. An officer jumped from one of the vehicles with his gun drawn and the open car door as his shield. The other policemen did the same.

With a shake of his curly Italian head, Officer Ancona called out, "Stand down. It's only Big Lou causing trouble again." He holstered his weapon and buttoned it down. "Can you get up, ma'am, or do you need an ambulance?"

Lou pushed to her feet, but stood there swaying. The back of her head displayed a mass of bloody, unkempt hair. "That bitch there tried to strangle me just when me and Tommy were about to get it on."

"Tom?" asked the officer who'd talked Xochi into a lunch or two when she went to translate at police headquarters. Somehow, he always showed up when trouble involved a Billodeaux. Maybe it was just his beat. Probably, he wanted to impress Xo. Tom thought the latter more likely.

"Tony, she had a machete. It's under my car. Wanted me to—um—eat her out."

By his side, Alix made a gagging noise. "You were going to do that? Good thing I came along to save you."

"I figured I had two options: do what she asked and

274

have a penicillin shot afterwards or get down on my knees and make a grab at her ankles while hoping she wouldn't behead or neuter me as I jumped over her to escape. Hadn't made up my mind when you arrived here."

A little embarrassed, Alix said, "I saw what was happening from our condo window and dashed over here to break it up. I got her in a horse collar."

"Illegal in a football game, but not in self-defense for a civilian. She must have hit her head in the fall, huh?" Officer Ancona hinted.

Not catching on, Alix shook her head. "No, I bashed her against the concrete. I really thought she'd try to get up again and hurt Tom."

"Okay, no more for now. We'll take her by the emergency room and see if her brains are scrambled any more than usual, then over to the station. Tom, you want to press charges?"

"I think I must. Maybe if she spends some time in jail, she'll leave the Billodeaux family alone."

Officer Ancona shook his head. "I wouldn't bet on that. We've picked her up for disturbing the peace, soliciting, prostitution, you name it. Someone always bails her out. Maybe since a weapon is involved, the judge will refuse to set a bond and you can rest easy for a while. Come on, Lou. Pull up your pants and let's go for a ride. Watch your head, there. One of you, collect the knife." Gingerly touching her filthy clothes, Ancona cuffed his perp and pressed her into the rear of the cruiser.

A young, slim policeman with the fresh, dewy look of a rookie lay on the oil-stained floor and retrieved the knife for evidence. Awestruck, he stared at Alix.

"You're the Sinners' punter. Might I say you are even more beautiful in person and out of uniform?"

"But she has a mean temper certain days of the month." Tom discouraged her adoring fan. Alix shot an elbow into his ribs. "Okay, she has wicked temper all the time."

Peering at his nametag, Alix said, "I do not! Thank you, Officer Pratt."

"Pratt! Stop gawking. You can get her autograph when they come in to make their statements. We get lots of celebrities in the Quarter. Try to learn not to drool around them." Ancona pointedly slammed the rear car door and got into the front seat. The squad cars took their time going down the ramp.

"We didn't tell them Lou might be Layla Devlin," Tom said.

"If she is, I'll bet that female impersonator in the French Quarter is the one bailing her out. No one else remembers her, and he clearly adored the actress."

"We can share the information when we make our statements."

Tom removed the roses from the shopping cart and pushed it against a wall out of the way. "These were for you, but I did use them as bargaining tool. I figured they might distract her, and I could make a run for it. I'm pretty sure I could outdistance her, but Big Lou is fairly cunning. She just pulled her cart closer and boxed me in even more."

Alix accepted the roses, inhaling their scent to clear her nostrils of the bag lady's odor clinging to her hands. "You never considered punching her or wrestling for the weapon before I got here?"

"What can I say? I'm a wimp. And I would never

hit a woman, even one like her."

"No, I think you are a kind and gentle man, Tom Billodeaux." One of Alix's wide smiles expanded across her face just above the scarlet bouquet. "I'm the savage."

"Maybe you could be my bodyguard?"

"I want to be more than that."

"My permanent roommate?" He returned a tentative, hopeful grin.

"More."

"My full-time lover?"

"More. Your lawfully wedded wife."

Tom's russet brows shot up. "Alix, did you just propose to me? Here in a parking garage with oil and blood on the floor?" He fanned his face like a flustered southern belle and put on the accent. "I surely expected you to court me properly, Miss Alix, with flowers and fine words as we strolled beneath the live oaks, then go down on one knee and—"

Alix thrust the roses at him and took a knee like a football player returning one his kickoffs. "I'm not a proper lady, Tom. So, yes or no?" Waiting for the answer, her insides shook more than they had when she feared he might die.

He continued doing his Miss Scarlett routine. "Why, I'm so flustered by your kind offer that—"

"Cut it out, Tom, or I'll put *you* in the horse collar." The concrete was hard and cold under her knee. If he didn't answer soon, she'd do it, too.

"I feel I must accept," he said in his own light voice. "Alix, you could have asked me to marry you when we met on Rookie Day and gotten the same answer." Tom offered his hand to help her up.

"Then stop gabbing and kiss me."

Their lips joined perfectly, their bodies melded together at the hip, their big feet tangled. Every part of them matched.

## Chapter Twenty-Seven

Tom and Alix planned to keep things low-key: the attack, the identity of Big Lou, their engagement. No big splash in the newspapers. No grand announcements. They would quietly tell Dean and Stacy about Big Lou since she'd also stalked the quarterback, but after the arraignment when they knew more. Maybe by Thanksgiving they'd reveal their personal intentions to the family, but in the meantime they planned to hug the knowledge to themselves alone. It wasn't to be.

They went hand in hand to give their statements to Officer Ancona and learned the police department must have leaks as big as a breached levee. News of the assault trickled out, first scooped up by reporters assigned to the police beat. Even the *Times-Picayune* felt the story warranted a mention under the sedate headline *Sinners Attacked by Street Person.* The gossip rags souped it up with *Sinners Savaged by Bag Lady* and *Kickers Cornered by Crazy Woman*, both displaying Lou's belligerent mug shot bracketed by very attractive publicity photos of Tom and Alix provided by the Sinners PR department.

Feeling obligated to attend Lou's arraignment they put on disguises to prevent being mobbed. Tom shoved his curly red locks under a black watch cap and shielded his Billodeaux brown eyes with dark glasses. A long-sleeved black T-shirt with no sign of a Sinners' insignia covered his freckled arms and blended with black jeans and athletic shoes.

Alix drew a pale blue knitted cap bordered with white reindeer and topped with a pom-pom over her bright hair. A white silk turtleneck, gray slacks, and wrap-around sunglasses completed her anonymous outfit. She eyed Tom. "Going to rob a convenience store?"

"Heading for the slopes?" he shot back.

"I wish."

Regardless, they were asked to remove their dark glasses and hats as they passed through the metal detector at the courthouse and turn over their phones. "So much for disguises," Alix muttered as she straightened her hair with her fingers. Tom's curls stood on end, wild and crazy. She patted them down.

Slouched in the very rear of the chamber, the couple observed Big Lou enter in a clean orange prison jumpsuit that did nothing to flatter her sunken violet eyes. Her court appointed attorney, a weary-looking woman dressed in gray, stood to address the judge after he read the assault with a deadly weapon charge against Louise Dillman alias Big Lou alias Layla Devlin and called for the plea.

"Not guilty," roared Big Lou, making her lawyer flinch. "He wanted my body!"

The attorney flushed, bringing some color to her washed-out face. "Pardon me, your honor, but the defendant is not capable of entering a plea. We have verified she never returned to a facility for the mentally ill in Iowa after a Christmas visit to her mother. As she isn't responsible for her actions, we ask that Ms. Dillman be remanded to the state mental hospital in

Pineville until other arrangements can be made by her family."

"Who the hell is Louise Dillman?" Big Lou spat. Her attorney leaned away to avoid the spray. "Everyone knows I am the fabulous Layla Devlin." She struck a pose with a hand on a jutting, bony hip and raised the other to uplift her dirty dreads, letting her locks cascade down again as if every man in the courtroom desired to stroke her hair.

"You are. Be quiet. Your Honor…" Her harried lawyer began again.

"Yes, yes, I see your point." The judge, his keen dark eyes parked on either side of a beaky nose beneath a white head of hair, resembled an eagle about to dive at prey. He zeroed in on Tom and Alix. "Mr. Billodeaux, Miss Lindstrom, I see you back there. Please rise. Is this satisfactory to you?"

Tom answered. "As long as she doesn't get out again. If so, our family must be notified at once." Alix nodded, throwing in her future with Tom's family.

"Reasonable." The judge raised his gavel to make it so, but a man so nondescript he would have made a superior spy had he not called attention to himself by standing, cried out "May I address the court, please?"

"You have something pertinent to add, Mr…"

"Smith, Lee Smith. Much of this is my fault." He raked a hand through thinning brown hair. "I am a friend of Miss Devlin's, her most ardent admirer actually."

Big Lou covered her ruined mouth and emitted a girlish giggle. "Lee-Lee is one of my biggest fans. He wants to be me."

The judge raised his brows in a doubting

expression. "Go on, Mr. Smith."

"Layla, Miss Devlin, contacted me just before the New Year saying she'd been cured and released. She asked for money to come to New Orleans and start over. I agreed and offered to provide a place to live while she pursued her career as an actress. She stayed with me only a short time before disappearing. You see I work nights in the Quarter and couldn't keep a good eye on her. In the past, a heavy dose of hydrocodone would pacify her and put her out for the night, but…she went on the streets and developed a taste for crystal meth. I bailed her out whenever she called, but she wouldn't stay with me and let me protect her. That drug has ruined her. Once she possessed a lush body, a brilliant smile, and those violet eyes…"

"Do you have a point to make, Mr. Smith? Others are waiting."

"Yes, I ask she be placed in a facility closer to New Orleans so I might help in her recovery with frequent visits. I truly believe I am the only one who cares about her any more. Even her mother appears to have given up." Lee's pale, watering blue eyes pleaded with the judge, then turned to the back of the courtroom to appeal to Tom and Alix.

"What do the victims have to say?" the judge asked.

"I guess that's okay," Tom answered.

"As long as she doesn't get out again," Alix said.

"I cannot guarantee that if she should show improvement, but the court will notify you if that occurs."

"All right, I guess." Eager to be gone, Alix shifted her feet and twirled her knitted cap around one finger in impatience.

Lee Smith rushed to their row and kissed their hands, their cheeks. "Thank you. Thank you for your compassion toward one of the greatest actresses of our time."

"Damn right!" Big Lou crowed.

"So ordered. Bailiff, take the defendant away." The gavel slammed. "Next case."

The paparazzi lay in wait just outside the courthouse doors. Despite uttering, "No comment" every few feet, cameras flashed and caught Tom with his arm protectively around Alix's waist. They grabbed a cab home.

Alix settled back in the seat as they sped away. "Hard to believe Big Lou was once Layla Devlin, or that Lee looks so much like her in his act. Strange world."

"Well, this is New Orleans, honey. You aren't in Madison any more." Tom put his arm around her shoulders and snuggled her in for the ride.

At the condo, they let off steam racing up the stairs. Tom keyed in the lock numbers. "Bye week is nearly over." The way he said it implied something else entirely.

"Yeah, it is. I know how I'd like to spend the rest of it."

"Me, too. Your bedroom or mine?" About time for some action after days and nights of doing nothing but cuddling and talking out their problems. Eagerly, Tom backed Alix into their living room, his hands on her firm rump, his mouth on her wide lips—only to find their space awash in Billodeauxs overflowing the brown couch and occupying the floor in front of the fireplace.

"About time you got home. I called a team meeting," said Daddy Joe.

## Chapter Twenty-Eight

Alix and Tom moved to the center of the living room. Xochi ducked her head since she'd obviously let the horde inside the condo. Joe slapped down a tabloid featuring their pictures and Big Lou on the coffee table. "Exactly why didn't you call after this happened? We had to find out from our housekeeper's trashy magazine that the two of you were attacked by a maniac...and not just any maniac."

"Um, didn't want to worry you. It's all over now, anyhow. Layla Devlin is on her way back to an asylum," Tom offered, his ears turning that telltale shade of red.

Alix knew her face flushed as she turned overly warm and tossed the ski cap to lie beside the scandal sheet, but deep inside, she felt a tiny thrill to be included in a real Billodeaux family team meeting where serious decisions were made and childhood punishments had been meted out.

The legendary Joe Billodeaux paced before her, waving his arms in agitation. With worry deepening the soft lines in her face, Mama Nell sat on the sofa next to Stacy who took up much more room than usual with her seven-month-size belly. Dean kept a comforting arm around her shoulders since her waist had disappeared long ago. Teddy sat in his red wheelchair off to one side while long-legged Lorena and Mack lounged in the recliners. The rest and shorter part of the clan settled on the area rug. Alix wished she could take a picture for her album.

"This is partly my fault," Joe admitted.

"It is?" Tom's red brows raised at this small reprieve.

"Yes, I got word when Layla went missing in Iowa after Christmas, but she had no ID, no resources. I thought they'd pick her up fairly soon. The last thing I expected, me, was to have her show up in New Orleans and stalk my children. Knox kept an eye out for her if she tried to get onto the ranch, and we let anyone else who might care know."

Dean interrupted his father. "Dad, I should have recognized her from years ago and had her arrested instead of just getting the cops to remove her all the time. Truly, I thought the woman was harmless, not the person who nearly killed Mom."

Stacy nudged her husband with an elbow. "All you had eyes for the single time Layla visited the ranch was her Mustang convertible. Now, you own one, but we'd better be thinking of a family car pretty soon."

Mama Nell held up her hands. "Enough trying to take the blame, though I do appreciate you not heaping it all on Tom. Layla is locked away again. We came mainly to provide support in case a messy trial loomed ahead and to ask you to keep us in the loop of your life. Alix, dear, I'm so sorry you were drawn into past Billodeaux drama and might have been hurt."

Alix tried to keep her excitement under wraps. "I keep telling Tom I'm a big, hearty girl who can take care of herself. He finally found that out when I helped take down Big Lou. Actually, I'm the one who identified her by her violet eyes."

"See," said Xochi. "I told you Alix could handle anything this family can dish out."

"I can!" Alix shouted with enthusiasm.

Mama Nell stood and opened her arms. "Come get a hug."

Alix stooped to accept the embrace. As she bent, her phone, still on manners mode from the courthouse, vibrated in a pocket. Nell released her. "It's my Mom. I'll go into the kitchen. You keep on with the meeting."

"Not much more to say, but I tell you me, boy, you call us first when something like this happens." Joe wagged a finger at Tom.

"I guess I just wanted to be the grown-up and handle it myself for a change."

"As Mawmaw Nadine would say, you never get too big for your family," Dean added. "We have some happy news since everyone is gathered. Stacy and I have decided on a name for the baby. I wanted to call her Nellwyn after Mom."

Alix, only half listening to her mother, stuck her head out in time to see Nell look at her eldest son with enough warmth to melt chocolate. Then, Stacy spoke up and lowered the heat to tepid. "I said the child should have her own special name."

"Certainly," Mama Nell said. "That's only right." If any hurt bubbled to the surface, the woman hid it quickly.

"We compromised. See, we're getting good at this. We settled on Wynn, part of Mom's name. And I like to win, we both do, so there you go," Dean revealed.

Regaining his cockiness, Tom asked, "Would her middle name be Tomasina?"

"We haven't gotten that far yet. We'll take it under consideration," his brother said diplomatically.

"No, we won't," Stacy replied.

Alix stepped out in full view grinning at the assemblage, enjoying the byplay and paying no heed to her mother's voice until she heard the admonition, "You have to move away from that dangerous city, across the lake at the very least. Those Billodeauxs attract trouble, and it's obvious from what the papers are saying Tom can't take care of you. You had to fight that lunatic off practically by yourself. Your father feels the same way. We'll come down there and help you find a place."

"I'm not moving, Mom." The words came out more forcefully than she intended. "Yes, I'll give you one good reason why. Tom and I are getting married!"

Oops. All those brown eyes turned her way. Teddy wheeled his chair around to stare at her with his baby blues. A void of silence surrounded her in the room and from the phone pressed to her ear. Then, the congratulations and questions and suggestions burst into the air like fireworks at a Billodeaux family Fourth of July celebration.

Her mother screeched into her ear, "Nels, Tille, Alix is marrying Tom Billodeaux!"

"So happy for you both," from Mama Nell, a "Perfect" from Xochi, an offer to help plan the wedding from Stacy, and a demand to see the ring from Lorena. The twins muttered something about another bridesmaid's dress, and little Edie jumped up and down at the prospect of being flower girl again. The men simply seemed stunned at the abrupt announcement.

"Tom, what did I say about keeping us in the

loop?" Joe finally said.

"We were going to keep it quiet until after the season. There is no ring yet. We're going to go together to pick it out."

"I can recommend Leslie at Schifferman's. He has great taste," Dean offered. "I call best man!"

"Wouldn't have anyone else, bro. Right now I only know the ring must be a blue-white diamond with the depth to match her eyes and the sparkle of sunlight on the snow in Wisconsin."

A collective "awww" went up from the women, Alix included. "Nothing, Mom. Tom just said something so nice. Sure." Alix held out her phone. "Repeat that for your future mother-in-law."

Tom did, though embarrassment set in when the three youngest boys snickered. He aimed a finger at them. "Your day will come. No, not you, Mrs. Lindstrom. Ah, sure, I'd like to ask Mr. Lindstrom's permission to marry his daughter." Not helping that Dean, Teddy, and his dad joined in the laughter. Still, he got the words out, received the consent, and tossed the phone back to Alix like a hot *ebelskiver* burning his hands.

"Look, Mom. Nothing has been planned without you. I'm certain the diamond will be as big as Stacy's, but we want to keep this out of the news until the end of the football season, okay? Sure, start looking for reception venues, but don't tell anyone else yet except Rika and *Morfar*. Yes, I'll call him shortly. I've got company. Gotta go…bye." Alix exhaled.

"I mean it about helping with the wedding," Stacy said. "I love planning special occasions."

Tom's forehead wrinkled. "You don't want one of

those big white weddings, do you?"

"Oh, no! I want the full Swedish in Wisconsin when the weather warms up, probably June. It'll have to be a Lutheran service. I hope that won't upset anyone."

"Only Mawmaw Nadine. She'll get used to the idea," Nell murmured.

"What else does a full Swedish require?" the future groom asked, a little worried.

"Nothing too strange, but I will have to teach you to polka and how to hold your aquavit. You, too, Dean."

"Okay, sounds like fun. No rush. We have plenty of time."

"No, you don't," Stacy told him, and all the women nodded in agreement.

"Fine, but let's try to keep this to ourselves until the end of December. Looks like we're headed to the playoffs again, and we don't need the distraction."

"Exactly what I was about to say." Dean stood and hoisted his pregnant wife out of the soft cushions. "I guess we should let the lovebirds alone now that everything is settled."

"Oh, I thought with the family together, we could go out to lunch at Commander's Palace," Mama Nell suggested.

"*Mais,* yeah, I already made the reservations for a large table." Daddy Joe checked his watch.

"I could eat," Alix said.

"But what about…never mind. Lunch it is." If they could get them fed and on their way, all would be well. Tom motioned his family toward the door.

## Chapter Twenty-Nine

As Dean said, the Sinners had a season to finish. Alix and Tom still sat side by side on the bench, took turns kicking into the practice net, and tried very hard to keep their PDA's to a discreet minimum on the field, in the locker room, and around town. Driving for the playoffs, the Sinners dropped one game but won the others. Alix got roughed a few times, but nothing serious. Tom managed to keep his cool.

She gave him lots of extra credit points for spending their brief Thanksgiving break in Wisconsin scouting reception locations with her mom, dad, and Tille who had been persuaded to act as their decoy on one condition. Vince Barbaro must be included among their groomsmen. Agreed. So, they slogged from place to place with Tille masquerading as the bride-to-be.

"Too small, too small, too small," her mother kept saying. "We must be able to seat three hundred." Where those three hundred would come from, Alix had no idea. Even if the entire team and management showed up as well as most of the town where she'd spent her childhood, she doubted they'd need a hall that large.

Finally, they found a venue big as a barn. In fact, it had been a barn at one time, a very old one with stone walls and hand-hewn beams. The owner, Lina Holmquist, a sturdy and convincing woman who'd devoted years converting the ancestral dairy farm into a wedding destination and the farmhouse to a B & B, showed pictures of previous receptions with the open rafters festooned in floral garlands. Plenty of room for a band and dancing, rows of trestle tables, and a long buffet line. In fact, she'd throw in the use of the replica Swedish church, which sat on a knoll above the barn and seated two hundred. "I know the area appears gray and muddy now, but imagine it in June, a walkway lined with white peonies connecting the two buildings. Of course, you can have your hometown minister preside. Plenty of parking in the pastures, too." Lina patted the thick gray-blonde braids wrapped around her head as if a stray wisp might change their minds about her efficiency. "I will be here to oversee everything. No need for a wedding planner."

Standing between Tom and her father and as bored as both of them, Alix said, "I like it fine. We should book it."

"I think a city wedding in Madison might be better," Tille said. "Maybe in the art museum. That would be so chic."

Alix glanced sidelong at Tom. Both burst into laughter at their private joke. The owner quickly added, "We sow the meadows with wildflowers. No city can complete with that natural beauty."

Alix placed her large hand on Tille's small shoulder and squeezed. "It's perfect for you and what's-his-name, don'tcha think?"

"I guess." Her sister sighed.

In the interest of keeping the secret as long as possible, Nels Lindstrom signed the contract and nailed down the date for the first week in June. "This is dry work. I could use a beer. Saw a tavern down the road.

Anyone interested?"

All but Tille were. She requested wine. They shared a "mission completed" toast. As for Alix, she dreamed of next November when she'd be sharing fried turkey at Lorena Ranch and all this fuss would be behind her.

****

The Sinners earned themselves a bye week and a home field advantage in the playoffs as might be expected from a team who'd lost only two games. They crushed their wild card opponent and moved on to the next, a more crucial challenge with tough opposition. The game came down to seconds with the Sinners three points behind, and so far Dean was unable to shake free and find an uncovered receiver in the end zone. Fourth down and one timeout saved for just such an occasion.

Coach Buck called for the field goal team to trot out. He fooled no one. Trick play in progress, and Alix knew which he'd choose. In fact, she argued to carry the ball as no one would suspect her, but Tom gained that privilege. Her orders were to lean back instead of catching the high snap and stand aside as the kicker took the ball over the top of the wall formed by the two lines just a couple of yards in front of the goal.

Alix had never feared for Tom during a game—in that parking garage confronted by a mad woman, sure, but not on the field. He caught the ball and surged into the solid pack of bodies. His long legs propelled him over the top, only to meet resistance from two stalwart linemen shoving him back. He held out the ball, trying to break the plane by squeezing between them. From the rear, Vince and Beef shoved at his slender hips, then boosted his thighs. With one massive effort, Tom shot over the top of the pack, head first, legs in the air, and disappeared.

The officials signaled a touchdown, but where was Tom? Why didn't he stand up? Broken arm, broken leg—broken neck? Fear squeezed her lungs, deflating them like a pair of illegal footballs. Had Tom felt this way when she lay on the bottom of that dog pile protecting the ball? She understood fully for the first time.

Alix pushed through the throng of celebratory Sinners, using her elbows at will. Tom still sat on the ground—laughing. He stood up a little wobbly but obviously not hurt and shook his red hair free of the helmet. Teammates mobbed him. Alix shoved one broad shoulder aside, and then another until she got to her man. Ripping off her helmet she laid a kiss on Tom that set him off balance. She grabbed his shoulder pads and heaved him upright again as her hands tangled in his curls and her hips ground against his.

Vaguely, she heard Beef Bolivar say, "Hey, ain't that on the forbidden list? I thought only helmet bumps and back pats were allowed."

Dean, not the hero of the minute, answered, "I think management overlooked kissing since it's never happened between players before—at least not like this." He tapped Alix on the back. "Ah, maybe you should break it up."

"Go away. You know we're engaged." She'd dropped the bomb, or maybe the football. The photographers continued to get shots from all angles. The press demanded an interview. They got it. The two flushed kickers faced the reporters.

"Alix, how did you feel when the man you so

obviously love went over the top with the ball?"

"Afraid, very afraid—but I know it's part of the game. We have to live with it."

"Tom, how did it feel to score?"

"Fantastic!"

"When's the wedding, Alix?"

"June. We'll let you know more later."

"Do you have a ring yet?" a female reporter shouted from the rear as she pointed frantically toward her finger.

Alix fished under her jersey and drew out a thin chain. She held up the ten-carat emerald cut blue-white diamond in its platinum setting with two brilliants on either side. Large but not fussy or ornate, it suited her big hands. She'd picked it out with Tom's—and Leslie's—approval over the Christmas holidays. Tom unfastened the clasp and placed it on her finger. Applause from the audience and a few "awwws" from the women ensued.

The Sinners did their best to capture the division title, but this year, it wasn't to be. They lost their final playoff in double overtime on a field goal. A kicker saved the game again, but not for their team. Alix breathed easy at last. She'd survived her first year as an NFL punter and been a credit to her team. Neither she nor Tom had been seriously hurt. And in June, she'd marry the man she'd met and loved through her albums and only come to know less than a year ago.

## Chapter Thirty

"If I'd known how much trouble the full Swedish was going to be, I'd have eloped. We still can, you know. The wedding isn't for another month." Alix splayed belly-down across her bed with Tom beside her. She flipped a few pages of the album containing all the minutia of Dean and Stacy's wedding that had entranced the press. "I could put on the white lace dress you like, and we'd sneak off to Vegas the way your parents did."

Tom kissed her cheek. "We're close to the goal line. Don't give up now. Besides, we've had some fun with the planning. I especially enjoyed seeing my sisters' faces when you showed them the bridesmaid's gown."

"Your idea to hit them with the picture of the Swedish national dress first was sheer genius." Alix let loose with a loud guffaw. She opened another album that traced their wedding journey. "Here it is." She poked the photo of the long dark skirt covered with an equally long bright yellow apron, blue embroidered folk vest, long sleeved white blouse—and the big, white Swedish cap that would have made them all look like the Flying Nun.

"Only Edie loved it. She thought she'd get to dress up like a little Dutch girl and could wear the costume for Halloween. Stacy turned even paler than usual, and

Xochi had to cover her face to hide her horror. Then, Jude shouts, 'No way!' and Annie tells her to be kind. Lorena says, 'I guess I can pull it off because I'm tall—and I owe my life to Alix, but the twins are going to look like souvenir dolls.' Oh, it was great!" Tears of laughter gathered in the corners of Tom's brown eyes as he enjoyed the rehash of the conversation and mimicking each sisterly voice.

Alix flipped to the next page. "You pegged it right. They were so relieved that when I showed them the real dress I didn't get a bit of flack." Lovingly, she ran a finger over the white dresses with full knee-length skirts embroidered with wildflowers. Deep blue corsets bearing the same pattern covered the bodice with its scooped neckline and puffed sleeves. "They didn't even grumble when I asked for white stockings and black shoes. Too bad we gave it all away by snickering. Xochi said we were perfect for each other again."

"Yes, same warped sense of humor. Hey, the guys are still thanking me for the standard black tux with a red waistcoat. I think they worried we might choose knee socks and short pants. That would have been a hoot."

"Come on, they wear stockings and knee pants when they play football, and most of them are vain about their legs. We could have gotten them to do it. All the girls will be lovely with the floral circlets for their hair and matching bouquets, only I didn't figure on eight bridesmaids."

Letting the fine blonde strands sift through his fingers, Tom toyed with her hair grown well below her shoulders now. He'd asked to have it long for the wedding, and she'd done that to please him. When training camp started, she planned to whack it off to shoulder-length again.

Her groom said, "That's what you get for marrying a Billodeaux—lots of immediate relatives—plus your two sisters. I never thought I'd have to add Vince Barbaro and Beef Bolivar to the wedding party along with your brother-in-law."

Alix squeezed Tom's arm. "Call him Barton, please. He asked so sweetly if he could be a groomsman, and we needed another. Lorena is being a good sport about being paired with him. It's good to have someone in your eternal debt, but I'm sure he'll be fine."

"Says you." Tom squinched all his freckles together in a frown.

"Rika and Tille are still upset that I chose Xochi to be my maid of honor. Heck, Rika didn't want me in *her* wedding because I'm too tall and would ruin the group wedding pictures, but Mom made her accept me. I've never gotten along with Tille, but Xo is the reason we're still together."

"Yeah, I almost asked her to be best man, but you beat me to it."

"You did not!" Alix cuffed Tom on the shoulder. She flipped to their wedding invitation rimmed with colorful folk art designs. "I guess it is too late to run away since we mailed these two weeks ago."

"Are the preparations getting to you that badly?" He lightly rubbed her tense back.

"Sure, your part is finished. You pick a tuxedo, line up the groomsmen, buy them a gift, and you're done. If Mrs. Holmquist doesn't stop calling me about every little detail, she'll drive me mad as Big Lou. About the flowers, besides the wildflower bouquets with red poppy accents, did I want to add astilbe for some fluff and muscari for whimsy? Any idea what those frickin' things are?"

Tom shrugged. "Flowers are my best guess, but I'm all about whimsy." He drilled a dimple into his freckled cheek.

"You're a big help. I told her yes and looked them up later. Yesterday, she wanted to know if I'd like brass chargers under the dinner plates since we have brass candlesticks and the brass pitchers filled with flowers."

"What the hell is a charger?"

Alix pointed a finger at Tom. "My words exactly. It's this metal plate that goes under a regular dish. As far as I can tell they are just for pretty, but I said, '*Ja*, sure.' Then, I asked her if we could have black and white spotted cows, Holsteins, ya know, in the meadows."

"She could tell you were joking, right? You usually are when you use *Ja*, sure, but she might not get it."

Alix shrugged. "We'll see when we arrive. Cows are pretty if you aren't close enough to smell them."

Tom closed the albums, laid them aside, and straddled her hips. "We will survive all this together exactly like playing a game in foul weather. Here, let me give you a massage to ease the tension."

"Your massages always lead to one thing." Still, she relaxed under his kneading hands that had already made their way under her T-shirt and unsnapped her bra.

"Right. Any objections?"

"None at all."

"See, we do think alike. By the time we're married

twenty years, we'll be able to read each other's thoughts." He moved to her thighs, worked the yoga pants off her hips, and placed a kiss on each beautiful, firm buttock. "I think these are my favorite parts of your anatomy."

"What, not my legs?"

"Everyone gets to see those. Only I get to do this." Tom, hard and ready, slid between her legs and removed all of Alix's prenuptial jitters.

## Chapter Thirty-One

Their wedding day arrived with far north sunshine bound to last well into the evening along with the reception and black and white cows grazing in the wildflower meadows. Knox Polk, who seemed to know law enforcement personnel everywhere, stalked the grounds with a rifle and vowed to shoot down any drones mounted with GoPro cameras like a bunch of clay pigeons. In fact, he sent out a press release stating this. His hired cohorts kept the press at bay.

Inside the farmhouse, the wedding party changed into their finery. The men trooped to the church on foot with a photographer impeding their progress for candid shots. The ladies rode the short distance in white limos with very dark windows. No seeing the bride beforehand.

The antique organ pumped out the processional and one by one the eight bridesmaids bobbed down the aisle. Tom, lined up with his brothers and teammates at the altar, craned to see Alix in her wedding gown, the one thing she'd kept top-secret from him. The wedding march began and the rather over-crowded guests rose. Alix entered on her father's arm. She paused as the photographer got his shot.

Her filmy long sleeves were embroidered with flowers and the same fabric filled in the bodice of what would have been a strapless gown otherwise. Neither poufy nor tight, the soft white material of the dress swirled down her long body to her very valuable toes. A transparent veil covered half her face and flowed down her back to the floor with only a plain, green myrtle wreath to anchor it on her straight, white-blonde hair. Solemn as only Swedes could be, Nels escorted his somber daughter down the aisle and turned her over to Tom, still dazzled by her simple beauty. When Alix turned to give her bouquet to Xochi and he saw her back, bare nearly to the waistline, the shimmering cloth molding to her hips, the groom burst out in a grin that his bride answered immediately.

Alix pronounced her vows in a clear and steady voice and boomed out her "I do" in a volume that rattled the rafters and some of the guests. Tom, forewarned by Ancient Andy about this old world custom that would determine who wore the pants in the family, answered her decibel for decibel. The Lutheran minister rocked back on his heels. "Well now, I think this is a match of equals—as it should be." He pronounced them man and wife. The kiss that followed impressed the applauding congregation, too. "Like whooping cranes with their necks entwined," Dean muttered from his place as best man. When the newlyweds untangled, Tom replied, "I heard that."

The couple led the procession from the church. Edie, escorted by T-Rex, strewed flower petals with wild abandon. The bridesmaids and groomsmen paired off beginning with a very pleased Tille and Vince who wore a tuxedo with unexpected élan, ending with Stacy and her closest brother, Teddy, who toiled along on his armband crutches, then Dean with Xochi on his arm. Caught off guard, they mindlessly followed Alix and

Tom when they veered from the peony-lined path and tromped to the meadow to have pictures taken with the curious cows that came to the fence to observe. From the couple's shared laughter, another private joke.

In the reception hall with its garlanded rafters and gleaming brass, the overflow guests had taken advantage of the open bar, but left the amber bottles of aquavit sitting on runners of blue and white Swedish weaving and spaced along the tables for the many toasts to follow. Instead of settling into the bower designed for the bride and groom, Alix batted away the photographer and headed for the smorgasbord that began with an array of fish—fresh, smoked and pickled—moved on to meats carved to order, a myriad of hot dishes, and ended with a mountain of cheeses the size of Timms Hill, Wisconsin.

"I'm starving," she said.

Tom followed, and everyone else got in line while she piled her plate. On a separate table sat two cakes. T-Rex stood staring at them with the concentration of a little boy who wanted dessert first. The bride paused on her way back to the bower. "Pretty tempting, huh?"

"What's that one?" T-Rex pointed to a conical creation three feet tall and topped with flowers.

"A *spettekaka*, a spit cake."

"No foolin'? They make it with spit?" His eyes went wide with boyishly gross delight.

"No, no! It's made on a cone-shaped spit like your dad uses to rotisserie chickens. See, they dribble the batter on to make the cake all light and fluffy. Balancing her full plate on one hand, she pinched off a morsel and fed him a piece. "Good, *Ja*?"

"Real good. What about the other cake?"

"Under all that white icing and sugar poppies, it's chocolate."

T-Rex hugged the bride hard around the waist. "I love you, Alix."

"Beat it. She's mine, kid." Tom gave his youngest brother a light swat on the behind. "Go eat something, or Mom will say no cake for you, spit or otherwise."

They ate, they drank and endured many toasts growing more elaborate and sometimes involving song as the aquavit bottles emptied. At one point, Beef Bolivar stood gripping his shot glass in a mighty paw. "Alix is like a sister to me. You better take good care of her, Tom, or you answer to me." He swayed a little and sat abruptly. That toast was as good as any other excuse to down more liquor. Ancient Andy had said something similar earlier.

Andy Mortenson sat with one arm slung around Mariah Coy dressed in cleavage revealing poppy red to match the décor. Oxygen tank or not, Mariah never missed a good party. Sharing a bottle of aquavit with Andy suited her just fine. She opened her sequined handbag and handed several pages of sheet music to the bride and groom. "Here you go. Have fun out there."

The couple dropped off the music, got the approval of the bandleader, and continued on their rounds to the table of redheads that included his birth mother and step-father, Howdy. After tears and embraces there, Tom said, "I guess we have to say hey to Prince and Ilsa. At least, they didn't haul the babies along this time."

"No need to compete since Stacy decided not to bring Wynn," Alix whispered as they approached the table where most of the single Sinners' players hung out hoping to score with her Swedish blonde Lindstrom cousins. Ilsa and Prince held a place at the end of the table.

There were baby pictures to be admired, however, the latest of little Princess Dobbs. "Oh, so sweet and cute." Alix did her best to coo over them.

"Not so sweet. She made me wait an extra two weeks to be born. *Mein Gott*, what a labor and nine pounds, she was. Months to take off that weight to fit into my mermaid gown for our wedding. You look very nice, Alix, but mine will be tight with a big ruffle on the bottom. Seeing your bridesmaids, I am thinking dirndls for mine. Folk dress does not suit Stacy very well, *nein*?"

Prince winced the slightest bit. "Well, baby, the Temple of the Dreadlocked Jesus ain't near finished yet. We got plenty of time to figure that out." He stared at his child's pictures before pocketing them. "What I want to know is how Dean got a blue-eyed, blonde baby girl, and I got one with fuzzy brown hair and amber eyes."

"Because she is like her papa," Ilsa spit out. "Her very handsome papa," she added quickly enough to allow Prince Dobbs to preen by fluffing his dreads.

"Princess is adorable," Tom said, ever the diplomat. "Have a good time this evening."

"I know *you* will!" Prince shouted after them.

Tom moved Alix away by her elbow and leaned toward her ear. "Ours will be prettier, all strawberry blondes."

"You'll have to wait a few years to find out.'

"You ready for the dancing?"

"As I will ever be."

The carefully selected band that assured them they could play romantic songs and fast contemporary pieces as well as frisky polkas got the cue from Tom, and the leader announced the bride would now dance with her father. Straight and stately, and not yet as drunk as many of his relatives, Nels Lindstrom guided his daughter around the floor. Joe Billodeaux cut in and showed off his footwork. When Dean took a turn with the bride, his father gathered Nell in her perky yellow suit and tucked her against his lapel like a bright sunflower boutonniere. He could still get a woman to follow him anywhere. Other members of the wedding party joined in. Beef Bolivar proved fairly adept at staying off Lorena's toes, and Vince and Tille, expert enough together to try out for a revival of *Cats*.

Tom hung back until the slow song ended and the dance floor cleared. He gave the bandleader the signal. "The bride and groom will now perform their special dance together—the *Whooping Crane*. You might recognize it as another popular song, but the steps are original."

The music of their first dance together at Mariah's Place pulsed with a strong beat that rocked to the rafters. Starting out in the middle of the floor, Tom jerked his knees and flapped his arms pretty much the way he always danced. Alix lifted her skirt and held out her veil in her fingertips, swooping around him as if she flew on great white wings.

In the audience, Dean covered his handsome face with his hands and shook his head. Stacy pulled them away as the couple galloped by with knees and elbows flailing. She cupped her mouth to shout good wishes over the loud music. "I think you've mated for life!"

Laughing at their own antics, Alix called back, "You betcha!"

Epilogue

Alix "Legs" Lindstrom Billodeaux punted for the Sinners for six years, longer than most men who held that position in the NFL. During that time, she was consistently ranked among the top five punters in the league and often number one. She hung up her cleats as she approached thirty and turned her mind to the babies her husband, Tom, imagined and desired.

Mia arrived a year later made to order with her strawberry blonde hair and Billodeaux brown eyes. Two years after, Anders, named for his great-grandfather, came into the world kicking, and Nelson, so called for their grandfather who had only daughters of his own, followed a mere fourteen months later. As Tom remarked to any who wanted to hear, "They are as close as Dean and me always were." Both had those famous brown eyes, but fine blonde hair.

The boys idolized their cousins, Beck—who could bounce a soccer ball off his head and showed no interest in football—and Dean Joseph Billodeaux, Jr.— or D.J., already being groomed as a quarterback. "Let's hope with initials like that he doesn't decide to go into music," his mother, Stacy, quipped, greatly upsetting her husband and Daddy Joe.

Last came Xoxo with her bright red curls and big blue eyes. Aunt Xochi warned her parents this child glowed with an aqua light the likes of which she'd never seen before but assumed it to be a good sign.

Whenever a woman's sports group convinced Alix to address them despite her dislike of public speaking, she cited her children as her greatest achievement. "Oh, and playing in three Super Bowls and winning two rings, that was good, too."

The rest of the world disagreed. She'd made football history and opened the way for several more female punters and a place kicker as well as women referees who worked their way up in the system to officiate. They credited her for greater respect for their sex and much improved locker room conditions. Her advice to female athletes in a man's sport—"Work hard, be the best you can, and learn to get along with guys. That's all it takes."

Despite her modesty, Alix Lindstrom made the Hall of Fame on the first vote. Tom Billodeaux followed her there after a long career as a kicker that rivaled Ancient Andy Mortenson. When asked what he considered his greatest achievement, Tom said, "Being mated for life to my perfect woman."

## A word about the author...

Once a librarian, now a writer of romance, Lynn Shurr grew up in Pennsylvania Dutch country. She attended a state college and earned a very impractical B.A. in English Literature. Her first job out of school really was working as a cashier in a burger joint. Moving from one humble job to another, she traveled to North Carolina, then Germany, then California where she buckled down and studied for an M.A. in Librarianship.

New degree in hand, she found her first reference job in the Heart of Cajun Country, Lafayette, Louisiana. For her, the old saying, "Once you've tasted bayou water, you will always stay here" came true. She raised three children not far from the Bayou Teche and lives there still with her astronomer husband.

When not writing, Lynn likes to paint, cheer for the New Orleans Saints and LSU Tigers, and take long road trips nearly anywhere. Her love of the bayou country, its history and customs, often shows in the background for her books. Contact Lynn at www.lynnshurr.com or visit her blog—lynnshurr.blogspot.com

Also available from The Wild Rose Press, Inc. are:

The Sinners Series: *Goals for a Sinner, Wish for a Sinner, Kicks for a Sinner, Paradise for a Sinner, Love Letter for a Sinner*

A Sinner's Legacy Series: *Son of a Sinner*

The Mardi Gras Series: *Queen of the Mardi Gras Ball, Mardi Gras Madness, Courir de Mardi Gras*

The Roses Series: *The Convent Rose, A Wild Red Rose, Always Yellow Roses*

Single Title: *A Trashy Affair*

Thank you for purchasing
this publication of The Wild Rose Press, Inc.

If you enjoyed the story, we would appreciate your
letting others know by leaving a review.

For other wonderful stories,
please visit our on-line bookstore at
www.thewildrosepress.com.

For questions or more information
contact us at
info@thewildrosepress.com.

The Wild Rose Press, Inc.
www.thewildrosepress.com

Stay current with The Wild Rose Press, Inc.

Like us on Facebook

https://www.facebook.com/TheWildRosePress

And Follow us on Twitter
https://twitter.com/WildRosePress